# DARK DESIRE

## THE "DARK MADONNA" TRILOGY
## BOOK 1

**ELAINE MOORE**

**ibooks**
new york
**www.ibooks.net**

DISTRIBUTED BY SIMON & SCHUSTER, INC.

A Publication of ibooks, inc.

Copyright © 1999 Elaine Moore

Originally published under the title
*Madonna of the Dark: A Vampire Novel*

An ibooks, inc. Book

Distributed by Simon & Schuster, Inc.
1230 Avenue of the Americas, New York, NY 10020

ibooks, inc.
24 West 25th Street
New York, NY 10010

The ibooks World Wide Web Site Address is:
http://www.ibooks.net

ISBN 0-7434-7906-8
First ibooks, inc. printing March 2004
10 9 8 7 6 5 4 3 2 1

Printed in the U.S.A.

## Author's Notes

*Love is blood, it floods the heart*
*Need of it make the wishes start —*
*Wishes make the dreams begin,*
*In dreams we long for the flood again.*

—Ronald  Frazier

# Prologue

The whistle and crack of the whip rang out across the moor as the driver punished the horses mercilessly. In the distance a stone fortress rose out of the mist, crumbling ramparts clearly visible in dawn's paler gray, while night clung tenaciously round the base. But the close race between time and distance would mean nothing if fatigue should cut the legs from under one of the animals. Or the coach fail to withstand the punishment of the rutted track.

It had been a foolhardy decision to attempt the last leg of my journey without stopping. Even now, the sun rose over the mountain, rushing the world madly toward the hour I both loathed and grieved for.

An early spring had made our journey across the barren and desolate Highlands a nightmare. Traveling by night, and hiding the coach with its curious baggage by day had lowered me to such a degree of depravity I no longer felt the least bit human. A blackness bordering on oblivion threatened what little strength remained.

The coach skewed sharply to the left and slid to a halt. The door jerked and Rodrigo stood in the opening, black skin waxy in the near light. His hand on my wrist insisted I hurry.

Once outside the coach, the isolation was overwhelming. I staggered toward the lathered, heaving horses trembling in their traces and the stench of their pain washed over me, driving the splinter of need deeper into my heart.

Some strange compunction urged me to look back.

It was then I saw her. A wayward gypsy, astride a dappled gray mare, heavy red hair curling wildly about her face. She had ridden the mare hard for some distance, and I could hear both hearts pounding fiercely.

The sun charged the air at the top of the hill with brilliance, turning the last wisps of mist to rainbows, but nothing nature created dared compare with her beauty. The bloom of youth on fragile cheeks beguiled me. I watched, mesmerized, as the sun began its relentless march across the sky. Neither of us moved for an eternity. Then, abruptly she broke the spell, turning the horse and racing away. I, too, turned and limped up the short flight of steps to safety.

The days and nights that followed became one while I lay like a corpse in the grave. No single human traveled near enough to rouse me. On the third night I felt her presence again. Felt the sweet echo of her heartbeat calling me back from the brink of oblivion. Back to the only reality I knew. Blood calling to blood.

I knew I must have her—or cease to exist.

# Chapter One

"I swear to you, Duncan, he is not like other men."

Victoria MacKay stood in front of the black stallion her brother was grooming. The horse snorted and danced to the side. Squinting into the late afternoon sun, she reached up to gentle the restless animal. Victoria's flashing green eyes followed Duncan, daring him to go see for himself.

"If he wears breeches, little sister, he is like other men." Duncan smiled, glancing over to where she stood, feet firmly planted on rich Highland sod. The setting sun turned her hair to mahogany, streaking golden fire along a few loose strands. Fate might have brought her from their mother's womb first but she would always be his little sister. And if the outlander even glanced in her direction, his desire would indeed follow the same path all other men's had recently. She grabbed the rope halter and moved closer, looking up at him. He stood two inches above her but he knew she was capable of more than he could manage.

Duncan barely remembered their mother but the look on Victoria's face made him feel five-years-old again, seeing some secret fear on the sweet face that was as familiar as his own.

After their mother died, Angus MacKay had refused to let either of them out of his sight for years. They ate, drank, slept and went to war at his side.

For all her beauty, Victoria was tall for a woman and the training to weapons by Angus made her as fit as any man. She had taunted awkward, clumsy Duncan until his skills were as sharp as her own, but now her mother's gift of second sight warned this stranger should not be taken lightly.

"Just go with Moro and find out what he wants," she said. "Perhaps he's come to ask your hand in marriage, little sister. If you're not more willing to make a choice yourself, father might just favor marrying you off to an outlander." A wicked grin widened into a leer as he leaned toward her.

She punched him hard in the stomach. He remained standing but the grin vanished as he sucked for air.

"One day that tongue is going to get you killed and, if you're not careful, it might just be by me." She turned and strode away, one long braid swinging in time with her hips.

Duncan watched for a moment then grabbed a handful of mane and swung up on the horse. A quick nudge with his heel and he caught her.

"Victoria."

She continued across the hard-packed courtyard, straight for the entrance to the keep, chin stuck out like a battering ram.

"I'm sorry. I shouldn't have said that. I don't want you to get married. None of the men I know are good enough for you. They're like those rutting animals out there."

She stopped and looked up at him. "Oh, go on with you. All the men you know are boys like yourself. Love doesn't have to be like the barnyard for a man and a woman."

"You don't say? And which one of the kitchen girls might be telling you how it is?" He sat on the horse, legs dangling.

Victoria smiled and was rewarded with one in return. She crossed both arms under her breasts and shrugged. "I just haven't found anyone worth giving everything up for yet."

They moved across the bustling yard, horse and rider shadowing the red-haired girl.

"Will you go with us to speak to the outlander?" he asked.

She stopped and searched his puzzled face a moment. "No, Duncan. I must not." Victoria's ancient lineage of witches and long dead kings made her wary. Twice she had answered the summons. But darkness brought a command to obey that grew stronger with each passing night. Stomping away across the open courtyard, she swore he would have to come to her.

Duncan sat on his horse and stared at her arrogant retreat.

A full moon sat atop the craggy peak like a fiery opal. The vampire stood in the highest turret of the crumbling fortress feeling as ravaged by the centuries as his surroundings and watched for her shadow across the face of the glowing sphere. The spring breeze brushed his bare chest with a chill fingertip and soothed his scarred cheek. He didn't need a mirror to know the disfigurement was still visible.

It would be gone soon. Forever.

Stilling a compulsion to touch it, to compare it to the unspoiled cheek, he drew a dark cape close around a body weak from lack of nourishment.

*Tonight*. He savored the thought. *Tonight all her strength and beauty will flow in my veins*. His right hand strayed to the scar, caressed it lightly and stroked the dark moustache.

The sound of hooves in the distance reached his sensitive ears. Two, riding fast. *She is not alone. So much the better. Once my hunger is sated, I'll enjoy her offering even more.*

By the time the riders crested the hill, he knew it wasn't her. Two men, one young, one old, rode straight for the fortress, down the hillside and across the moor. He smiled and slipped quietly into the night to welcome his first guests.

The doors stood open and the vampire stepped out beside his body servant. The giant's skin gleamed wetly in the torch light, muscles rippling over the massive chest and arms.

Nikolai had found the young black boy in a Turkish hellhole a decade before, badly beaten. Some dark secret had been locked away when a previous owner cut out his tongue and left him for dead. In the beginning it was difficult to tell if he understood anything but the powerful body belied a quick mind. They worked with hand signs while his wounds healed and eventually Nikolai taught him to read and write. For lack of better understanding of his true name, Nikolai had christened him Rodrigo.

Now the look on his face said they were thinking the same thought. *Sacrifice, at last.*

The riders reined to a halt but neither moved to dismount. The younger of the two sat on a horse any man would kill to own. The powerful animal responded to a gentle pressure of knee signals, moving first right then left as the rider sought a better view. Nikolai stood in the shadows and took care to hide his scarred face.

"Who are you and how came you to be here?" the older man asked in soft burred English. The words were gentle enough but his left hand rested on the hilt of his broadsword.

"Johann Nikolai Valfrey." The vampire swept the cape aside to reveal his own weapon and bowed stiffly from the waist. "My—family has long held claim to this small corner of your country. I need fresh horses. Then I will be on my way to other more pleasant parts of the world."

The night wind gusted down the moor and set the torch dancing, pitching shadows across the ground at the feet of the horses. Warm blood so near sent a dagger of hunger slicing through the vampire's control. He stepped closer to the stallion and the flapping cape brushed a powerful shoulder. The horse backed away. Nikolai caught the bridle and looked directly into the boy's eyes. *This is blood of her blood. If I take him now, I will never have her.* Anger churned up from the pit of his need. The girl had found the strength to disobey his command.

The old man spoke harshly, drawing his attention from the boy. "If it's horses you seek, Angus MacKay may be willing to bargain. It's a long ride due north, but worthwhile." He turned his horse and, with a signal to his companion, galloped away.

The heartbeats diminished, blending with the thrum of hooves against turf, taking the vampire's anger away even as it did little to ease his desire.

"Well, Rodrigo. How shall we prepare for tomorrow evening? Is there still one shirt suitable for entertaining?"

Nikolai turned to go inside but the black man barred his path. With a low growl, Rodrigo raised a massive finger and touched the scarred cheek.

"Yes, my friend. Not quite a proper appearance for making a good first impression."

Nikolai pressed the hand close in a gesture of affection. Rodrigo had offered his own blood more than once, and though Nikolai needed his strength for other purposes, necessity demanded. The vampire's thin lips drew back, exposing enlarged incisors that sank easily into the tender flesh at the wrist. Rodrigo's heart raced, forcing blood into Nikolai's mouth faster than he could swallow. He staggered drunkenly as he broke away and saw his visitors silhouetted against the moonlight at the top of the hill.

Watching.

Nikolai moved a hand across the disfigured cheek. Not a trace of scar remained. He smiled, wiping blood from his chin as the Highlanders rode out of sight.


A week had passed since the vampire's arrival and this was his first encounter with the local inhabitants. The rest of the world was relatively civilized in the year 1570, but this Highland clan appeared to be a boorish, mauling tribe of illiterate drunks.

They sat at the many tables in the hall—one could hardly call it dining—in sheepskins and tattered woolens, screaming at each other in a language that lent itself well to profanities. Nikolai toyed with a horned flagon full of the potent brew they consumed.

Across the room, voices rose in jesting challenge, drawing an angry rebuke from the host's table. Nikolai had not formally

met Angus MacKay, but the most impressive man at the head
table must surely be the lord of the manor. Broad chested and
muscular, he wore the look of Viking kings, laughing loudly as
he slapped the table so hard the flagons shook. At his side sat
the only woman in the room, Nikolai's wild beauty.

A yellow-haired boy continued to taunt her, drawing his
sword foppishly as he advanced across the open space between
the trestles. The next moment Victoria stepped lightly to the
table top and leaped into the arena.

Her broadsword sang shrilly as it slipped from the scabbard,
silencing the crowd. She moved with confidence and grace, the
muscles in her upper arm tightening ever so little as she raised
the blade to point at her opponent's heart. He circled round her,
strutting prettily, cornsilk yellow hair floating off his shoulders
as his eyes ravished her.

Nikolai sat back and watched the battle begin.

The girl moved with assurance, handling the weapon like a
man. With both hands grasping the jeweled hilt, she hacked at
her opponent, once—twice. Here was no pampered princess but
a warrior queen fit to wed only the bravest and best. After some
teasing on the part of the yellow-haired lad, it became apparent
she was not playing. Suddenly forced to defend himself for real,
the ring of cold steel became a deadly counterpoint to the quick
shuffle of boots as he blocked her blows and tried to put her on
the defensive. But Victoria already had the upper hand. She
made short sport of him, swords clanging noisily, then floored
him with a booted foot behind his heel. Her victory resounded
around the room, the men hooting and pounding flagons on the
table tops. She put a foot on his heaving chest and nicked his
breast with the tip of her blade.

The would-be suitor lay on the floor in front of Nikolai,
blood welling from the small wound like an offering. Nikolai
watched the scarlet drops gather and pool like a precious gem
in the golden hair, very much aware she studied his every

move. His gaze traveled upward as she murmured a few unintelligible words.

Then she knelt. It was as though no one else in the room existed, just the two of them, warriors alone on some distant battlefield with one slain enemy. She lowered her lips to the gash and drank from the wound in the custom of all victors partaking of the blood of a vanquished foe. When she looked up, the tip of her tongue slowly swept her upper lip.

The conquered prince suddenly pulled her down, covering her bloody lips with his. The noisy throng intruded, banging flagons and weapons, egging him on as he rolled over and pinned her to the floor.

Across the way, three men rose together; Father, uncle and brother, warriors enough for any battle. But before they could advance, Nikolai stood to her rescue, saber drawn. Cold steel at the jugular dampened the loser's ardor quickly and when nudged with a booted foot he rolled to the side, rage contorting his handsome features. Nikolai offered his hand but Victoria rose without assistance.

The rough sheepskin vest she wore gaped open, and he swirled his cape round to cover her breast. She was breathing hard.

"You shall die a thousand deaths before dawn," Nikolai said in English, his saber tip still touching the prince's throat.

"Better you had died at her gentle hand," came a guttural growl from Angus MacKay. He spoke with a brogue so thick Nikolai could barely understand. "Count Valfrey," he said, acknowledging the vampire's presence at last.

Nikolai's saber shifted, allowing his prisoner to retreat. "Your Lordship," he said, deferring to Angus as the proven ruler of this small corner of the world.

The young woman had become very still.

"Unhand me," she whispered through clenched teeth. "Or I shall be forced to spill your blood, too."

Nikolai bowed slightly. "It would be my honor."

Victoria turned away without speaking and retrieved her sword. Angus and Nikolai watched her sheath the weapon and clutch at the torn vest before striding haughtily away.

"My daughter Victoria. I fear no man will ever prove worthy of her allegiance," Angus grumbled as she fled.

The tables had quickly emptied but Nikolai was aware of the chastised prince moving no further than camp just outside the fortress walls. There would be plenty of time to conclude his business here before attending to the brash young man.

"My kinsman tells me you have need for horses. What do you intend to use these animals for?" Angus asked.

They walked a circuit of the hall, ignoring the servants as they moved about, cleaning up.

"The horses, Lord MacKay, will be for pulling my coach. I would also like one for riding. I must soon travel far."

"I, too, have traveled. For many years with the court of the lady king and suffered much for it. I have learned it is better to remain at home with little than to have all the world could offer and no fine son or daughter."

"But what of your children? Do you not wish for them a larger world than you know?"

"My children do as they will. I have no fear, when I'm gone, they will continue to do as they please. I have taught them to be strong of body and of will. That should see them through most any hardship."

"I have no wish to be on the receiving end of Victoria's sword," Nikolai replied.

"A wise choice. And how will you pay for your horses?"

"How would you have me pay? I have gold coin. I have knowledge to pass on to others. Or I could simply do you a favor." Nikolai watched the old man's face for signs of betrayal.

"You would like the young pup punished? Give me one

gold coin and the insolent whelp before dawn, and you shall have your pick of my animals." Angus stopped walking and turned to face him. "You are not a man I would cross, Count Valfrey. I prefer to know when my back is turned you would be there to protect it. I will deal fairly with you if you do so with me."

"You have my word." Nikolai reached into a pocket and withdrew a newly minted coin. He bowed stiffly from the waist, tossed the gold piece to Angus and turned to leave.

"By dawn," the Scotsman growled.

The arrogant youth was camped nearby. Nikolai stood a moment, observing. Tents erected close with the restless horses tethered in the center gave a semblance of security.

Sounds of laughter and drunken revelry drifted from a large tent halfway round the line. The stupidity of youth had not even posted a guard. Not that it would have made a difference.

The vampire reached out and found the yellow-haired youth. In the middle of the entertainment, Ian MacLeod sat alone, brooding and drinking. Nikolai couldn't keep from smiling. An outrageous boy with black dreams of punishment.

*I shall give him a taste of his own cruelty*, Nikolai thought. He entered the camp, darkness spreading as he passed. On either side campfires burned, flames leaping high without lighting his path. Behind him the night swallowed everything, horses, dogs, the sounds of revelry. Time stretched out slowly, each moment an eternity until Nikolai reached the central tent.

Inside, carnage lay heaped around MacLeod's feet. Nikolai faced him down as the tent filled with smoke, creating a shadow world where tormented spirits writhed and dead brothers whispered.

Nikolai drew the boy close as he began to shake. "You think to punish me? For protecting a rare treasure from plunder? You who despoil all you touch? You are unworthy to clean her boots." The body continued to shake but the eyes were already dead.

"You are about to outlive your usefulness, little prince."

Ian MacLeod's body convulsed as the vampire wrapped both arms about his shoulders, much like a lover's embrace. There had been a time when blonde boys such as this appealed to Nikolai, but even now, ready for this kill, his mind overflowed with thoughts of Victoria. This beast deserved to die for merely having touched her. Hot blood gushing fed his frenzy. The vampire ripped at the boy until his passion had been sated as well as his hunger.

Nikolai released the body and it fell heavily to the floor. With one quick jerk he tore off the head and holding it by the long, now white hair, carried it away.

Outside, the entire campsite had been devastated, horses lay mutilated, twisted and torn as if by wolves. Dead men sprawled in a parody of battlefield postures. Nikolai walked amongst the debris and felt very satisfied. Cloaked in darkness, he slipped past Angus MacKay's watchful sentry into the fortress and found Victoria's room. He watched her sleep in dreamless innocence and cursed himself for not being a man.

Nikolai left her tucked in her virginal bed and moved down the hall to Angus' quarters. He walked unnoticed past the alert bodyguard and stepped over the sleeping body servant.

"My word," he whispered, dropping the MacLeod's head in the chamber pot. Then he leapt toward a high slit in the wall, dark wings swirling outward as he took flight, confident the Highlander would see his offering the moment he woke.

## Chapter Two

Victoria stood near the south tower while the men in her family looked out over the ravaged camp.

Moro leaned against the parapet. "You best do something about the remains. The stench will be unbearable."

Angus stalked back and forth.

"I never heard a sound, Father," Duncan said.

"I tried to warn you. No one listened," Victoria whispered. She gazed out over the verdant meadow. Gray heather just beginning to tinge purple brought no easy smile to her lips. Blood ran in the meadow as the day grew dark around her. The paralyzing scenes of the past evening played over again in her mind.

Victoria stared into the darkness and chewed her lip to hold back the terror. The moment she touched the MacLeod, she knew. Saw his past, watched him stab his brother a hundred times, witnessed this battle, and welcomed his death at the hands of the outlander. Victoria shuddered as blood filled her mouth but the sudden pain dissolved her vision. The walkway was deserted.

*How do I dare explain? Father will never understand what it's like to see and feel so much in a single moment.* Victoria had done a good job of avoiding personal contact all her life, and it had been a long lonely time.

The bustle in the courtyard drew her to the rail. Broken tents and human and animal remains were gathered and doused with pitch. The sickly sweet smell of charring flesh mingled with the stench of burning hair and horse hide. Victoria leaned over the rail and gagged. Angus walked slowly toward the fire, carrying the chamberpot that always stood by his bed. She turned away just as he swung the bucket high into the fire.

Duncan looked up from the dirty work of destruction to see Victoria ride out of the castle. He watched the dappled gray mare race across the meadow and disappear into the distance.

"Open! Open at once!" Victoria pounded on the iron bound door. "Open, I command you!" She raised both fists and brought them crashing down against the heavy wood.

The door swung inward silently. She strode forward, stopping when the servant stepped out of the darkness to block her path.

"Where is your master? If I must search all day, I'll find him."

The black giant placed a massive hand on her shoulder. A wave of agony and despair washed over Victoria, threatening to buckle her knees. She twisted away and drew her sword.

"Do not touch me!" She stood ready to defend herself if he tried again but he stepped back and dropped his arms.

"Merciful Jesus, did Nikolai do that to you? How could any man punish even a beast in such a manner?"

He shook his head.

"Take me to him. I mean him no harm." Victoria sheathed her weapon. "The MacLeod deserved to die."

She spoke slowly, eager for the servant to understand. He turned and walked away. Down the hall, he opened the door to an inner chamber and stood aside for her to enter. A single torch on the far wall flickered in the draft.

On a raised bier stood an ornate wooden casket. Victoria stepped inside the crypt and walked around the coffin. Its polished surface reflected her face like a dark mirror. She reached out, slipping her fingers along the cold, hard surface.

"Open it," she said, her voice whisper-thin in the silence.

Rodrigo moved to do her bidding, touched the catch and stepped back, allowing the lid to rise of its own accord.

Even the ruddy glow from the torch could not disguise his pallor. Nikolai lay in the casket like one recently dead, awaiting the first clods of soil to descend. But Victoria knew there was no truth in what she saw. Here lay a creature who hunted the night like a stalking animal, but had the tender mercy to rescue one almost beyond hope. Duncan spoke of seeing him drink blood. She gazed at his face. A hint of a smile caressed his thin lips and softened the harsh line of jaw. She actually wanted to reach out and touch him but her fear was suddenly different. More than just fear of knowing what future awaited him or what past had led him to this place. She was afraid for herself. Turning quickly, she bolted out the door.

The dark plume of smoke drifted north on the evening breeze. Victoria saw it long before the stench reached her. The mare had pulled up lame, the pain touching Victoria with remorse for treating the animal so poorly. She had no thought these days for anything but that man. So she dismounted and walked, leading the mare home. It would be hours before they got to familiar territory, but it didn't matter.

They reached the top of a rise and stopped. The setting sun created a play of light and shadow across the valley below. The stillness of twilight struck a lonely chord in her heart. Her self-imposed exile had lasted so long. She wanted, desperately needed, a touch of affection from someone. Suddenly the warrior princess was simply a young woman carrying a big burden. The landscape dimmed as her eyes filled with tears.

"Victoria." His soft whisper could have been the evening breeze. "I know what it is you seek."

The last rays of red faded to purple and rose. A shadow formed and Nikolai reached out a gloved finger to lift her chin. He looked into her eyes and gave her a glimpse of himself. Standing before a roaring fireplace, jeweled goblet in hand.

Alone and lonely.

Justly so, a true picture. A long lonely life his last one had been. This new one would be different. He removed the soft leather glove and cupped her chin in his hand. His lips brushed hers like the night shadows caressed the valley far below. And he filled her mind and heart with his love and passion. They stood together in a room filled with soft light. He dressed in white tie and tails, she gowned in scarlet silk, hair piled high in a mass of curls. He stroked her bare shoulders with his fingers as his lips slipped to the nape of her neck. Victoria turned trembling into his embrace, allowing herself to be wrapped in his darkness.

The hoarse baying of dogs echoed across the valley. Nikolai raised his lips from Victoria's neck. He sensed Duncan's approach in pursuit of the hounds.

He embraced her once again and whispered, "Not yet, my princess. We have all the time in the world."

Victoria opened her eyes to find herself alone. By the time Duncan arrived, her tears had dried and only a vague disquieting memory remained.

# Chapter Three

Moro approached the forge where Angus stood working, naked to the waist, sweat running off his powerful shoulders.

"The outlander finds no pleasure in our company. He sent the heathen to fetch his horses," Moro said.

"Good. Now the man has no reason to remain." Angus drew the short sword from the fire, placed it on the anvil and struck it repeatedly and plunged the glowing steel into a barrel of dark water. Clouds of steam rose, hissing around his face.

"Is it true the heathen has no tongue? Sometimes Victoria regales me with stories I find most difficult to believe. Where does she get all those strange notions?"

"It's true, Angus. But he knows what he wants and communicates that quite well. We may have a fight on our hands. He wants Duncan's stallion."

Angus put the broadsword aside and followed Moro into the courtyard, where a fair number of men stood around the corral, ordinary tasks forgotten as they watched Duncan work. Four fine animals already cut from the herd waited. Duncan stood between the black man and the black stallion, one hand on his dagger.

"Rodrigo!" Victoria shouted.

The body servant turned toward the gate where Victoria strode between the horses.

"No!"

Rodrigo walked away from Duncan without a glance and mounted one of the horses. She handed him the leads and he rode swiftly away.

Duncan caught up to her before she reached the castle. "Why do you do that? You make me look a fool." Anger burned in his red face and harsh words.

"You *are* a fool if you think to defeat Rodrigo. He has powers on his side you could never dream of owning." She walked beside him as he made no attempt to conceal his anger.

"And are you more powerful than I because he obeys you? What does that gain?"

She stopped and whirled to face him, suddenly very sad to see him so reckless. "Yes! Yes, I am more powerful, but it gains me nothing. You must learn to use your wits. I will not always be here to think for you and my going will be for nothing if you do not learn from it."

The anger and frustration left his face, replaced by a look of puzzlement.

"You speak as though the world will end, Victoria. I believe you will find that untrue. Marriage cannot be all that bad no matter the tales you have heard from the kitchen girls."

Victoria walked on in silence. In her heart she hoped Duncan could be right. Count Valfrey had touched her yet she could remember only pleasant visions.

Inside the castle, Victoria passed through the kitchen. Preparations for the evening meal were well underway, and she felt his presence. She turned from the roasting spit, expecting to see the Count standing behind her. A fleeting vision of herself dressed in a scarlet gown swirled through her mind, leaving her breathless. She glanced down at the tight leather breeches, and smoothed the front of her coarse woven shirt. She ran a hand through tangled hair.

*I have nothing to wear but men's clothing,* she thought. "Anne, have you a chemise and kirtle I could wear?"

The cook's daughter turned from her duties, a look of surprise brightening her face. "Whatever for? You never cared to wear a dress before, if you don't mind my saying."

"Just get me something now and be quick. I'll turn the spit."

"You'd best come with me so I can show you how to arrange it. Seeing you've never had one on before."

Both girls raced to Anne's room and then up the back stairs, laughing and giggling. Once in her room, Victoria threw off her clothes while Anne shook out the creamy white garments.

"Heaven forbid, Victoria. You've no breasts at all. It'll hang on you like a sack."

Victoria dropped long slip over her head. It hung so low it revealed more than the cleavage of her small, firm breasts. She stepped into the skirt and twisted while Anne wrapped the waist with a matching girdle, drawing the sash tight.

"Your father's plaid will be just the thing to hide your lack of bosom."

Victoria ran barefoot down the hallway to Angus' quarters. Muffled voices floated up the stairs from where her father and Moro greeted the Count. She could almost see Duncan standing in the wings, unsure of himself and what to do next.

Her father's heavy English chest held a wealth of clothing, including a dark green tartan with black bands and narrow yellow stripe. The heavy Tara brooch sparkling with rubies would be the finishing touch. Lifting her skirts, she hurried back to where Anne waited, hairbrush in hand. Victoria sighed. *Why didn't I just go to dinner the way I always look?*

She sat on the narrow bed while Anne brushed and pulled and tugged and twisted at the mass of wild curls.

"Heaven help us, Victoria, but you are a pretty girl." Anne reached out and hugged her. Without thinking, Victoria returned the embrace. Happiness overwhelmed her. She could barely see the blue skies and bright sunshine of the vision through her tears.

The two girls were chattering away when they reached the top of the stairs and the men glanced up at them. Anne crossed herself, rushing away when she saw the dark forbidding figure standing with the men, leaving Victoria to continue alone.

Angus and Moro simply stared, speechless at the change a dress made.

Nikolai met her at the bottom of the stone stairs. "Allow me," he insisted.

Victoria looked at him and saw blue eyes in a face so pale it had quite likely never seen the light of day. A dark moustache adorned his thin upper lip. Her gaze dropped to his extended hand, the long fingers deceptively fragile. She reached out and placed her hand on top of his—and was drawn into a moonlit night, all fear swept away by a warm breeze brushing her bare shoulders as she looked into the face of love. Smiling, they led the others in to supper.

"You cannot have my horse," Duncan said quietly, "but I'll give you a bargain. I'll find one such as he and break him for you. It'll be easier than parting with my own. You'll be wanting to train him to your touch for the finer points of horsemanship."

"It seems a fair pledge, Duncan. When will you begin? And how long will it take?"

Nikolai felt the shield of protection Victoria placed around her brother, stronger here in this place of their past togetherness. He no longer desired to breech that security. Once he had her the others would not matter.

Now that her seduction had begun, he eagerly sought its end. Then Victoria would be with him for eternity. The anticipation of her surrender brought a smile to his lips even as Duncan set the time limit for his commitment.

"A week to find the right horse and another to break him."

Angus finally found his voice. "That seems a short time to accomplish so much, son. Are you sure you can handle it?"

"When I set my mind to something, nothing can stand in my way, Father."

Moro spoke in an effort to lighten the mood around the table. "That's true, boy. You can be very stubborn on some points."

Their unexpected guest had spent the entire meal staring at Victoria, never touching the food, as though he fed on her beauty. Heavy tapestries softened the sound of their voices echoing off stone walls, making the small dining room much too intimate for such entertaining. Candlelight reflecting off the richly woven colors cast thin delicate shadows in which Moro could see the ghost of his long dead sister moving between Angus and Duncan. And each time he turned to address Victoria, it was as though she were already gone, she and the Count moving together as one. Moro didn't need a witch to tell him he would end this night drunk. His visions now most likely came from the amount he had already consumed.

"The hour is late. I must go. Lord MacKay, see that your son delivers on his pledge. Two weeks will be adequate time for my plans." Nikolai rose, bowed at the waist and lifted Victoria's fingers to his lips. *Soon, my sweet warrior, very soon I shall have you,* he promised.

No one accompanied him to the door and, after a moment, only Victoria was sure he had even been there.


The next four days passed in a flurry of excitement as Duncan made good his promise. The extraordinary horse was black as sin and possessed the devils own temperament. One could almost imagine it breathed fire. It took five men to subdue the creature and most times it acted like a demon straight out of hell. One man died, face and chest crushed by the flying hooves that wounded another before they reached the crumbling fortress.

Duncan's arrangements to stable the horse there, so Nikolai could take part in its training, fit splendidly with the vampire's plans. Angus had thought it another of Victoria's whims when she insisted on being at the campsite while Duncan worked the wild creature but he believed there was substance to her madness. He gave his permission finally, considering perhaps her presence would protect the boy from some scrape or another.

Victoria stood at the rail of a makeshift corral watching a dirty, haggard Duncan trying to stay on the bucking, stallion. Just when he brought the animal around to his way of doing things, the horse would send him flying into the air and he would start over again.

The sun lay well past its zenith when Victoria sensed the Count's awakening. Shutting her eyes to the clouds of dust and flying hooves in the corral, she allowed her inner sight to penetrate the room where he lay. No torch lit the crypt today, none was needed as Nikolai moved through the darkness. One hinge squeaked softly as he moved out into the brighter hall.

The harsh neighing of the stallion brought her attention back to the corral as Duncan wheeled the animal into a tight turn. The horse went down on its right fore leg as though kneeling before her then rolled to the side, pinning Duncan. The demon steed rolled back to its feet instantly. Duncan lay deathly still in the trampled dirt. Victoria slipped through the fence, her only thought to protect him from the fury of flashing hooves.

A shadow flowed past her, silent as a memory of moonless nights and those who hunt to survive. Then Nikolai stood before the rearing horse. A black cape hung loosely from the vampire's neck. One white sleeved arm reached out and a gloved hand caught the halter. The horse snorted and stamped but made no further move to attack. Victoria could hear Nikolai's whispers but could make no sense of the words.

"Dark one. Meet your master and obey." Nikolai released the halter and turned back to where Victoria stood between her fallen brother and the horse. And him. Rage burned bright in her eyes. Her posture spoke of carefully controlled fury.

"The boy will be all right. Allow me to help." Nikolai

stepped past her and knelt beside Duncan. "Rodrigo! Inside!"

The servant lifted Duncan. Nikolai hurried ahead, leaving Victoria to follow.

With a last malevolent look at the horse, she turned and rushed inside. She could hear them moving through the stronghold, down an unlighted hallway that grew darker with each step. Outside twilight still reigned, but here daylight had capitulated to dark of night. Victoria hesitated and turned in a circle. Completely disoriented, she shut her eyes and screamed.

"Duncan!"

Nikolai appeared, standing by a door, torch in hand.

"In here." He moved about, lighting torches until the narrow room trembled with a ruddy glow and flickering shadows.

"You need a brandy and I have none to offer. Accept my word of reassurance instead. Your brother is not injured badly. The leg is broken. Rodrigo is acquainted with such damage but I must assist him as he sets the bone."

"I would see my brother. Now!"

"As you wish." Nikolai moved quickly across the room and threw open a door. Victoria followed and saw Duncan lying on a narrow table, Rodrigo ripping the torn britches. The exposed leg was bruised and swollen. Rodrigo made a sharp sound deep in his throat. Nikolai handed her the torch and moved to pinion the upper thigh. Rodrigo grasped Duncan's foot and ankle, pulling as he twisted.

Victoria heard the grate of bones slipping back into place but could do nothing but watch while Rodrigo's huge hands gently bound the leg between two heavy pieces of wood.

She turned toward Nikolai. He spoke before she could ask.

"I have seen many such wounds. It is necessary to allow the bone to heal before putting weight on the leg. Rodrigo will prepare a potion to dull his senses and let him sleep. When he wakes the worse will be over."

"I must let my father know. He will send help." She moved

closer and looked down at her brothers' face. She didn't have to touch Duncan to know the agony he felt.

Nikolai took her hand.

"I will send a message. And Duncan will rest easier if you are here." *And I will fare much better if we are alone without the meddling of old fools and young boys.*

She watched Rodrigo lift Duncan's head and urge him to drink. Then she stepped willingly into Nikolai's embrace, eager to forget Duncan's pain in the gentle rain of kisses falling on her face. She stood quietly as his touch eased the all too real agony and filled her with more immediate longings.

"Take me away, Nikolai. Take me to a world where I no longer need fear the touch of others."

Nikolai's body tensed. He pushed her away and held her at arm's length. "Oh, no, my sweet warrior. You will not come to me to hide from yourself. You must want what I have to give with all your body and soul. No faint-hearted maiden could ever exist by my side, for our passion will be like the fury of battle. Devastation will ride in our wake. The entire world will provide for our amusement."

Then he vanished, his words leaving an ache in Victoria's heart like the bruises his fingers left on her shoulders.

# Chapter Four

Victoria spent the night curled in a corner of the narrow room, afraid to leave and yet afraid no one would come to their rescue. Only Duncan could dispel her fear, and he lay on the cot in a stupor.

She woke to brilliant sunlight streaming through a slit in the wall. Duncan lay propped on one elbow, watching her.

"Duncan, are you well?" She moved to the cot. "Do you need anything?"

"No, sister. My leg hurt like the promise of eternal damnation, but whatever the heathen gave me to drink took me beyond the point of caring." His eyes had a dull, glazed look, and he fell back on the bed.

"It's true. Nikolai said that would be the way. You'll be up to traveling in a few days if he sent for Father."

Duncan stretched out a hand, but she stepped beyond his reach. "Victoria. Be careful. I think the Count means you harm."

She smiled to hide her own misgivings. "Haven't I always been able to handle men?" She tried to face him and couldn't.

"You said yourself this one is different."

Victoria turned away and started for the door. "I'm going to see to the horses."

"Have a care, will you?" he called as she hurried out.

Victoria labored and sweated her way through the morning. She tossed hay to the Count's animals as well as hers and Duncan's, and carried water from the well across the courtyard to the stable. The hot still air and exercise dulled her senses. She welcomed the distraction from thoughts of herself dressed in fine gowns and the excitement of Nikolai's touch.

By mid-afternoon the combined foes of hunger and fatigue

defeated her. The battle of body over mind forced her to retreat to the dim, musty barn in search of food. Trembling limbs compelled her to rest as she rummaged through her near empty pack. With a stringy piece of dried meat in hand, she lay back in the hay, too tired to chew.

It was there the Count found her. A night breeze cooled the sweat on her body. Victoria shivered and opened her eyes. A single torch burning at the door cast a frail halo about the opening. Nikolai knelt in the hay beside her, clothed in a glow that had no connection to the ruddy light. He raised her hand to his lips and kissed her palm.

Victoria shivered and moaned softly. He released her hand and the soft blue imprint of his fingers and lips remained. He leaned down and traced the edge of her jaw with one finger, leaving a sliver of glowing residue all the way from her hairline down the neck to her breast. She moved to embrace him but he forced her back into the hay, his lips whispering against hers. For the merest moment, Nikolai savored the soft sweet warmth of her mouth. Then his lips moved to the hollow of her throat, where the salty taste of sweat teased him almost to distraction. The thin shirt she wore ripped easily at his touch. He followed the pounding vein in her throat with his lips and as his kiss caressed her breast, sharp incisors sank into the tender flesh.

*Just a taste of what eternity at my side will provide for both of us, my sweet.* Nikolai filled her mind with a vision of the two of them rolling in the hay, bodies joined in a lusty hunger. But the degree of his own desire stunned him, left him drowning in need. Not in all his long memory had he known anything like this wondrous creature. Her fingers in his hair pressed his lips to her breast and he wanted nothing more than to drink his fill now, to know the secret joy of having her so totally she would belong to him forever.

Reluctantly, he drew back. Now was not the time. Too much remained to be done.

Victoria woke. Nikolai knelt in the hay beside her, one hand resting lightly on her shoulder.

"You've been gone a long time. Duncan is quite agitated."

The torch still burned at the door behind him. She sat up too quickly and her vision clouded as the world tilted. She raised a hand to steady her head. A hand that held a piece of jerky.

"What's this?" he asked, taking it from her. "Food? Did you not eat today?"

"I—the heat—asleep. Dreaming. . . ."

Nikolai leaned forward, slipped his arms under her legs and shoulders, and lifted her.

Victoria put her arms around his neck. The dream had left her with a yearning she couldn't explain. A need to be close, to be held in his arms forever.

Nikolai kicked open the door and carried her toward the room where Duncan lay. "Rodrigo. Get food."

"What's wrong? Victoria?" Duncan clenched his fists. "What have you done to her?"

"Open your mouth, please, and tell the young fool you just forgot to eat." Nikolai set her down quickly by the cot.

She stood on trembling legs and spoke. "It was very hot in the stable and I fell asleep. I'll be fit as soon as I've eaten."

"Well, whatever you were about, you're dirty enough, and you've torn your shirt." Duncan's anxiety for her safety turned to a pout. "Father will be here soon. You'd best not let him see you like that."

All Victoria could think about was the smell of rabbit done to a turn. "I don't care what Father sees, I'm starving."

"Your supper awaits," Nikolai said, offering his arm. He led her off into the darkness, leaving Duncan alone with his misery.

Victoria sat at a crude wooden table in a kitchen that contained only the barest necessities. "I have never been so hungry." She tore meat from the bones with her fingers and ate greedily. Wiping her mouth with the back of a hand, she drank from a flagon by her plate and set it down with a thud.

"Milk! Do you have nothing more to drink?"

"Only water and that barely fit for bathing." Nikolai sat across from her, a smile playing about his lips from time to time as she consumed the meager meal. "Would you like a bath, now that your immediate needs are sated?"

"Am I such a sight?" She looked down at the torn shirt.

"You are the most beautiful woman in the world." Nikolai leaned across the table and looked into her eyes. "Our brief interlude today was but a taste of what we can have together, should you so decide."

She touched his hand where it lay on the table.

"I can see the future and the past with a single touch. It has always been most frightening. Until now. Until you." She took his hand in both of hers. "My father speaks of marriage, of babes and knows not why I hesitate. He knows not that a brave front is my only protection from myself." She drew Nikolai's hand to her lips and kissed the fingertips.

"I have no fear with you. I see only love and feel only tenderness. And now, this hunger that fills me with a longing I know only you can satisfy." She reached out and pressed her fingers to his cheek. It created a curious sensation in her heart, to use so casually a gesture that had always caused pain.

Nikolai stroked her hand then pulled away. "It is a flame, which once kindled, will burn forever. A raging inferno destined to consume all who grow intimate with you. But you must not come to me without knowledge." He rose, moving away from the table to stand by the hearth.

"Love does not come easily to me. I had not thought to even recognize it, but this must be love." He stared into the leaping flames. "I want you beside me. Forever. So you must understand what I am. Only then can you make the decision to join me."

The bench scraped against the floor as she rose from the

table. Even greater than the fire, the warmth of her body thrilled him as she stood close.

"I have heard tales of men who would not die." Her whispered words were like shouts in his ear. "Men who have a peculiar aversion to sunlight, sleep in coffins and drink the blood of those who serve them."

"I am such a man. My memory serves as far back as the days before the one men call Christ. I was immortal even then. I carried the cipher when Alexander commissioned his beloved city on the sea." Nikolai turned to face her. "I walked the road to Golgotha behind Jesus, saw His blood drip on the dust but even His blood could not make me a man again."

Nikolai placed his hands on Victoria's shoulders. She didn't flinch as her mind filled with his memories. A warrior plundering captive cities at the side of a golden haired man. A beggar in torn and tattered rags, standing in the shadows watching a screaming mob follow the cross up a hill to redemption. A knight in bright armor beside the Red Lion rampant, broadsword stained with the blood of a thousand infidels. Always a man alone.

Nikolai looked deep into her eyes and saw no anger or hate.

"I still remember the first time I came to drink blood. It began as a ritual, the victor partaking of the blood of his slain enemy in order to become stronger, more valiant. For a long time afterwards, I still functioned as a man. I walked in sunlight and ate red meat like those around me." Nikolai released her and walked to the door. His voice became harsh.

"Then came the day I met a foe mightier than all I had ever encountered. The carnage stretched as far as the eye could see across a battlefield. The enemy left me wounded. Dying. As the sun sank westward into oblivion, I fought a darkness I took to be death." He heard her swift intake of breath but didn't turn to face her.

"Some time later I awoke to the smell of fresh blood. My

nemesis walked alone on the battlefield, decapitating those few still living. I lay like one dead until he passed by, choosing the man moaning beside me. He took his head with one swift blow and tossed it away, allowing the blood of my fallen comrade to fall like rain on the parched desert of my face. Then I died—again."

He was silent for so long Victoria moved to the door and stood watching him. He stared up at the stars, as though puzzling out the patterns they created. She made no move to touch him, sensing some new and even more horrendous revelation.

"I woke to agony. The sun had completed its journey through hell and its rising brought forth an even more deadly enemy. The skin began to melt from my bones. The only shelter I could divine was beneath me, so I buried myself in the earth."

Victoria didn't need to touch him to know his pain. With eyes squeezed tight, she exhaled deeply and leaned against the door frame. She folded cold arms across her breasts like a shield, but her mind had become an enemy she could not flee.

"Nightfall brought renewed strength and I roused from my grave to search for food and water. My hearing and vision were unnaturally acute. I could smell campfires and hear muffled noises. The closer I got, the louder the noises became. A thousand heartbeats hammered inside my head. A distance that would have normally taken hours to cover passed in a blur. I swooped down upon the campsite unnoticed. They were all sleeping. The noise I heard was indeed heartbeats—man and animal—thundering against my senses to the point of madness. I found the tent of the commander and entered. No one could see me. As I stood by his bed, he woke, and to prevent his challenge of alarm, I took him by the throat and squeezed." Nikolai raised his hands and stared at the clenched the fists.

"I can still feel my hands closing around his neck. It was the first time I ever took another's life except in battle. I tore open his throat and drank. The hot liquid seared my throat like raw alcohol. My hands and forearms healed instantly. I left the tent and stood for a moment, sensing the wind. Then dropped on all fours and moved away through the camp, stampeding horses and rousing sleeping soldiers. I'm sure they blamed their commander's death on the lone wolf everyone saw."

Nikolai turned to face her. Tears glistening on her cheeks shimmered in the bright starlight. "My travels have taken me in diverse directions. I believe it was all meant to bring me here, now. To reach you, the one woman destined to share eternity with me. To share my life forever."

Victoria moved into his welcoming embrace. When she could finally speak, her whispered words were resolute.

"What's done is done and we cannot change it. But the future is ours to shape as we will. I want to be a part of your future. I swear to you, there will be no more loneliness. I will share everything with you." She held him close and saw only what he wanted her to see. The exotic places he spoke of and none of the harsh cruelty of death for survival's sake.

Nikolai returned her embrace and smiled.

## Chapter Five

"Victoria! For the love of Christ, girl, where are you?"

Angus MacKay's deep voice echoed down the dark hall. The heavy tread of boots and rattle of weapons filled the small space as he and Moro rushed into the kitchen.

From inside the dark kitchen only one shadow was visible against the starry night. Victoria's head lay cradled against the curve of the Count's shoulder. His arms wrapped around her.

"Angus, I don't believe the outlander means her harm." Moro sheathed the short sword he held.

Steel rasping against leather broke the reverie. Victoria raised her head to look at her father and uncle. The dim light from the fireplace cast deep shadows about their faces. For the first time in her life, she saw them old and vulnerable.

"Victoria, would you care to tell your poor father what this is about?" Angus put his own weapon away and stood quietly.

Victoria took Nikolai's hand and led him toward her father. A tender moment passed as she looked from one man to the other. Then she reached out and hugged Angus. A great sadness welled up from within him, but she dismissed it, unwilling to have her own happiness over-shadowed.

"I want your daughter for my own, Lord MacKay."

Angus straightened his shoulders, gently pushing Victoria aside.

"As do most of the men within a fortnight's ride. Have you nothing more to add, sir?"

"Father, I do love this man."

"Hush, girl. Let the Count speak for himself." Moro moved to the table and propped a foot on the bench. "Let's get on with this. It's been a long ride and I'm weary. Besides, someone really should put Duncan out of his misery. And soon."

"See to your brother, girl. Moro and I will tend to this."

With a last glance at the three of them, Victoria moved down the hall to where Duncan lay moaning and tossing about. A flush of fever colored his face.

"Don't go, little sister. I beg you, do not go."

Victoria's cool hand to his brow quieted the tossing and turning. Some inner alarm died as he sensed her return from the far away, unreachable place of his mind to his bedside.

"Just a touch of fever, Duncan. It'll be gone by morning."

Beads of sweat glistened on his brow. Strong fingers grasped hers when she reached for the hand dangling off the bed. The face she stared into was so much like her own. Torches guttered and flared in the long room, and in that moment she watched him mature gracefully into a man. The comfort he found in the arms of a lovely dark-eyed woman brought an end to some long period of grief. The sun warmed the world the day he became the father of two fine sons and a harsh winter punished men and animals as he survived a battle in a country she did not know. He gave up the land he loved only to find the sea an unsatisfying mistress. Victoria saw the daughter of his old age grow up in her own image. The young woman knelt at his bedside, just as she did now, a tender look on her face when he died calling her Victoria.

Victoria placed the hand she held across his chest and leaned against his shoulder for a moment. A lifetime of love and strength flowed into that simple touch. She realized she would likely never see him again.

Moro stood in the doorway and watched the ghost of his dead sister hover about her children. The pain she radiated tormented him but he had learned long ago what it was like to be helpless in the face of fate. She turned and beckoned him to enter before fading away.

"Victoria, do you truly mean to wed this man?" he asked.

"I do," she answered.

"And nothing short of imprisonment will hold you back?"

"Even death will not keep me from this love, Moro." She rose to stand before him.

"Then your Father and I have no choice but to agree to the arrangement. All that's left is the marriage settlement— "

"There will be no marriage settlement." Nikolai interrupted as he and Angus entered the room. "I would have Victoria with me without delay and with as little fuss as possible. Though I have little here, riches wait in my own country."

"Am I to be allowed no word in this matter?" Victoria asked. "I know that marriage proposals move slowly in the Church and I, too, wish to have this done quickly. Could we not have the ceremony in the old way, Father? Would that not please you?" Victoria moved away from her family and stood beside Nikolai.

"The Church does not recognize the old ceremonies as lawful, but I will accept it if that is what you want. It must still be done proper. We'll set the time a month from now," Angus said.

"Two weeks, Father. Two weeks is time enough." Victoria moved closer to Nikolai and put an arm around his waist. Angus took a step as though to separate them but Moro placed a hand on his shoulder.

"It's settled then. Tomorrow we leave for home. Journey with us if you will, Count," Moro said, closing the matter.

"I have duties here," Nikolai said, "perhaps when all is in order." He leaned toward Victoria and whispered in her ear. "Come to me at dawn, my love." He bowed slightly and left the four of them together.

Rodrigo had brought in their meager supplies. Moro stomped about the room, kicking at the blankets and cursing.

"The Count's hospitality leaves a great deal to be desired."

He grabbed up a blanket and started for the door. "My old bones cannot take a night on these cold stones. I'll sleep with the horses, if you don't mind."

"And where did you sleep last night, girl?" Angus asked.

Victoria drew her attention from the doorway and spoke.

"In that corner, father. With less comfort than you have tonight. Not even a blanket to warm my cold bed."

The disapproving hardness in his face melted as she watched. She wanted to go to him, to reassure him, but her courage failed. Instead she turned to the cot where Duncan slept. The fever was gone. A soft snore escaped his parted lips.

So like a child while sleeping. The dark-eyed woman who would share his bed made Victoria smile. She knew his passion lay just below the surface of innocence. Waiting, like her own had been, for the right touch to wake it.

"It's late, Father and tomorrow will be long. I'm afraid we'll find little comfort here for either of us." She covered Duncan with a blanket and took one to the corner she claimed for herself.


Victoria sat up and looked about. It seemed barely a moment had passed but the feeble light from a small crescent moon puddled near her feet. She loosened her hair. Without the heavy braid, she stood light and free and moved dreamily through the patch of moonlight into darkness. Traveling blindly down the hall, the invitation of an open door took her into the inner chamber she now knew well. She hesitated a moment at the threshold. Then Nikolai spoke.

His soft words held the promise of heaven and hell. "Come, my sweet." He lay in the coffin, a faint smile curving his lips.

Victoria slipped in beside him, resting her head on his shoulder.

Nikolai shivered, trembling under the warm burden of her

body. The vampire buried his face in the cascade of her hair as the coffin lid silently closed on the rest of the world.

The sun boldly rose in the sky. The heat of its passion burned away the shroud of mist. Spring was fast passing into summer, the time to harvest the tender fruit of carefully cultivated vines.

Victoria waited astride the dappled gray mare while the men propped Duncan against blankets piled in the wagon. The journey would be rougher for all the care they would take to go slowly. An hour's journey by fast horse would take all day at the pace her father intended to set. Figuring her young body would suffer less in the wagon, she had offered to drive but Angus refused.

The dark pall of the evening was gone. Even Duncan appeared in high spirits. The Count had not made his presence known and everyone, including Rodrigo, seemed at ease in his absence. No one escaped the fact that the servant fussed over Victoria more than the invalid.

The small group moved slowly away, Moro taking the lead and Victoria falling back to keep watch on her brother.

## Chapter Six

Victoria stood alone near the tower. The evening breeze swept away the remaining heat and tugged gently at her dress. Anne had spent the last three days working on her wedding trousseau and this creamy yellow gown was Victoria's favorite. It had once belonged to her mother and the barest alterations made it a perfect fit.

Victoria could remember her mother wearing this dress. As a child, she had come to the tower one night. Her mother stood here looking out across the moor. Did she watch for Angus then just as Victoria now watched for Nikolai?

Something compelled her to look at the doorway. She turned and caught a fleeting glimpse of herself, five years old, standing alone, silently entreating her mother to look her way. But the older woman had not moved, had simply continued to stare into the darkness. Victoria watched the child turn away. The small body already showed signs of the loneliness the future would bring.

Victoria shivered, feeling the wind eddy around her body and was suddenly surrounded by warmth and peace. A beloved voice spoke from a past long dead and buried.

"My sweet gentle child. Even then you possessed my gift. Had I acknowledged your presence, I would have been forced to take you in my arms and comfort you. It was my fear that woke you. I could not bear for you to know what the morrow would bring. I only wanted you to love me and forgive me the legacy I passed to you." The warm embrace faded.

"I love you, mother. I do love you," Victoria shouted. The wind whipped loose hair into her eyes, causing more tears to flow as she pressed her cold body against the warm stones.

"Mother, come back. I forgive you," she sobbed.

Nikolai stood nearby, wrapped in darkness. Watching Victoria make peace with her mother. It took a great deal of concentration to hide himself from her sight, so powerful was her gift to call forth even the dead.

*What a wondrous talent. Will it survive the mortal death?* He would soon know the answer. He let her cry a moment longer then approached. He reached a hand out, but she whirled to face him before he could touch her.

"How dare you spy on me!" Her eyes sparkled, putting the pitiful starlight to shame.

"Go!" She slowly raised an arm, pointing in the direction from which he had arrived.

*I must take this power from her soon,* he thought. *Before she grows too strong for even my will to conquer.* He unfolded his cloak and obeyed her command, soaring silently into the night.


Victoria turned back to her post at the castle wall and stood staring across the moor. Watching the massacre that took her mother's life.

The frail moon hung high in the sky when the ghosts ceased their haunting. Fatigue washed over Victoria in waves. Her fingers cramped from clutching at the parapet. Her mother had left this very spot that night knowing nothing could save her. She had drugged Victoria and Duncan and hidden them away. Moro found them days later, silent, dirty and starving, but safe in a place only he and his beloved sister knew existed.

Victoria willed her knees to stop trembling and started down the stairs. Duncan struggled upward on crutches.

"It's about time you got out of bed, brother." She stood above him, looking down.

Duncan stopped and stared at her. "That pretty dress has improved your looks, but not your tongue, little sister." He raised his good leg to another step, lost his balance and began to sway.

Victoria rushed down the steps and grabbed his arm.

"Curse you, Duncan MacKay. What kind of wedding day would I have if we were all in mourning." She looked into his eyes and caught her breath. A glimpse of herself, in her mother's wedding dress, lying in a coffin.

"I can manage without your help." He shook off her grasp.

"Have it your own way," she said, running down the staircase, the long skirt held high. She removed the clothes the best way she could without help and dressed in britches and loose vest. Duncan made it to the landing when she rushed past.

"Victoria, where are you going? It's late."

"None of your business." She stopped long enough on the way out to buckle on her broadsword.

The gusting wind chased debris across the courtyard as she hurried to the stables and chose Duncan's black stallion. The huge horse stood calm enough while she saddled up and climbed on the rail to mount. But when they tore out of the barn and headed into the wind, he reared and pawed at the ground, snorting and shaking his head in refusal. The bridle jerked, but Victoria held hard. The moment she had him under control they struck out across the moor.

Dark clouds obscured the tiny sliver of moon, but Victoria knew the way. Bent low over the neck of the stallion, the wind mixed the black mane with her own red hair. The miles disappeared under thundering hooves as lightning transformed the familiar countryside into a forbidding landscape.

Horse and rider plunged down the hill to the fortress midst a symphony of thunder and lightning. The doors stood wide in welcome. Heart pounding, she rushed in. Nikolai waited in the long, narrow weapons room, a fire raging in the hearth behind him. Outside the storm struck, thunder and lightning and torrents of rain echoing her turbulent confusion.

"Must I die to be your bride?" she demanded.

"There is no other way."

"No man will be so much my master that I lay down my life at his whim. If it is to be, then you will have it only by force."

Drawing the broadsword, she waited, ability and intent visible in her very posture and attitude.

Nikolai thought her a witch, standing there, wild eyed and disheveled from the hard ride and the storm.

*This is what she wants. To be conquered and thusly surrender. And that is exactly as I would have it. She is indeed a witch, to know so surely how it must be.* He removed his jacket and draped it across a chair. With a black gloved hand he drew the thin bladed rapier. Nikolai could see the tension in her body. The vein at her temple pulsed with racing blood. Muscles stood out in her upper arms as she held the heavy sword in both hands, ready for battle.

"Take me, then! If you can!" She advanced on him quickly, the sword swinging from left to right in a sudden graceful deadly arc.

Nikolai sidestepped the opening gambit as she whirled to attack again, sword high. He had forgotten she fought like a heathen. There was no time for the proper etiquette of fencing. Her next blow came crashing down with the speed of the lightning that flashed outside. He threw the rapier up in defense. And caught the heavy blade with the hilt. The force of her effort vibrated against his hand for an instant. Then she drew back.

Nikolai recovered quickly and pursued her. She met his quick thrusts and parried with a speed and agility that amazed him. The clash of steel on steel rang out in the long hall, blending with the crash of thunder from outside. A fine sheen of perspiration broke out on her arms and face. Even as he attacked, he watched a drop of sweat trickle down her neck and run between her breasts.

Victoria saw his moment of inattention and dropped her blade. A simple ruse, but it caught him off guard as she cut upward with the broadsword.

Nikolai realized his mistake immediately and thrust forward in counterpoint. His thin blade caught her in the upper arm, slicing through flesh and muscle. The heavy sword slipped from her grasp, falling to the floor where her blood dripped and pooled. She stood defiant, chest heaving as she gasped for breath.

Nikolai stepped closer and grasped a handful of her hair. She leaned into his body as he kissed her hard. The saber dropped from his hand, and he wrapped her in a crushing embrace. Her injured arm forgotten, he pulled her to the floor.

Outside the raging storm matched their own frenzy. Inside, the blazing fire lighted a scene of passion much as any man and woman in love might endure.

The hard core of Nikolai's lingering humanity pierced Victoria's maidenhood as he bit into the jugular and drank deeply of the blood of his most crucial conquest.

She arched her back, eager for all he offered, even as he filled her with a loathing she could not name.

## Chapter Seven

The fury of the storm passed, its passion gone the way of all lovers. Only the rain continued to fall in a gentle show of grief.

Nikolai sat on the black stallion, quietly urging him on through the drizzle. Barely conscious, Victoria lay cradled in his arms, the fever of death already burning her life away. Confident he had drained enough blood so she would die a mortal death within hours, Nikolai drew the dark cape close around her shivering body.

"Soon, my love, we shall be together soon." He stopped the horse and lowered her to the ground.

"Close enough. This great fellow will have no trouble getting you home from here." He dismounted and lifted her back into the saddle. Carefully securing the reins about her wrist and leaning her close to the horse's neck, he sent the horse on its way with a slap on the rump.

Nikolai rose in the air, and circled toward the castle. The hounds began to bay before the horse with its precious burden moved into view. The gates opened and anxious hands lifted the girl down. Satisfied all was well, he made speed for the fortress to prepare for the summons from Angus.

Rodrigo had taken care to execute his plans to the letter. A rough casket had been filled with soil and attached to the coach floor as his own would soon be. The two extra horses and the matched pair would be teamed to the coach to insure a speedy departure. There would be no time to lose getting out of the country, in the event someone prematurely discovered Victoria did not lie in her grave. Rodrigo had seen to everything.

The vampire went to his rest pleased with the events of the evening.

Nikolai opened his eyes the moment Rodrigo lifted the coffin lid. Angus MacKay had wasted no time in sending for the prospective bridegroom.

The sun still rode the crest of the hill when Nikolai confronted the messenger. The boy related his bad tidings fearfully.

"Lord MacKay begs you come quickly. The Lady Victoria is taken ill." The lad bowed and backed toward the door, as though eager to be done and away.

"Tell your master I leave within the hour." Nikolai turned away so the boy would not see his smile. "Rodrigo, see to the coach. Our stay here is soon over."

The women bathed Victoria's body but cool water did nothing to quell the raging fever. Death hovered about her, a dark angel with no mercy.

Duncan stumbled around in the hallway, cursing himself for allowing her to leave. Like a madman, he pounded on the door until he was allowed entry and then struggled clumsily to the bedside.

"Sweet merciful Jesus, Victoria, a ride in the rain cannot have caused this." He sat on the bed and placed a hand on her brow.

"What has happened to you?" His voice lowered as he realized she indeed lay dying.

Anne had dressed Victoria in their mother's wedding dress.

"How cruel, to become the bride of death on the eve of your wedding day." Duncan's mind reeled suddenly with the logic of his words. "So this is how the outlander would take a woman for his own."

Hardly daring to breathe, he moved aside a row of ivory lace at her neck. A dark bruise almost hid the two small puncture wounds.

"Noooo! Victoria, come back!" His anguish reverberated through the room and echoed down the hall.

Outside the women began to wail.

Duncan lifted the limp body into a close embrace. His tears fell on her pale face as the fever burned ever hotter.

"If I cannot keep you from death itself, then this life you have chosen must be enough. I swear, dear sister, no matter the miles or years come between us, if you ever need me, I will be there."

Duncan held her feverish body for a long time, unaware his father and Moro had joined them.

"Come away, boy. There is nothing more we can do."

The heavy hand on Duncan's shoulder gave him no comfort. The tears had dried, but his heart was filled with a pain that would remain forever.

Duncan looked from his father to his uncle. Both stood impassive as he lay Victoria's still body back on the bed. Touching the feverish cheek one last time, he arranged a curl of hair at her throat to hide the bruise.

The torches gutted and flamed bright. Wailing from the hall grew louder as Duncan rose unsteadily and took the crutches from Moro. Nikolai appeared just as Duncan reached the door.

"Victoria?" Nikolai voiced the question and was met with Duncan's look of hatred.

Nikolai pushed past him and moved to her bed.

"Leave us." He did not look at the older men who moved to do his bidding without question, taking the boy with them.

The door closed quietly, muffling the noise from the hall. He removed the heavy gold ring from his finger. A moment passed as he stared at the ring then, bending close, he slid it on the index finger of her left hand.

He spoke softly.

"With this ring I thee wed. I do take thee to be mine own for eternity. Thou art bound to me by blood. Forever."

Through the fever haze, Victoria was dimly aware of Nikolai leaning close. Brown hair curled about his neck framing a face softened by emotion. A sweet, acrid smell of cloves and smoke filled the air. She could barely make out the wailing of women in the hall. The voice she heard whispered in her mind as much as in her ear.

"Have no fear for what lies beyond this night. Three days hence and we shall be parted no more, until the universe subsides into darkness."

Nikolai placed her hands tenderly across her breast and closed her eyes as Victoria breathed her last.

He remained by the bed the rest of the night. Dwelling in the darkness that filled her mind, knowing she was indeed dead, yet loath to leave.


Angus watched stonily as the deep mahogany hair was brushed into place and adorned with a wreath of delicate white flowers.

The bereaved family agreed without visibly consulting the Count. There would be no formal lying in state. The women saw to the corpse, carrying the body down the long staircase and arranging the bier in a small antechamber near the chapel.

Her mother's body had been far too mutilated for ceremony. Angus himself had placed that torn, shattered form on the funeral pyre, agonizing over the savagery that turned such beauty to so much unrecognizable meat. Angus had spread the pitch, but it took Moro's hand to touch the trembling torch to the pyre. The black oily smoke had filled Angus' nostrils and his heart as he clung to Duncan and Victoria.

Now Victoria was gone. The broken heart Angus had lived with for so many years turned to stone. No funeral pyre for this wild beauty. These precious remains would be preserved as long as possible in the stone sarcophagus waiting in the dry cool earth. For as long as it took to no longer matter to Angus.

The full skirt of the silk gown flowed off the side of the bier to the floor. Angus blinked tear-filled eyes and in the ruddy flame of torches, the dead flesh seemed to glow with life. He blinked again and swore long lashes fluttered against ivory cheeks, still lips smiled ever so slightly.

The keening women finished their task by spreading a thin veil over her body. Then they moved away and took up places around the small room, the rise and fall of their voices creating a dismal song as Angus stared at the shroud.

The mourners could be heard all the way down to the kitchen where Moro sat across the table from Duncan, murmuring a word now and again, filling the boy's cup more often than his own. The more Duncan drank, the more sober he became.

"It's not death that robs her of life. It's her own choice to join the dark shadow that plagues us." He lifted the cup once again and drank it dry.

"It's a hard thing to accept, the death of one so close" Moro said. "Believe me, I know. Even strong drink cannot drive the ghosts away. You may see your dead sister from time to time, but you cannot allow it to take away your zest for living." Moro filled both cups again, splashing the strong brew on the table.

"The hardest time is still to be seen. We must go down to your father where he sits with our darling." Moro rose unsteadily from the table. He handed the crutches to Duncan, who ignored them and limped away. The crutches fell to the floor, the sound loud in the long hall. The two drunken men followed the song of mourning to the chapel.

The Count stood near the inner wall, where the shadows were deepest. He watched the scene of sorrow unfold like a petty drama across the stage of disbelief. Not one of the three could believe Victoria had died and Nikolai wanted to laugh in their sad faces and tell them they were right. Not dead, not really, but gone from them all-the-same. Gone to resurrect the hopes and dreams he had buried long ago. Buried and effectively forgotten until the day she rode into his life. Nothing would ever stand before his power now. The entire world waited to welcome Victoria and Nikolai with its splendor. Every eye that looked upon them would know their love and beauty. Riches and blood alike would flow at their bequest. Men and women both would give freely for one moment of glory at their lips. Nikolai smiled in the darkness, heavy canine teeth contorting his thin upper lip and disappeared in a wisp of mist, leaving the bereaved to their own black fantasies.

The ritual of internment began early. A lone piper greeted the dawn as mist rose across the moor. The melancholy lament sounded from the parapets as the slow, steady cadence marched through the halls from tower to dungeon. Each face turned away at his approach. Every eye averted to avoid acknowledgment of his presence. Those who believed, crossed themselves in reverence for the dead and promise of the glory of heaven. Those who swore by older gods, made other signs of protection against images only the superstitious mind could conjure.

The hours passed quickly as the shrill keening wavered and trilled through the castle to finally localize in the crypt.

Nikolai watched from the shadows as the stage was set for the next act. As if on cue, the litter appeared, borne on the shoulders of four strong men. Angus and Moro led the long line of mourners but nothing was to be seen of Duncan. Nikolai joined the line parading before the bier. At last he stood with the final participants, arranged around the open grave. The pall bearers reached for the body.

"Leave this to me." Angus pushed the nearest man aside and hovered protectively over his daughter.

A simple glance from Nikolai sent the men away. He placed a hand on the old man's wrist.

"This is no task for you, Father."

Angus turned away without responding and left.

Nikolai lifted the body of his bride, taking a moment to hold her close before laying her in the open stone coffin. Lifting aside the sheer veil, he looked long at the lovely face. Dark hair shimmered with fiery highlights from the torches. Long lashes created deep shadows on pale cheeks. He took a clod of earth from his pocket, crushed it and sifted fine soil over her body.

"Ashes to ashes," he murmured, "dust to dust in the sure knowledge of resurrection to everlasting life . . . ." The words trailed away as he lifted the heavy lid and closed the tomb.

Always a creature of darkness, Johann Nikolai Valfrey, Count Drache, stepped back into the shadows and began the loneliest vigil of his long existence.

Even deep within the mausoleum the sun made its presence felt. Nikolai had not fed nor rested for three days and his bones ached with a weariness that spoke softly of deprivation. Lethargy crept in as he relaxed.

## Chapter Eight

The sound of footsteps on the stairs woke him. Duncan appeared, limping slightly. The torch he carried low cast a circle of light in which he moved. Three days spent drinking had left him ill. Red-rimmed eyes, wild hair and a shadow of a beard gave him the look of a madman. He stood staring at the coffin as the torch fell forgotten from his hand.

With all the strength he could muster, Duncan leaned against the heavy lid. After a moment, it began to scrape and move.

Nikolai stepped up behind him and spoke.

"Do not disturb her, Duncan. You will not like what you see."

Duncan turned to face him in the dim light.

"She will always be my sister and the love we have for each other will never be displaced by you. I cannot fight you now. She told me that much weeks ago. But the tie that binds us will last through the ages. As long as is necessary for the day to come when the two of us will defeat you." Duncan stood tall and looked Nikolai in the eye.

Something in Duncan's voice alarmed Nikolai. He shivered, a scene from the future passing through his mind. An expanse of dark green water so vast it could only be the ocean, far away a tiny speck of white dwindling in the distance as he stood on the shore, those very words passing through his mind.

The scrape of the coffin lid startled them both. Duncan jumped aside and stared at the widening gap. Nikolai hurried to the coffin and lifted the heavy lid easily to the floor. A pale hand reached out to caress his cheek. He turned his head slightly and kissed the palm.

Victoria sat up in the coffin and looked about.

In the dim light she appeared perfectly normal. Duncan saw the familiar eyes shining and dared to hope. He smiled, the tension in his jaw easing. She smiled back and what he saw was his face as though reflected in a pool of stagnant water. The upper lip looked tender and swollen. Fear stole his breath as he saw the enlarged teeth. Nikolai helped her rise from the coffin, then Duncan stood frozen while she approached, hand outstretched, inviting. It had been so long since he had touched her, held her, kissed her.

Victoria touched his face tenderly and uttered a small cry as he cringed away.

"Duncan. Please. Don't hate me." The words were slow and deliberate, her mind sluggish on reawakening. His fear made her angry. The gentle touch became a paralyzing blow that sent him reeling into the wall.

Duncan lay dazed, unable to move away from her next attack. But it never came.

Nikolai spoke, his voice commanding her attention.

"My blood, Victoria. It must be my blood. I have chosen you, and only my blood can fulfill your destiny."

Duncan shook his head to clear away the haze. The dimly lit scene swam in and out of focus.

Victoria moved across the crypt like a wraith. The long, pale dress swept the dusty floor, filling the air with motes that intensified the cloud in Duncan's mind. Nikolai draped the black cape across the half-open coffin and stepped out to meet her, opening the neck of his immaculate white shirt. Fine powder swirled in the small ring of light around the torch where it lay abandoned on the floor.

Duncan watched the two of them embrace. Saw their lips meet, saw Nikolai's hands slide down Victoria's back to cup her buttocks through the clinging dress. The lovers turned slowly in the spotlight, moving to a song only they could hear.

The Count broke away from her embrace, drew Victoria to

his side and taking her hand in his, punctured the artery in his throat with her fingernail.

Victoria placed the finger in her mouth and smiled as dark blood spurted from the small wound to fall on the white shirt. She reached up and grasped Nikolai behind the neck, drew the wound to her mouth and sucked greedily.

Nikolai closed his eyes and tilted his head back, a look of pleasure on his face as he pressed her close.

The picture faded from view as the torch flared one last time and died, plunging the crypt into darkness. Duncan leaned his head into trembling hands and wept as he heard the ring of Victoria's laughter from the stairs.

"Goodbye, Duncan," she called. "I love you."

Then they were gone.

# Chapter Nine

The coach was ready and waiting. Night had come to the moor and although the moon hung low in the sky it could be clearly seen while the road was practically invisible, obscured by heavy mist. Rodrigo sat hunched in the driver's seat, the horses snorting and stamping in their impatience to be away. The fog effectively muffled all normal sounds, creating a silent world in which only the foulest creatures of night and the bravest creatures of day dared confront each other.

Far away the cry of a wolf broke the mute reverie, to be answered immediately by the call of another. Rodrigo smiled and straightened his shoulders under the heavy hooded coat. A ripple of anticipation from the horses jingled the trappings. Sweet music to ears that listened as the rousing chorus of yelps and baying of two wild animals broke through the fog.

A small, sleek wolf halted at sight of the coach as a heavy muscled black and silver animal ran circles around it, nipping at its flanks and calling softly. It stopped and nuzzled the other's face and Nikolai and Victoria stood before the coach. They were laughing and smiling as Nikolai draped his cape around her shoulders. He lifted her up to Rodrigo's waiting arms and with a bound, took his place beside them on the driver's seat. Rodrigo handed him the reins. With a flick of his wrist the horses moved out and were swallowed up by the mist.

Dawn halted the travelers long enough for the eloping lovers to move into the privacy of the coach. Rodrigo secured the heavy leather drapes allowing the seclusion they sought, and under his direction, the coach once again traveled onward.

Victoria lifted her hair and Nikolai helped her undress. He opened her coffin, removed a handful of soil and rubbed it over her soft skin.

Though they were safely removed from the sun, its approach created a slow, somnolent atmosphere inside the dark coach. With a slight movement of his head, her coffin closed silently and his opened. Nikolai lay back inside the gray silk surround and pulled a lethargic Victoria into his embrace. Her legs spread around his hips and exploring lips created sources of wonder in the darkness until that small death overtook each in its own time.

Victoria lay sleeping, her weight a soothing reminder that he no longer faced the world alone. Nikolai drifted off and the coffin sealed once more.

The heavy coach and four traveled on. The miles rolled by beneath its wheels as day after day found them further from Scotland and closer to Nikolai's homeland. The small party passed through England, pausing only to rest the valiant beasts that bore their burden, uncomplaining, and to feed the beast within that demanded its due.

By the time the coach had been hauled across the English channel to Calais, Victoria had become a true vampire.

Six months at the side of the master taught her what was necessary to survive. The short side trip to the country of his birth provided a new coffin for Victoria and a fortune in gold coins for Nikolai, but little more. So they headed for France and a new life.

Rodrigo abandoned the Count to be of service to Victoria. It became a situation Nikolai found laughable until he decided the silent black man was very much in love with her.

Their vagabond mode of living continued until they reached Paris. A late autumn sunset streaked the sky orange and faded to gray. Rodrigo stopped the slow-moving horses on a cobble stone street in front of a narrow two story house. The quiet street near the river was the same as Nikolai remembered. Fifty years before he had left this place in a hurry.

He had lived here quietly for a number of years in the

company of another lovely young woman. Nikolai had simply walked out early one evening for his usual tour and had the unfortunate luck to pick a royal victim. The young man literally died of fright in his arms. The bodyguard caught Nikolai by surprise and he barely escaped with his head still attached to his shoulders. He never returned to Paris or to the bed of Claire Tobias, one of the few women in his life.

Drawing aside the leather curtain, Nikolai watched the house for signs of occupancy.

"She's inside, resting." Victoria spoke from a dark corner in answer to his unspoken question. "Nikolai, she is very old."

Nikolai remained silent, staring at the house.

"Let me go."

He dropped the curtain and spoke curtly.

"You do not speak the language."

The gray twilight faded and Nikolai stepped out of the coach, a shadow in the darker night as he approached the house.

Victoria leaned back in the seat and mentally followed his progress to the front door. The soft rapping was barely discernible, even to her acute hearing. Did the old woman hear? A feeble light appeared in an upstairs window, then disappeared. Victoria sensed the narrow stairs, the dim circle of light from a single candle. Then the door opened. She felt Claire's fear. A dark shadow stood at her door, the upturned collar of a cape partially obscuring the face. Then the old woman gave a startled gasp of recognition.

"Nikolai." The candle trembled in her shaking hand. "I have waited for your return."

"I am pleased you are still here." Many years had passed since he last spoke French but the words flowed softly from his lips. Nikolai took the old woman's free hand and kissed it. The fingers were gnarled and shook continually.

"Come in, I have kept everything as it once was." She moved away so he could enter.

He stopped inside the small vestibule.

"I am not alone."

She peered out into the deepening night. Rodrigo held the coach door open and helped Victoria out.

"Of course. A man such as yourself must always have—a companion."

"Victoria is my bride." Nikolai saw the hurt on Claire's face and chose to ignore it.

"I see. Then she is like you, yes? A creature of the night? You must ask her in. This is your house. I am but your devoted servant."

The old woman curtseyed stiffly and stood aside.

Nikolai stepped outside, swept Victoria off her feet and carried her through the doorway. The old woman watched as he strode boldly up the stairs. Kicking open one of the doors at the top of the stairs, he paused at the entrance of a room he had not slept in for a long time. The large four poster bed had been turned back for the evening. A candle standing on a nearby table had not yet burned quarter way down. The bed linens were new enough to smell fresh and a white nightshirt lay across a dark dressing gown. He took a few steps and lay a smiling Victoria on the bed.

"This will be our home for now. You will stay here until I return."

Victoria threw off her cloak.

"There is much to be done before morning. I will help Rodrigo."

Nikolai stopped at the door. "You will do no such thing. You are now the wife of a Count and you will put aside your uncivilized upbringing and act like a lady."

Even as he glared, Victoria straightened her shoulders and spoke quietly. "There is more royal position in my bloodline than your simple family title can ever confer on you."

She could have been the queen of Scotland or the queen of

witches. Nikolai appraised her soberly, as she stood beside the richly ornate bed, a haughty regal expression on her face belying the tattered state of the dress she had worn for months. He went to her and wiped a smudge of travel stain from her cheek.

"I see where Mary and Elizabeth get their backbone. They clearly come from the same stock as you, my sweet warrior." He took her chin in his hand and kissed her possessively. "But they have a failing when it comes to their men. Do not make the mistake to think it will be so with me." He shoved her harshly but instead of falling on the bed, she stood against his rough treatment. He whirled sharply and was gone before he reached the door.

The room immediately filled with echoes from the past. Sounds of a man and a woman in this big bed, his harsh grunts of exertion mingled with her sharp protests. The sound of blows from an open hand on soft flesh. Victoria moved silently to the door, never looking back as the screams turned to whimpers of surrender. She pulled the door quietly to behind her as though not to challenge the ghosts within and came face to face with Claire on the small landing.

The memory of what had taken place in that room was reflected in her demeanor. Fear hung round her like the odor of an old wound. Victoria took one of the gnarled hands in her own, gently tucked a wisp of thin white hair back underneath the ruffled cap Claire wore and spoke in English.

"Those days are gone forever. He must deal with me now."

The old woman led the young one down the stairs to the back of the house. Claire went to a cupboard and took out a towel and a small jar. She spoke, the soft sibilant words no more than whispers in the half light from a flickering candle. A knock sounded at the door and Claire opened it to admit Rodrigo. She spoke to the black man, gesturing to Victoria and the towel.

Rodrigo took the jar, stuck his finger inside and rubbed at the dark spot on Victoria's cheek. Then he handed her the bottle.

She inhaled a mild lemon scent and dipped two fingers into the lotion. "Even you understand this beautiful language. I must learn."

"And so you shall." Nikolai stood in the open door. Beside him stood a young man dressed in hose, pants that came only to the knee and a short jacket.

Victoria stopped smoothing lotion on her face. The young man was hardly more than a boy. Fine brown hair swept back from a high forehead and hung to his shoulders. The clean shaven good looks were marred by a crooked nose.

Nikolai handed his hat and cape to Claire along with a bottle of wine.

"Allow me to present my wife, the Contessa Victoria Valfrey."

The young man swept a wide brimmed hat in a flourish and spoke in English.

"Gascon Sorel, at your service, Madame."

"Rodrigo, see to the horses. I have brought Gascon to teach you French, Victoria," Nikolai said and moved to her side.

"I will teach you to speak French like a native though I doubt you will ever be mistaken for such." He looked first at Nikolai and then at Victoria. "It is not a good time for one of her origin to be in Paris."

"We are aware of the religious strife in your country but she is my wife and I will not come under scrutiny as long as we do not take sides."

"The way King Henry feels, there is no middle ground. You are either one or the other." The young man approached the table where Victoria sat.

Nikolai picked up the towel and wiped her cheek.

"In my service, you shall also enjoy my protection."

"Even your protection may prove less than adequate, Count. Frenchmen are never more brutal than when fighting each other." Gascon placed his hat on the table and sat down.

Victoria reached across and placed her hand on Gascon's. "You must teach me the history of France, as well as its language."

"French is the language of love, Madame, but I fear it is heard most often these days raised in anger and protest."

"And you, Gascon? Do you support the Catholics or the Protestants?" Nikolai asked the question, watching his guest through narrowed eyes.

"I must confess to being simply a poor scholar, educated in languages and the arts. I do not believe in God." He stared defiantly at the two strangers sitting across the table.

Nikolai laughed, easing the tension in the room. "We three are probably the only true skeptics in the whole of France. So what say we make a bargain." He called to Claire. "Bring glasses and the wine." Nikolai faced Gascon once more and waited until goblets were placed on the table. He poured the rich red liquid and lifted his glass.

"We shall play both sides against the other, always to the advancement of our own purposes."

The trio raised their glasses together and drank. Rodrigo stood careful watch at the back door, and Claire trembled in the corner from her own personal fear, as well as the calamity their words might bring.

Gascon was persuaded to return each day at twilight for Victoria's lessons. The sum of money he settled for was paltry, convincing Nikolai the young man would soon become so enamored of Victoria it would be unnecessary to pay him at all.

## Chapter Ten

Victoria refused to allow Claire to act as her maid, insisting Nikolai find someone of stronger mind and body. She knew the old woman was not long for this world and vowed to make her last days as pleasant as possible. Victoria was not surprised when Nikolai brought in a bent and crooked crone of a girl. The perversity of his nature made him cruel in ways she already found familiar. Rather than being repelled by the twisted spine and shoulder, she was drawn to the angelic beauty of the girl's face. Long graceful fingers proved quick to fasten tiny hooks and smooth curly hair into the bouffant coiffures of the day.

When Chloe spoke, the eye of the beholder was drawn from her deformity to a face so lovely it took one's breath away. A God who would afflict any creature in such a manner was far more perverse than Nikolai could ever dream of being. Because everyone ignored her, Chloe moved about in places Nikolai and Victoria could never freely go. Within a week she had procured the services of a dressmaker for Victoria, adding to the simple designs of the quiet woman embellishments that turned ordinary gowns into queenly garments.

The downstairs parlor turned into a brightly lit study and workshop. Victoria and Chloe fingered bolts of fine silk and brocade while Gascon recited in French the description of each, then translated the voluble explanations of the seamstress on how each would be constructed. Victoria proved to be a quick student, learning to speak the language within weeks.

Nikolai watched, amused at the display of three ordinary humans vying for the attention of his wife until he became bored with the tedium, then he would disappear for the remainder of the evening. He returned just before dawn each day, calling silently to Victoria, urging her to join him as he drank of the potent narcotic that insured youth and happiness.

Often she refused, acknowledging no need for the warm, fresh blood. Sometimes she felt his anger, and what she knew to be his fear, for days afterward. Most often he simply acquiesced to her wishes. Dawn always found them wrapped in each others arms; lost in their world of darkness bounded by the four strong walls of Nikolai's coffin.

Each evening the seamstress brought her finished garments. First were the soft silk nightgowns and *peignoirs*. Chloe spent a part of each evening embroidering seed pearls to the bodice of each of the soft green, dark garnet and white gowns.

Nikolai often expressed his pleasure at the feel of the sensuous fabric on his bare skin so Victoria quickly fell into the habit of donning one of the beautiful garments before joining him in the coffin.

Somber-hued day dresses, in shades of black, gray and dark red, were finished next. Chloe and the seamstress both commented on Victoria's figure being well suited to the style. The fashion forced most women to bind their breasts in an effort to achieve the flat chested look of Louise of Lorraine.

Chloe laughed and the seamstress tittered as they shared court gossip with Victoria about King Henry's *mignons*. His preference for beautiful boys might have influenced his decision to marry a woman with a definite lack of female endowments. But who could account for the tastes of a man who couldn't make up his own mind about something so simple as religion. Both women agreed King Henry felt the only thing a Protestant was good for was keeping the fires of hell burning. A great portion of the population shared his philosophy.

Secretly Victoria preferred the older gods her mother had worshiped to the relative newcomer, this one almighty supreme being. How could a God as powerful as they proclaimed Him to be not be merciful to those who worshiped Him?

Three months in Paris found the weary travelers settled in for a long stay. Gascon still attended his institute of higher learning each day, but had taken up residence in the small house on the *Rue de Playa*. Sweet Chloe also spent her few hours of sleep on the topmost floor of the house. Claire had taken to her bed and much to Nikolai's chagrin, Victoria undertook the care of the old woman herself.

Everyone, including Rodrigo had a fashionable wardrobe by now and Victoria was fluent in the language. Gascon, unwilling to forgo the evenings closely spent with Victoria, embarked on what he thought would be a monumental task to teach her to read and write.

She found the assignment quite simple; marveling at the way she read Gascon's mind and learned to recognize the letters almost without visible effort on his part. The books he brought her to read were dark heavy tomes of history and philosophy but Victoria didn't care. She devoured every work like a dying man in search of an antidote for the poison that threatened to take the light from his life. She wondered how her father could never have taught her this marvelous thing. Then she realized the man she had thought to be the smartest person in the world had not known how to read himself. Poor Duncan, how limited his world would be without this ability.

The harsh winter sapped Claire's remaining strength and she died in her sleep in February. Gascon and Chloe saw to her burial. Victoria did not go to her grave, instead she spent that first evening alone immersed in a volume of poetry, her hearing still tuned for the light tinkle of Claire's bell from upstairs.

Six months in Paris and Victoria had become a native. Nikolai watched patiently as she learned to walk in the high heeled shoes popular with the men as well as the women. He showed his approval when she at last behaved in a manner he thought appropriate for his wife by presenting her with jewelry. It was a role she played well.

Spring came to Paris. Gascon became more attentive than ever of Victoria. Chloe stood straighter, laughed more often and preened in the mirror as she dressed Victoria's hair. Rodrigo and Nikolai left one night in the coach and did not return before dawn. The next afternoon Victoria rose to find Gascon waiting by her coffin.

"A message. From the Master." He handed her a small rolled scroll. It was tied with dark green ribbon and sealed with the Valfrey crest.

Gascon helped her from the coffin. Victoria stood before him, oblivious of the thin silk gown she wore, and tore open the note. It was the first time she had ever seen Nikolai's handwriting. Thin spiky script covered the parchment. There was no signature, only a small drop of sealing wax pressed thin by the heavy signet ring he wore.

The hand holding the note dropped to her side. She looked at Gascon.

"Nikolai will not return until the end of the week. And he expects me to stay here while he gallivants around the country-side for his own pleasure."

"I would prefer you to stay here," Gascon entreated.

"Because the Master wills it?" She glared at him.

"Because I would be alone with you." He lowered his gaze to her breasts. The nipples stood out sharply against the thin white silk gown.

"We are often alone, you and I." She did not touch him though he stood so close she could feel his breath ruffle the fine hair on her bare arms.

"Nikolai was always here," he gestured in the narrow space separating the two of them before continuing, "—between us."

Victoria took the last step necessary to close the emptiness and spoke, her lips almost touching his.

"Nikolai will always be here between us. You must not let that stop you from taking what you want."

He leaned down the fraction of an inch it took for their lips to meet and kissed her. His tongue probed gently between her teeth until it filled her eager mouth with a fullness not unlike that which also longed to be inside her.

Two pair of enthusiastic hands left a trail of discarded clothing from the coffin to the bed. Nikolai's note lay forgotten on the floor.

Caught in the heat of passion, Gascon barely heard the soft knock at the door. Victoria beckoned faintly with her thoughts and Chloe entered. Twilight rushed toward dusk as the lovers slowed their pace long enough for Chloe to catch up. Gascon tenderly removed her cap and dress while Victoria loosed the long blonde hair to stream over her humped back.

The silky fall of hair hid her deformity. The rustle of sheets mingled with gasps of pleasure as the three lovers moved about on the bed. Each maneuvered for the position they thought best for the joy they wished to bestow on the other. In the final moments, Chloe lay between Victoria's spread legs, leaning back against her breasts as Victoria half sat, half reclined against the pillows. Gascon kissed first one, then the other as he entered the hot sticky center of Chloe's pleasure. At the moment of release, Victoria bit into the vein pulsing madly in Chloe's throat and drank. All three shuddered slowly down from the plateau of excitement. Victoria lifted her face from Chloe's neck as Gascon pressed forward and kissed her. The taste of blood mingled with sweat turned the gentle after-passion caress into lust. She broke away and pressed his lips against the still dripping wounds. Chloe clutched his head to her neck. The bed creaked and groaned as both shared a thrill of forbidden pleasure.

The two young people slept, cooling in the spring breeze from an open window while Victoria took a hooded cape from the wardrobe and disappeared into the darkness.

The residential street was deserted, the hour apparently later than she imagined. Six months had passed since she'd last been on this street but time counted by a different pace for Victoria these days. It seemed like yesterday she had driven down this avenue with Rodrigo and Nikolai but now she thought and spoke in French and dressed like the natives. She walked for some distance without meeting anyone so she wrapped the cloak tightly around her and once again shifted shape. The sleek black wolf moved quickly away from the river, sounds of a loud discussion drawing her to a small tavern. The odor attacked her senses as she materialized across the narrow street from the source of the disturbance. Something cold and pulpy slid between her toes. She stepped back into the shadows as an angry mob billowed out of the tavern. Some of the men carried torches, others brandished far more hazardous weapons. She followed at a distance, flitting from darkened doorway to shadow until they reached a modest shop several streets away. The mob yelled and screamed as one man pounded on the door. A woman opened an upstairs window, stuck her head out and screamed obscenities. A rock sailed out of the crowd, hitting her in the face, knocking her backwards into the room.

The door broke in quickly and several men rushed inside. They returned in less than a moment, dragging a portly man in a nightshirt between them. He begged, pleaded with them to remember he was their neighbor, their friend, but to no avail.

Victoria watched in growing horror while the mob stripped him of his clothing and his dignity, hung him from a lamppost and before he stopped kicking, ripped his torso open from the chest to the groin with a short bladed weapon.

The hot scent of blood filled the air. The mob cooled quickly, dispersing in all directions as someone hung a placard from the post labeling the dead man a protestant. Victoria stood silent, hidden from prying eyes, hands clasped over her mouth to keep from vomiting as several bloodied men hurried past.

Being familiar with the history of France had not prepared

her for this savagery. The things men did in the name of religion were not the same on paper as in reality. She left the scene of murder feeling coated with the slime clinging to her foot.

The river still flowed freely with the aftermath of spring rains, but the cold water could not cleanse the feeling of despair as easily as it washed her bare feet.

She slipped off her cloak and slid into the bed with Chloe and Gascon, afraid for the first time in her life of being alone with her thoughts. Gascon turned sleepily to embrace her.

"Where have you been? You're cold and you smell of the sewer."

She settled close to his body, fitting into his warm embrace as he slipped back into stillness. She lay awake until just before dawn.

## Chapter Eleven

Nothing more was said of the evening, not even when Nikolai and Rodrigo returned. The household bubbled with excitement as Nikolai announced the purchase of a larger house on the outskirts of Paris. The time had come for entertaining, for showing off his wife at court, so they were to move immediately. One set of coffins would remain here in the event Nikolai or Victoria should be caught away at the wrong time and unable to return to the other house.

Wardrobes were packed quickly. They rode in a new black coach pulled by four matched horses through the same area Victoria had explored three nights before. Chloe sat beside her. Victoria stared out into the night, glad the rough passage on the cobbled street prevented conversation. The corpse no longer hung from the lamp post but the stench of filth and rotting meat made her shudder. Chloe offered a small square of lace filled with dried spices. She waved it aside and forced herself to breath deeply, so she might never forget what happened here.

The carriage left the main boulevard much later in the evening, turning into a circular drive fronting the property. The stone edifice was grand as any castle. Lights blazed in welcome. Nikolai took Victoria's hand as she stepped from the coach and led her into the entrance hall. Marble floors sparkled under a massive crystal chandelier. A line of servants stood quietly awaiting introduction. Nikolai barely acknowledged the group as he barked instructions and they scattered to do his bidding.

"Upstairs first, my dear," he said, leading Victoria toward the landing. Gascon and Chloe followed, wide eyed at the splendor. They strolled through rooms fit for royalty. No one questioned how Nikolai had come into the fortune necessary to for provide such riches. Only Victoria had any inkling of how many souls had shed blood to provide this extravagant display.

On the third floor they entered a large room with one floor-to-ceiling window. Chloe rushed across the room, flung the french doors wide to the starry night and stepped out onto a small private balcony.

Victoria moved casually across a pale blue rug to a large bed hung with ice blue brocade. Ivory-handled brushes lay in perfect symmetry on a nearby dressing table. Crystal perfume bottles shared the space with containers of powder and rouge.

"It's very lovely, Nikolai," she said, speaking in English.

"You will speak only French please."

"Very well," she said, slipping into the other language with ease. She continued to gaze around the room. "Where are the coffins?"

"Later. When we are alone."

Noise from the hall announced the arrival of Victoria's trunks. Gascon stood near the door, quietly appraising the room and its contents. As soon as the servants left, Nikolai closed the door.

"Chloe," Nikolai called to the girl still standing on the balcony. She turned back into the room, smiling. "See to Madame's things."

"Yes, Master." She curtseyed and hurried to carry out his orders, the smile gone from her face as she looked about the room, really seeing it for the first time.

"Gascon, your domain is on the fourth floor. There's a schoolroom that will easily convert to your needs. You and Chloe will have rooms there. The other servants will see to the lower level of the house. No one is to be permitted above the ground floor but the five of us. Rodrigo, as always, will see to my needs. Chloe need only see to Victoria. You may do much as you please until your task is finished."

"We still have far to go with the reading and writing,

Nikolai," Victoria lied, masking her thoughts from him, choosing not to relinquish the company of Gascon for yet a while. "Now, if I may have a moment with Chloe, I will join you later to tour the remainder of the house."

"As you wish, my dear."

Gascon opened the door and followed him out, glancing back at Victoria with a wink and a shrug as he pulled the door shut.

"I did not realize he meant this room for you, ma'am." Chloe paused in unpacking the colorful dresses. "It is not right. Look how pale and wan these colors are. Not nearly enough warmth to make you look your best."

"I will not spend many hours here, Chloe. The room adjoining this one shall be my salon. You and I will see it is decorated it in quite a different manner."

"Oh, Madame. It will be just like the ladies at court. Holding their little candlelight dinners. I shall pass the word to their maids and all the ladies will come." She clapped her hands in delight. "The ladies will bring their gentleman friends, too. No husbands allowed."

Victoria wandered to the balcony.

"Is it true that the de Medici woman actually greets her guests in a dressing gown?"

"If you can believe her personal maid, it is." Chloe and Victoria both giggled wildly.

"Help me change into another dress, so Nikolai will not be angry with me for not accompanying him earlier. I must look at the rest of this mausoleum to keep him happy."

The evening aged rapidly as Nikolai and Victoria wandered hallways filled with portraits of dead men and women. When birdsong brought warning of daybreak, Nikolai escorted her to a chamber hidden between thick stone walls. A narrow staircase disappeared into the bowels of the building. Victoria listened to the jumble of sounds coming from different areas of the house. Secrets would not survive long in this place. She would have to be very careful that her own plans not be discovered too soon.

The next months passed in a blur of activity. Nikolai and Rodrigo continued to travel. Nikolai, now rich by any standard, became richer. Gascon taught Victoria to speak Latin. The Count and Countess became well known at court functions.

The upstairs salons conducted by Victoria were the talk of Paris. Chloe confirmed this news over and over, based on the gossip of the other maids. Occasionally Nikolai would rise to find the early evening party in progress. The cultured young woman his warrior princess had become would welcome him with a kiss on the cheek and then return to her latest verbal debate. Thus leaving him to move through the group, speaking or not speaking to those notables present as he desired. Sometimes stragglers still remained at dawn when he returned to escort his wife to bed.

After three years, the city still endured civil strife over its religious differences. Victoria and Gascon initiated many a discussion on the cause and possible solution throughout the salons but those most in a position to solve the problem didn't realize there was one.

Nikolai was adamant about staying within the confines of proper behavior for one of her station so Victoria would bide her time until he left on one of his many trips. Then she and Gascon, sometimes accompanied by Chloe, would go abroad in the night. Mostly they listened to those gathered in taverns speak harshly of the government. Occasionally Gascon would interject a few scholarly words, but these only seemed to inflame the rabble more. He could hardly be considered a part of the upper class, but they hated his education almost as much as they despised the rich.

Business called Nikolai out of the city for the second time in August of 1582. The weather had been stifling hot for months. The river had dried to sludge, the smell of human and animal refuse lay over Paris like a storm, threatening to drown rich and poor alike.

Unable to bear the closeness of the house another moment, Victoria called Gascon to her chambers shortly after waking.

"I must leave this place, if only for a short while." She paced the floor like a restless animal.

Gascon went to her, attempted to lay an arm across her shoulder in an effort to calm her but she shrugged it away. A fever burned in her that had nothing to do with the heat.

"There is fighting in the city as well as the countryside. I do not think it wise to go abroad tonight."

"I can take care of myself. It is not necessary for you to go. Stay with Chloe if you are afraid."

"I am frightened only for you."

Victoria turned on him.

"Frightened for me? Do you dare forget who I am? What I am?" She laughed, the shrill sound alarming. "You are but a frail human locked inside a body doomed from the day you came into this world kicking and screaming. Doomed to a life as brief as the burning of one candle in the night. Would that you could taste what I have come to know." She stopped at the open balcony, lifted the mass of hair from her neck, then bowed her head. "Sweet Jesus, what has become of me. I have been too long without sustenance. The need upon me is too great to delay further."

She felt Gascon standing close—so close she could sense his apprehension.

"I would welcome this darkness that is upon you, but only at your hands. I would lay down my life to live at your side forever. The Master knows I love you. That is why he does not send me away, though my task was finished long ago."

"He has spoken to you of this?" She turned to face him, her frenzy barely controlled.

"Yes. But I have not yet agreed. I desire to belong to you alone. I will have no other master."

"Nikolai would never allow it."

"Do it now. We will face his wrath together on his return."

Sweat curled the hair around his temple damply as she reached out and grasped his shirt in her fists. The ripping fabric sounded far away to her ears as she tore it from his shoulders and arms. With a low growl and bared fangs, a distinctly less than human Victoria bit and scratched at his body.

Overcome by a madness he could not control, Gascon fought her, tearing at her hair and clothes until they both writhed on the floor. Neither one was completely human. The act they both desired was consummated with a cruelty that could hardly be mistaken for love. They lay on the rug, side by side, Gascon bleeding from countless minor wounds.

Victoria gasped for air. The room sweltered, refusing to cool even as the last rays of daylight disappeared.

"Phwheeeew," Gascon breathed deeply. "What will happen now," he asked softly. Every muscle in his body ached but he knew the discomfort stemmed from the violent act they had just committed.

"I think perhaps you will die, but this is my first attempt to create a vampire. How do you feel?" She sat up and looked him over.

"Quite like a woman who has been raped by a conquering army, but I do not believe I'm dying. Perhaps you did not drink enough blood."

"Then I will never manage. One more drop and I'll vomit."

"I shall most likely bleed to death from all the scratches." He rolled over and presented his back to her.

She jumped up and returned with a basin of tepid water and began to wash his injuries.

"I still want to get out of the house. Do you think we might take the coach . . . ?"

"No! It will be safer on foot." He groaned and rose from the rug. "Wear something plain." He picked up their torn clothing. "I'll send Chloe to help you."

Early evening found them far from home. They had already been part of one crowd, listening as a priest inflamed the group with words of hatred and violence. Victoria and Gascon hung back at the last moment as the others were led away like sheep to senseless slaughter.

They were less fortunate later. Traveling home, they heard sounds of fighting from the direction they were headed. Gascon pulled Victoria into an alley and stumbled onto a fresh corpse. They hurriedly moved away, hiding in shadows and doorways, as the sound of battle grew louder in the night. A cross street merged with the alley in the darkness and suddenly the mob rushed in from both directions. Sounds of boots on the cobbles were drowned out by cries of anger and fear. The crowd carried primitive but deadly weapons.

Gascon pulled Victoria back, moving to hide her from the crowd. In the dim illumination from a few scattered torches, the scene resembled a ghastly revelry of dancers. Blood poured blackly from the wounds of those struck down and coated the cobbled street. There was no way to tell one side from the other. Brother might have been slaughtering brother in the confusion.

Gascon stepped back, pinning Victoria against the building. For a moment the fighting moved away, then as swiftly as a storm wind shifts direction, the alley filled with men rushing through the dark toward each other.

"Go! Now! There is no escape!" Gascon pressed closer to the wall. "They must not find you."

"I cannot leave you. I will not leave you." Victoria shouted above the fury of the fighting.

"I will not die, you have created a vampire tonight. Go now, return for my body later." He stepped into the mob.

"Gascon, No!" Victoria cried out once, then leapt skyward, disappearing in a flash of dark wings spreading in the night. She circled overhead, watching as he was struck down from both sides.

The massacre that had begun early that day with the wedding of Catherine de Medici's daughter to Henry of Navarre lasted well into the night. The streets were filled with dead Huguenots—and Gascon lay among them, struck down by his fellow Frenchmen. Victoria alone moved in the street to Gascon's body. Blood tangled the fine brown hair, plastering it to his torn face. His wounds had indeed proved fatal. Blood no longer gushed from a great gaping cavity near his heart. She knelt, and vampire strength allowed her to lift him easily. No one watched or cared as she carried him home.

The house on the *Rue de Playa* waited. The cool darkness of the stable made Victoria homesick. Musty odors of old manure and stale grain brought back memories of hours spent in hard work, Duncan at her side, mucking out the fresher refuse of their own mounts. She lay Gascon's murdered corpse on the ground and looked around the gloomy building for some sort of coffin. On the far wall, a grain storage bin stood out in the dimness. Victoria hurriedly emptied it, seeking its soil floor. It was very small but she folded his body into the space, then scooped handfuls of dirt over his remains. She then spread hay over everything and closed the lid. Barring the stable door from the inside, she disappeared.

Victoria reappeared inside the house, in the room with her own coffin. After a fleeting moment of apprehension about Nikolai, she lay down to rest fully clothed, determined to find a proper casket for Gascon as soon as night came.

As always, Victoria woke before the sun had completely set. She moved through the still house, stood in the parlor remembering the many hours of study spent in the company of Gascon. She had matured greatly in the past years. Had become more of a woman and a scholar than she had ever dreamed possible. Gascon had grown from an awkward young man into a self-assured individual. She could only hope she had indeed completed the steps necessary to make him a vampire.

The distant sound of a carriage moved slowly down the street. She listened to it drive past the house and turn into the stable yard. Rodrigo. She ran to the back door, flung it open and threw herself into his arms. Victoria buried her face against his shoulder, and he carried her out to the carriage. They sat, both mutely waiting for the advancing darkness to wake Nikolai. One moment Victoria stared at the empty seat across the way and the next Nikolai sat there, his sudden appearance startling her.

"Where is Gascon?" There was no emotion in his words. Before Victoria could speak, Rodrigo growled, a low rumbling noise. Nikolai's eyes flashed in the dimness.

"Victoria," he spoke, softer than before. "Where is Gascon?"

Leaning forward in the seat, Victoria forced her fear to the background and spoke.

"He has been mortally wounded. I have attempted to make him a vampire. I am not sure I have succeeded."

"You did well to bring him here. Please show me what you have done and I will take steps to see the ritual is completed."

"I would prefer to fulfill this obligation myself if you will only instruct me further."

"Very well." Nikolai remained seated. "You must show me where he is so we can get on with the ritual."

Rodrigo was the first to move. He left the coach and helped Victoria out into the dark. He stood at the door of the stable while Victoria disappeared through the closed entryway. Nikolai went straight from the coach to the interior of the barn where she waited beside the improvised coffin.

Nikolai lay a hand on her arm.

"How long?"

"Less than 24 hours."

"It is not time to open the tomb. The coffin must not be breeched until three days have passed. He will rise on the third evening. Then he must drink of my blood to complete the ritual."

"No, Nikolai. It was his final wish. To belong only to me."

"Very well. Perhaps it will be better. Then there will always be someone to protect you, should we be parted."

Nikolai strode toward the closed door, cape hanging loose from his shoulders. He paused, not looking back.

"How did this happen?"

"We were on the street. A mob attacked. Gascon was wounded shielding me. His injury was harsh."

"Was he disfigured?"

"There is a great deal of damage to his face."

"Do not be frightened when he rises. It will heal once he has fed." Nikolai turned and looked at her standing alone in the dark barn, so young and vulnerable. "Shall I stay?"

"No. I will do this thing alone. Whether I do it well remains to be seen."

With a swift motion, he returned and embraced her. He kissed her, gently at first, then more and more passionately as she responded.

"I must know this man will never take my place in your life. I need you, Victoria. I love you. I will never love anyone but you."

Overcome by the intensity of his declaration, Victoria allowed herself to be comforted; to be held in his strong arms. This was all she had ever really wanted. Why had she let Gascon complicate things with his pledge of allegiance. Soon there would be no drawing back. She would have to continue on this course she had chosen. But for now, she surrendered to Nikolai's need, putting all thought of Gascon and the future from her mind. Seeing only herself and Nikolai, forever in love. Forever devoted to one another. It was what Nikolai wanted and needed. Let fate decide what would happen three days from now.


The next evening, she found Rodrigo had returned with fresh clothes for both her and Gascon. There was a note from Nikolai. Short and to the point, it read: *Be strong. Return to me, my love.*

The next day she stayed in the barn, reluctant to leave for any reason. She cowered in the darkest recess of the old building, wrapped in her cloak and a heavy blanket as the sun tread slowly across the desert of the day. Toward mid-afternoon her weariness faded and Victoria rose. She sat on the loose hay in a stall near Gascon. A golden ray of sunlight found its way through a crack in the door. She watched its progress across the floor, dust motes floating in its sparkling wake. It flowed closer as its source fell toward the horizon. Without thinking Victoria casually reached out her hand toward the paling stream. It blinked out of existence before touching her flesh. She smiled slightly. Her sensitive hearing told her Rodrigo stood between the golden orb settling to the west and the barn door. Nikolai would observe her wishes to complete this task without his help, but Rodrigo's presence lent her a strength she sorely needed.

The ability to see well at night without aid was one of the things Victoria had grown accustomed to early. She sat in the darkness and clearly saw the lid rise on Gascon's makeshift coffin. His clothes were stained dark with old blood, and the wound on his face looked unreal. The flesh of his cheekbone and part of the scalp were torn away. She stood and called to him.

"Gascon. I am here."

He moved slowly toward her.

"Am . . . I . . . truly a . . . vampire?" he asked.

"Not yet. This is the most important part." She slipped the loose blouse off her shoulder, baring an expanse of pale flesh from the throat all the way down to her breast.

They moved together. Gascon twined his fingers in her hair. The other hand moved trembling down her throat and caressed her breast. He hesitated, lips drawn back from fangs.

She drew him close, pulling his head toward her neck. Still he resisted. She pulled him down into the hay and lay beside him, loosening his shirt. She spoke softly.

"This is the act of our passion. Our pleasure. When our kind make love, we drink the blood of each other." She continued to unbutton his shirt. The deep wound stood out starkly against his pale skin. Her hand moved down his belly.

"So beautiful," Gascon groaned. He reached for her bare breast. She leaned toward him, biting hard on her lower lip. Bright blood flowed freely from the gash.

"I need you." His words were lost in the movement of his lips on her mouth. He sucked the blood from her split lip until she broke away, panting.

"I know what you need, Gascon. Come. Take it."

He rose to a sitting position, pulling her close.

"You are so beautiful. I would do anything for you."

She tossed her loose hair away from her neck, stretching her chin upward to display the pulsing vein.

"You have already died for me; now live for me."

With no more hesitation, Gascon bit into Victoria's neck. He gasped at the ease in which his teeth pierced the soft flesh. Her body stiffened for a moment then relaxed as she pressed his face closer. He closed his lips about the wound and sucked. The world whirled in and out of focus and finally righted. He could hear the frantic beating of her heart and his own as his head cleared. *I must stop now.* He drew away.

Victoria knelt beside him, smiling. The two small pricks on her neck were healing even as he reached out to touch them.

"Did I hurt you?"

"Only for the barest moment. Like a virgin, once penetrated, there is only pleasure. Come," she took his hand, "there is much more to learn."

He dressed quickly, fastened the long cloak and turned to find Rodrigo in the open door helping Victoria with her cape. He heard another heartbeat sounding in his ears. It had been there all along. Gascon looked at the mute giant with respect. He, too, loved her.

"We have no need for the coach. I will show Gascon the way home from here."

The two young vampires touched hands. Victoria filled his mind with visions of the night sky, high above the fog, where stars dotted the darkness with diamond brilliance, and they were gone. Victoria reveled in the wind in her face and hair, and in the dizzying heights, the way the avenues wound through the city, some brightly lit, others dark with intrigue, and the plotting of neighbor against neighbor. Then they were there. Far below Nikolai stood on the balcony of Victoria's bedroom, patiently awaiting her return. She felt Gascon's apprehension, wrapped his mind with her love and they left the freedom of the night for the world of mortals and a chosen few like themselves.

They materialized on the balcony beside Nikolai still holding hands. He smiled and moved to embrace them both.

## Chapter Twelve

The years passed quickly. Henry III died without an heir, and Henry of Navarre became King Henry IV. The people of France loved him for his impoverished upbringing. With his reign came an internal peace, an end to the constant fighting between the Catholics and the Protestants.

Rodrigo aged, and still his strong shoulders bore the coffins as Nikolai, Victoria and Gascon moved from the first mansion to another even finer.

To keep abreast of the costs of his extravagant tastes, Henry IV sold titles and offices to people of wealth. Among those first to purchase such position and lands was Nikolai. Not for himself, of course, but for his young nephew, Gascon.

Twenty years in Paris brought about many changes. New dictates in fashion made it easy for Nikolai and Victoria to age. Seldom were they seen in public. People who moved in their circles gossiped constantly about affairs of court, and occasionally about the close relationship between the two men and the young wife. Her salons happened less and less frequently. To be invited to Countess Victoria Valfrey's boudoir for an evening of light dining and music was to join the social elite.

Chloe entered Victoria's apartment just before dusk and moved across the room to throw wide the french doors. A soft evening breeze billowed the filmy drapes.

"Gascon's young friend is downstairs."

"Which one," Victoria asked.

"Jean. Du Plessis."

Victoria laughed. "Oh, that one! Tell him Gascon has gone to the country."

"I did. He insists you see him."

Victoria turned and slipped into the satin robe Chloe offered, tying the ribbons high under her small breasts. The last few years had not been kind to Chloe, fading her beautiful hair to pale gold. Today her deformed back forced her into a more pronounced stoop and she moved slowly. Her angelic face seemed haggard, dark circles making shadows under her eyes.

"Chloe? Are you ill?"

"No, Madame."

"You look so tired. Do you need help? I can set some of your tasks to one of the downstairs girls."

"Madame! Their hands are too rough to even wash your lingerie! I would never allow them to touch your dresses or your hair! The boy, Madame?"

"Oh, very well, send him up."

The young man appeared in the door almost immediately. He could have been little more than fifteen or sixteen, but he rushed to Victoria and took her hand. She snatched it from his grasp before he could kiss it.

"Ah, Jean. What mischief are you about this evening?" Victoria asked, frowning at the sudden glimpse of his future after so long a time of touching others without fear of ghastly revelation. "Gascon has been called out of the city."

"I know, Madame. Only you can help me in this matter." He tossed his hat on the bed with a gallant flourish and dropped to one knee before her. "I want you to come away from this dreary place with me. I will take you to a court where you belong. With you at my side, all France will bow before us."

He reached for her hand again but Victoria shook her head.

"Silly boy. You have nothing that I do not already own. Youth and beauty and wealth. All this and more are mine now—" her voice dropped to a whisper, "and forever."

"I love you, Victoria. I must have you! I will die if I do not have you!"

She clapped her hands in mock delight.

"Oh, but Jean, that is much better. A girl will always be much more willing if you profess undying devotion."

He looked up at her. "You play with me, Madame!"

He looked as if he might cry, then his face hardened and she caught a glimpse of the man he would become, the man she had seen in her vision.

"Jean. There will be many women in your life. Beautiful women. Powerful women. And you should get down on your knees every day of your existence and thank your God that I am not one of them."

Moving to the bed, she retrieved his wide brimmed hat.

"Go! And do not come back to this place, ever again!"

The boy walked stiffly to the door where he turned and bowed slightly to her. For a moment the scarlet jacket and trousers became the papal robes of the Cardinal Richelieu Victoria had glimpsed in her vision. Then he was just a boy again, pride and anger twisting his face into the mask he would wear until he died.

Three days later Nikolai and Gascon returned to find Victoria packing.

"We must leave Paris now. Trouble is coming and I have made an enemy who will never forget what I have done."

"We cannot simply leave, Victoria," Nikolai countered. "I have business here."

"Nikolai, perhaps Victoria is right," Gascon spoke in her defense. "We have been in this place a long while."

"No," Nikolai commanded. "There is too much at stake to leave so quickly."

Victoria continued to give orders to the two girls moving about her bedroom, and refused to hear his arguments. "Do not deny me this, Nikolai. Or I shall go without you! Chloe is sick. She's losing weight and I cannot persuade her to eat."

Gascon and Nikolai stopped quarreling and Victoria paused to look at them. "What? Nikolai, do you know what is wrong?

What have you done to Chloe? Gascon?"

"Nothing. I have done nothing to my sweet Chloe." Gascon declared. "I love her. Just as I love you."

"And there you have your answer, my dear." Nikolai moved to the bed and lounged against the ornate headboard, his travel stained boots streaking the silk sheets. "Gascon has not yet learned that our lust destroys even as we share pleasure without equal."

"Chloe is dying? Because she and Gascon make love? How can this be?" Victoria asked.

She stood at the side of the bed.

Nikolai took her hand and caressed it gently as he spoke. "Human flesh is weak. It cannot withstand the violation of the vampire coupling."

Victoria turned to stare at Gascon. "You drank her blood?"

"Of course. She said it made her satisfaction greater."

"When one is taken to the point of death, reprieve is always so much sweeter. But to do so repeatedly becomes abusive, damaging the frail human constitution to the point it cannot repair itself. It is far more devastating and visible when it is a man who must do the giving, my dear."

"Heal her, Nikolai! Bring her into our family now."

He pulled her down to sit beside him.

"Victoria. How can you condemn our dear Chloe to eternity trapped in a—less than perfect—body," Nikolai admonished.

"Change her." Victoria's voice was hardly more than a whisper. "Make her young and beautiful."

"Look at Gascon. Look at yourself." Nikolai's words were soft but unyielding. "There is no changing our physical nature. We are always what we were in life."

She tried to rise but he held her close. He could feel her anguish and for a moment it caused a fierce ache in his breast. Then with all the power he could summon, he forced her to see what he wanted her to see and nothing more but she would not be put aside from her purpose.

She rose from the bed and spoke sharply to the maids in the hall. "We must be ready to leave before dawn."

The entire household departed Paris leaving no sign for when they might return.

Within a fortnight Chloe was gone. They buried her quietly and moved on to another country estate, the house and lands a legacy of some aristocrat unfortunate enough to have been born on the wrong side of France's religious differences.

A new century was celebrated without their return to Paris. Ten short years later, Henry IV was assassinated and another power hungry de Medici woman held the reins of the kingdom for a child king. Once again the country struggled against disorder.

Victoria repeatedly warned Nikolai of a rushing tide of discontent that would soon sweep through France. Her obsession with the written history of France, coupled with her one glimpse of the Cardinal's future, told her those in control would never learn from the mistakes of those who had come before them. In a final attempt to be free of her nagging, Nikolai consented to leave the country.

The fine furniture, gifts, and inheritances were shipped ahead in the company of Rodrigo to a place Nikolai had found a century before, another house left in the keeping of a trusted retainer.

Just outside Toledo, Spain. The house sat high above the city, on the river where the summer months were at least bearable. A haven where they could spend some time alone and not be constantly subjected to civil warfare.

Spain would be good for them. A time of rest. A time for peace. A time to find love again.

The moon had set, and the dark night was alive with the sound of a thousand cicadas when the coach and two riders on horseback approached the *palacio*. The low, rambling, white stone house surrounded by trees had stood in just this manner for over one hundred years when Nikolai first traveled this way.

A single lantern now burned at the door. Nikolai dismounted and made for the entry. The door opened and Victoria watched Nikolai embrace Rodrigo where he stood in the shadows.

With a small cry, she threw her leg over the saddle horn and slid off the horse.

"Rodrigo!" she cried. Rushing up the walk, she practically threw herself into his embrace. The once strong arms had grown frail and he staggered under her weight. Nikolai and Victoria helped him inside the house.

"My old friend. You have not fared well this trip." A young boy stood in the foyer, holding a lantern as high as his short arm would reach.

"The old man let no one watch but himself. Mama say he wait for the Master then he die." The dark haired, wide eyed boy edged closer.

"Where does he sleep, boy? Show me. Be quick!" Nikolai lifted the big bag of bones that Rodrigo had become and followed the child down a long hall. He led them across an open patio and pushed aside a curtain to enter a small, windowless area. A narrow cot filled one side of the room. Nikolai lay Rodrigo down, aware the labored breathing had become more and more shallow.

Victoria knelt at his side. He fumbled for her hand and brought it to his lips. A habit of affection he had picked up in Paris, when he saw others kiss her hand as they bowed in awe of her beauty.

"Nikolai! Do something." Victoria turned to him, wishing for once she could cry.

Nikolai gave the boy a push out the door, then moved to her side. Rodrigo made an uncertain noise in his throat.

"Where is it, my friend? Where have you put it?" Nikolai looked sadly at the dying man. "In the small trunk, by the side board in the main salon. Yes, it will be safe now. Do not worry further." He smiled at Rodrigo.

A last, shuddering breath escaped Rodrigo's lips with a sigh and he breathed no more. He still held Victoria's hand.

"Your fortune bought with blood was more important than your friend? How could this be? I loved this man more than my own father and now he's dead."

She railed against Nikolai with more emotion than he had seen in years.

"Why didn't we hurry? Why didn't you do something? How could we not know he was dying?" She looked at first one man and then the other.

Nikolai turned his back to her and stepped outside the door.

"The caretakers will see to his burial tomorrow while we are resting."

"Are you so unfeeling you cannot even honor him by burying him yourself?"

"We cannot entomb him at night. It would not be proper for this place and time."

"I don't care! I want to be there for the burial."

The fury of her anger drew Nikolai to her side. He took her hand, forcing her to rise and step away from the bed.

"All we know and love will pass away and still we will remain. It is part of what we are. It is why I have you and you have Gascon. I could not bear for you to be alone should we be parted." He wrapped his arms about her unyielding body and drew her close. Just to touch her filled him with joy. "You cannot go to the burial. There is no way to protect you here and if you should be destroyed, my life would have no meaning."

She stopped struggling and relaxed against his body.

"There is much to be done before dawn, Victoria. We must hurry." Nikolai led her away from the deathbed.

Gascon waited outside the door, curiously at ease in the strange surroundings.

Victoria saw for the first time what a lovely place she stood in. The sound of running water soothed, and a soft night breeze filled the air with the smell of roses and almonds.

"I have moved the coffins, Nikolai. The boy has eyes like a hawk. See, he watches even now." Gascon led the way to the front entry.

The small boy sat waiting at the door, the lantern on a table beside him.

"Go to bed, boy." Nikolai cuffed him gently on the ear.

"Grandfather tell me, he watch long time, his father watch long time, for Master to come in the night. Grandfather old, tell me watch for Master in the night." The boy smiled proudly, pleased with his responsibility.

"Watch no more, boy. I am your Master." Nikolai took a gold coin from his pocket. "Tell your Mother, bury the old man with respect."

The child caught the coin in his fist and hurried away.


For the first time in years, Victoria slept alone by choice. And dreamed of those she had loved, and lost. Her father, his long dead bones now dried in their limestone sarcophagus; sweet Chloe, victim of her affection for Gascon, forced to pay a terrible price for loving a vampire before they realized the depth of destruction it caused the fragile human body. Rodrigo, even now being laid to rest in a land as foreign to her as the place of his birth. A moment of doubt clouded her dream but peace returned with the knowledge Duncan still walked in the sunlight somewhere in the world.

Early the next evening she rose from the coffin still dressed in her traveling clothes. Dark green tight waisted jacket, skintight black britches and knee-high riding boots, the spill of dark red curls caught back in one long braid. As usual, she woke before the others. The same internal clock they all functioned by marked time at a different pace for her.

Though it was late afternoon, bright sunlight flooded the wide *piazza*. She squinted, shielding her eyes from the glare with one gloved hand and pulled the hood of her cape close with the other.

*Nikolai was right. I could not have survived in this sun. It is not at all like France with its cool cloudy days and rainy afternoons.* Victoria paused in the shade of a deep overhanging roof to look out over the river. The smell of water nearby gave some semblance of refreshment. Trees with long low hanging branches invited her to walk along the edge of the river, but she craved escape and made her way across the yard to the stable.

The animals had been well tended, so she took the trim brown mare from a stall and saddled her. Victoria guided the little horse under the trees to the river bank and looked at the city across the way. The lure of the river pulled her in the direction of its flow, bringing her to the end of the trees.

She urged the horse up a steep embankment in hopes of a better view of Toledo. Horse and rider plunged over the rise to a grassy knoll, much to the surprise of a man sitting with sketch pad and pencil in hand. Victoria jerked the horse aside quickly to avoid trampling him.

The man jumped up yelling in a language Victoria did not understand.

She brought the horse around and he caught the halter as she spoke, in Spanish.

"Are you hurt?" she inquired.

"No, but I have waited most of the day for the light to be just so and now it is gone." The voice was deep and harsh but he answered in Spanish. The man, tall and thin, wore a dirty white robe belted at the waist. He turned aside and began picking up scattered equipment.

Victoria looked out the way he had faced. Twilight cast purple shadows as a backdrop to the city. White stone buildings rose high against the darkening sky. The spire of a cathedral seemed to pierce dark clouds rimed in bright light.

"It's very beautiful," she whispered, the awe in her voice catching his attention.

He turned back to the scene he had watched so patiently most of the day.

"It is exactly what I have waited to see." He stood and watched for several long minutes as the sky shifted and changed with the dying light, then shut his eyes tightly as though to commit the vision to memory.

"Now tomorrow I shall finish my painting." He turned back to horse and rider, squinting. He peered intently at Victoria's face. Pale skin appeared to glow within the shadowy confines of the hood.

"Who are you?" he asked. "Another dark angel to brood about? My wife will not appreciate my return tonight if I do not satisfy my curiosity about you."

"Then come with me," Victoria said with a laugh. "I welcome you to my home for the evening. You are free to continue your painting here whenever you wish. Where is your horse?"

"My feet are the only transport this starving painter can afford." He lifted the long robe to show dusty feet in rope sandals.

"We are fortunate it is not far." Victoria kicked a foot from the stirrup and offered a hand to help him mount behind her.

It proved a clumsy maneuver, Victoria holding the reins and his equipment in one hand while practically lifting him bodily from the ground with the other. He grasped her around the waist like a man afraid of falling.

The ride back went swiftly in the deepening dusk. They rode into the courtyard of the *palacio* to find the house bright with light. The same boy from the night before ran out to take her horse to the stable. The painter dismounted with relief, and Victoria handed the reins to the child.

"What is your name, boy?" she asked.

"Felix, Senora," he answered, intent on his task.

The artist turned and stared. Her hood had fallen, revealing curling wisps of hair slipping from the long braid and her cape thrown back over her shoulders. She had removed her gloves and slim fingers unlaced the tight jacket. Underneath, a white silk shirt flared open to the waist revealing a hint of small firm breasts.

The painter laughed and moved closer.

"I see you are indeed a woman. I thought you to be some strange, effeminate young man." His gaze moved to her hands, searching for a wedding ring and saw only the heavy signet on her left hand. "Am I to have the honor of meeting your husband this evening?"

"Johann Nikolai Valfrey, at your service." The Count stood in the open doorway, the soft glow of lamps inside delineating his body with light, creating deep shadows around his eyes. He extended a hand to Victoria, drawing her within range of his protection.

"My wife, Victoria." She joined him on the steps, extending her hand to the artist, beckoning him to enter.

"I am not from this fine country and the locals find my name unpronounceable, so they simply refer to me as Dominie," he said, inclining his head and shrugging his shoulders at the same time.

"I interrupted his work earlier and, having caused him much consternation, invited him to dine with us. He watched the city, awaiting for the perfect moment to catch the light and . . . ."

Nikolai escorted the tall, thin man inside. "You are a

painter, Senor? Have I heard of you? We have only just recently arrived from France. Are you well known here?"

"Alas, it has been my fate to offend those who might offer me patronage. But I will not compromise what I see as beauty for the mere sake of coin. My poor wife and child do sometimes suffer because of my unhappy patrons."

The three of them walked through to the patio where Gascon reclined on a low sofa. He rose as they entered, a well muscled body very much evident in tight britches and blue eyes made more vivid by the loose blue shirt he wore.

Victoria moved to his side. He took her hand and raised it to his lips.

"Gascon, we have a guest," she said.

He lingered a moment too long over her hand and then released it.

"You do have a way of finding the most extraordinary people," he said, smiling at her. He motioned to the man standing some distance away. "Come, be comfortable and I shall find some refreshment. We prefer to dine late, but I believe there is may be some fowl left from lunch."

The artist folded his long legs and half lay, half sat on the white wicker chaise.

"Will you help me in the kitchen, Victoria?" Gascon asked, taking her cape.

"I would be delighted, if you will allow me a moment to change into something more appropriate for entertaining." She glanced at their guest, who appeared to study her intently.

"I assure you, Senora, what you are wearing is entertaining enough for me." The serious look on his face belied the humor in his voice.

"Very well, for your pleasure I shall remain as I am." She glanced at Nikolai and caught his nod of approval as she followed Gascon to the kitchen.

"My wife is very young and I spoil her shamelessly,"

Nikolai said, moving a small table near his guest and seating himself opposite. "I would like very much to see your work. I may be interested in giving you a commission."

The painter studied the man sitting across the way. He was older than the woman by many years and his appearance, compared to the younger man, was quite staid. He wore a rusty black fitted jacket, fastened at the left shoulder, over trousers of the same fabric. In spite of the warmth of the evening, he seemed at ease.

"My work lately has dealt with commissions from the Church and local nobles. I am cursed with a sinner's vision of good and evil, and these mortals are not always pleased with the way I see them. Some deny me payment even when they know I live on the edge of poverty. The Church gives me as much support as they dare, although my Saints sometimes appear a bit too worldly. Even this piece of clothing is donated from their supply." Dominie picked at the dirty hem of his robe with paint stained fingers.

"The Holy Catholic Church finds favor with painters these days?" Nikolai sat forward, interested in what this man said. "I thought their only desire was to rid the world of heretics, not commission the creation of art."

"There are certain sects that still prefer to interpret the scriptures through art forms, although they are becoming fewer and harder to find. The Inquisition passed through Toledo some years ago, casting out those considered undesirable and, though their influence is still felt occasionally, we are relatively free of their burden." The painter crossed himself quickly.

Victoria and Gascon reappeared, he bearing a tray laden with fresh fruit, goats' cheese, and half a roast chicken. Victoria carried a small silver basin filled with water and, draped over her shoulder, a white towel. The jacket had been removed and in the place of the slim riding boots she now wore sandals. The heavy braid had been loosed, allowing dark red hair to fall in lazy waves over her breasts and down her back.

"For your comfort, Senor. Will you wash?" She knelt before him, the rose-scented water offered like a balm.

Smiling, he sat up, swung his feet to the floor and laved cool water over hands stained with the struggle of twenty years devoted to his art. He reached for the towel and dripped water on her shirt. The wet material clung to the pale skin underneath.

Gascon placed the food on the table and sat on the end of the chaise, watching their guest as his smile shifted to a look of puzzlement. Victoria placed the basin on the floor near his feet and bent to unlace his sandals.

Heavy hair curtained Victoria's face as she placed one foot in the basin and washed, reaching up the calf to splash water almost to the knee. She sat back on her heels and reached for the towel still hanging from the painters hand.

The artist's gaze traveled from the cleft of her breasts upward to the hollow of her throat, pausing like a drowning man to draw breath before sinking into the oblivion of her eyes. He stared at the top of her head as she finished the ablutions and handed the towel to Gascon. A wordless message passed between the two beautiful young people.

He glanced around the patio to find Nikolai gone. Gascon stood behind Victoria, hands gently caressing her shoulders. He whispered in her ear.

"May I join you later?"

She leaned back, pressing against his body.

"Much later," she boldly teased, watching the face of the man reclining on the small sofa.

"Are you hungry?" Victoria asked, sitting beside Dominie. She leaned across his body and drew his right hand to her lips.

"I am," she whispered, biting into the delicate collection of veins just above the wrist.

## Chapter Thirteen

Bright daylight woke Dominie. He lay in his own bed wondering how he came to be there. The happenings of the past evening blurred together, but he did remember drinking a large quantity of very fine wine while eating some exotic dish his hostess provided for dinner. A bad taste filled his mouth and a thousand cicadas beat against the back of his eyes in an effort to escape the ache in his head.

Far below, someone pounded on the outer door. The shrew of a woman he had married shouted some reply and eventually opened the bedroom door. He wrapped himself from head to toe in the bedclothes to tone down the high-pitched screech of her voice, telling him a client had come to pick up a portrait.

"It isn't finished." He croaked, trying to clear his throat. "Tell him it will be done next week. Bring me some wine, I have work to do." The woman left to do his bidding.

Dominie sat uneasily on the side of the bed, steadying his head with both hands. When the vertigo subsided, he opened his eyes and saw the two small tears in the inside of his right forearm. He shut his eyes quickly, sanity threatened by the image of Victoria bending close, the curtain of her dark hair shutting out the world, lamplight illuminating her pale face. Only the color of blood stained lips, and green eyes flecked with gold gave life to the picture. He stood abruptly, the world tilting as he staggered to the easel for charcoal. The sketch was completed in scant minutes. Deep within the vortex of his brain, he knew his wife mustn't see this woman. She was not like the others. This dark angel would steal his soul if he wasn't careful. He slid the sketch under a paint-stained pallet.

His wife returned to find him standing naked at the work table, searching in the haphazard array of tools. Screaming that he was not to be disturbed, he chased her from the room and bolted the door. Several glasses of wine eased his throbbing head to the point of allowing him to function and he found the object of his search. The day passed in a flurry of activity, which included more drinking of wine and with the approach of evening came the completion of his project.

The stench of his unwashed body overpowered him as he began to dress. Calling repeatedly for his wife with no response, he wandered through the dark house and found water and soap. He retired to the upstairs balcony with his bath and wondered why he had never felt it necessary to be clean before. He soaped lank hair, beard, and body; sluicing away the suds and dirt with a pitcher of tepid water. He stood at the edge of the balcony, gazing across the empty square to the house on the hillside. The evening breeze dried his body and fluffed the fine brown hair. He dressed in black britches and jacket. Holding the still damp miniature safely in one hand, he rushed out. He made for the gate of the city and, for the first time in his life, wished he owned a horse.

"Senor! Senor Painter!" He turned back to see the boy, Felix, leading the brown mare.

"The Senora sent me to fetch you for dinner." The boy held the small horse steady and Dominie mounted with an agility he had never felt around animals. He grasped the boy's arm and swung him up behind.

The horse, being an animal of great common sense, found its own way home while the artist gazed tenderly at the small portrait in his hand until the light faded.

The painter began to exist on a feverish plane. His nights were spent in the company of those he came to see as his family, their *menage-a-trois* life expanding to include him. Sometimes there were other folk from the city present, and those evenings passed quite normally. Once there was even a gathering of the local church officials, providing an abundance of political and religious arguments. Dominie sat and listened, astounded by the realm of education Victoria possessed.

The years passed in a hectic collection of days filled with work and nights filled with a joy he had never known. Painting after painting was finished at a level of mastery he had never before achieved. He tried many times to capture the elusive quality of his friends on canvas, but never found quite the same interpretation as with the first miniature of Victoria. The beauty that beguiled in Victoria was almost distasteful in his portraits of Nikolai and Gascon.

Felix had long ago entrenched himself in their lives through his loyalty and devotion. Although Nikolai sought to keep their secrets from the boy, he had proven he could be trusted time and again. He carried out many of the errands none of them were capable of handling during the daylight hours of this hot, bright land. Because of Victoria's special interest in the painter, Felix elected from the very beginning to see that the preoccupation caused by his work did not cause problems for her. As a boy, jealousy sometimes created a rage that threatened to consume Felix when he saw her with Dominie, but as he grew into adolescence, he too felt the dominating power of her presence. When she was near, one had no choice but to please her.

Through the years, Nikolai watched the entertainment with a jaded eye. When he grew bored with the story line, he would draw the players into his own passionate scene for a time and then retreat for a better view of the outcome. Gascon still had not learned when to surrender without suffering humiliation, and his anger and resentment provided many hours of enjoyment for Nikolai. Victoria always emerged the winner; mere mortals willing to shed blood for her, and the men in the family more than eager to cause warfare to accomplish it.

If the flow of strangers to the *palacio* created gossip, word never passed to the ears of those most concerned. Having learned too late to save Chloe from the ravages of affection, Victoria protected Dominie from Nikolai and Gascon, insisting they all spend their passion further from home.

Life sustained itself; sometimes hesitating, sometimes simply persevering but continuing as resolutely as the rise and set of the sun. No one gave thought to the future, content to exist in whatever manner presented itself next.

Then one day Dominie returned from his errands and found his wife hysterical. The Inquisition had returned to Toledo. The priest had sent word of warning. The men in black sought the artist for questioning with regards to the conduct of the gentleman from France. He rushed to pass the information along to his friends.

Victoria sat on the arm of Nikolai's chair.

"The Inquisition? In Toledo?" she asked. Tales of unspeakable deeds committed in the name of the church came quickly in her mind. A cold shiver settled over her.

"How do you know this, Dominie?" Nikolai inquired, slipping his arm around Victoria and drawing her close.

"My wife. They came, seeking me. I had gone to pick up your commission." He held a long package, wrapped in soft leather under his arm. He continued to stand in the doorway. Flight hovered at the edge of his mind while staying seemed of the utmost importance. He looked first at one and then the other, unsure of what to do next.

"I cannot go back, Nikolai," he stated flatly. "I survived the Inquisition once. I do not wish to come under their scrutiny again."

"You need never return to the city. Stay with us. You are welcome here," Victoria said. She rose and went to the painter. She embraced the man, now old enough in years to be her father.

"Do not be so formal, my friend. The Inquisition has no informer in this household." Nikolai added his welcome to

Victoria's in a more reserved manner. He took the slender package from the painter.

"Is it perfect?" he asked, balancing it in his hand.

Dominie smiled at last.

"It is the most exquisite instrument of pain and death I have ever seen," he whispered.

"What mischief are you up to now. What have you there? Let me see." Victoria playfully reached for the package and Nikolai moved away, teasing. "Help me, Dominie," she called.

Gascon entered the room and joined her in the chase. Felix stepped out of their way and continued lighting the lamps.

Nikolai shook off the leather wrappings and the jeweled hilt shimmered in the lamplight, throwing out a thousand pinpoints of brilliance. With a barely perceptible motion, he unsheathed the sword, tossing the scabbard aside. Cold steel of the narrow blade flashed white in the artificial light. The sun flared in one final blaze of sunset glory as Nikolai raised the sword in traditional salute to the enemy. The edge of the blade ran red, a bright omen of disaster, chilling the moment with a reminder of the bloody history of the Inquisition.

The group stood transfixed as Nikolai began the rigorous ballet of fencing. The blade sliced the still air with a shrill whine. The slap of boots on the stone floor settled into rhythm as his body performed moves learned by rote years before. His path took him straight to the painter.

Victoria saw a deadly intent in the cold, hard gleam in his eyes. His face contorted grimly as the sequence of moves carried him closer to his target. Dominie smiled at her, unaware of the destruction plunging toward him. She rushed across the patio to throw her body between the Toledo blade and her favorite. She wrapped her arms about the painter's neck and pressed her body close to his. She felt the white hot sear of tearing flesh as the sword pierced her flesh, the force of Nikolai's thrust driving the blade all the way through her body and into the heart of Dominie. Only her vampire strength held him upright. She watched the smile fade from his lips as blood trickled from the corner of his mouth. She screamed and lost consciousness as Nikolai withdrew the blade as quickly as he had driven it home.

"Felix, see to Victoria." Nikolai walked to the table and wiped the blade clean on the leather wrappings. He looked up. Both Felix and Gascon stood frozen, staring at him.

"Nikolai, have you lost your mind? What have you done?" Gascon hesitated, not daring to move closer.

"It's the Inquisition. We must hurry. Take only those things of the greatest value. The paintings, small statuettes, all the gold and jewels." Nikolai slipped the sword back into the scabbard. "Felix! She isn't dead, you fool. You can't kill a vampire with Toledo steel."

The young man moved woodenly to where Victoria lay, her blood mingling with the painter's on the white stones. Felix lifted her, cradling her head against his shoulder.

"You didn't hear his confession. Dominie admitted he could hold nothing back from the Inquisition and just one word, one breath, of what we are would mean the true death for us all."

For a brief moment the hardness in Nikolai's face lessened. He reached out and touched Victoria's cheek. "We are all strangers in this strange land, Felix. We—Victoria, Gascon and I—we carry our existence with us but to make Dominie a vampire requires life-giving soil from his birthplace."

His hand dropped to his side and he was once again the Master. "Take the body. We will dispose of it along the way. Now hurry, we must be well gone from here by dawn."

With a last glance at Victoria, he moved into the house and began dismantling paintings.

Gascon hurried to help Felix. They lay her inside the coffin and carried it to the coach. Midnight found them away, heading south, bound for Gibraltar and the dark continent.

## Chapter Fourteen

Felix watched the moon wan, wax full and wan again, and still Victoria lay silent in the coffin. Searing hot days melded into steaming, sultry nights. The fleeing party traveled as close to the sea as possible, their objective to reach Algiers quickly and drop completely out of sight for a time.

The shift changed. Gascon took the reins for the evening and Felix climbed inside to rest. He lifted the lid to Victoria's coffin. Somewhere along the route someone had replaced the torn, bloodied dress with a black silk shirt buttoned high on the shoulder. It was much too large for her delicate frame and Felix was sure he had seen Nikolai wear it before.

"She is only sleeping." Nikolai's quiet voice from a dark corner startled Felix. He could just make out a pale face in the darkness.

"Master," he acquiesced.

"We have no secrets from you, do we, Felix?"

"No, Master."

"When the body or mind can no longer justify existence, the only answer is oblivion. The sleep of oblivion. The nearest thing to the true death a vampire can know." Nikolai paused, drawing back the curtain to peer out into the night. "I once slept for a hundred years. Time washed over me like a deep, dark ocean, as vast as the unknown reaches beyond those stars."

The soft monotone continued, soothing Felix as he watched Victoria. His gaze never left her face, barely visible in the shadowy box.

"The longer I slept the more reluctant I became to wake. It took all the courage I could muster to bring myself back to reality. Even hunger had fled in the face of the ages."

Nikolai turned back to Felix, keeping his voice low.

"She is only sleeping. But you can wake her. I am the cause of this retreat into oblivion and I have not the means to call her back. Love alone will not suffice."

"How, Master? If your power is not enough, then how could a poor human like myself reach into that great darkness and free her?" Felix raised his face and looked straight into the eyes of the devil. Dark fire smoldered behind the pupils, the upper lip curled back over enlarged teeth in a semblance of a smile. One hairy hand reached across the open coffin, offering a short jeweled dagger. The shape-shift change was nearly complete, but Nikolai forced the words.

"When the time comes, you will know what to do." The dagger dropped into the coffin as the black and silver wolf bounded out the window of the slow-moving coach.

Felix, the man, leaned over and chastely kissed Victoria's cold lips. Felix, the boy, shut the lid and lay across the coffin, arms stretched wide to rest his head over the unbeating heart. Lulled by the gentle sway of the coach, he slept. And dreamed. Of a time he had not yet lived and a place he did not yet know.

By the age of 27, Felix knew Algiers intimately. He had become a man capable of going anywhere unnoticed and doing anything. Dark skin and hair allowed him to mix easily with the natives. He rarely slept, using darkness as cover for a multitude of sins. Thievery had always been part of his life, and he had now become a master.

In the beginning he feared the two male vampires, caught as he was between the force of their passion for each other and the intensity of their desire to wake Victoria.

As he grew older, he realized none of their hostility was directed at him. So he bore silent witness to their unspeakable deeds, compelled to do their bidding by his own desire to see Victoria live again.

Now, Nikolai and Gascon existed by his hand alone. Hidden away from the world, they had become prisoners by their own choice, slaves to the shrine built for Victoria. Their lack of contact with humanity had reduced them to the behavior of animals.

It actually took very little effort for Felix, with his rugged good looks, to procure victim after victim for sacrifice, leading them to destruction as easily as he stole the necessities for his own existence.

Gascon's sacrifices grew more bizarre daily in hopes of breaking through the barrier of oblivion but still Victoria slept. Nikolai took only enough nourishment to survive, venting his cruelty in ways Felix had come to accept as normal.

The power Felix held over the two vampires encouraged him to take chances even when unnecessary. He watched, year after year, the pathetic display of sadism employed in an effort to revive Victoria, and lived his life on the hectic edge of insanity. For he knew the truth. Knew it would take his blood to raise her from the dead. It had been revealed to him that night in the coach on the road to Algiers. He had dreamed of the jeweled dagger and its ultimate purpose.

The time for its fulfillment approached far too quickly, so he rushed through the hours left to him like a madman. He courted death even as he denied its existence.

Felix returned late in the day. The blood of last evening's offering congealed on the dais before Victoria's coffin. A severed head lay a short distance away, thrown there by the force of the decapitating blow. The thin-bladed sword stood upright, imbedded several inches in the dirt floor where Gascon had left it. Dried blood stained the fine Toledo steel.

The rest of the body was gone. Felix had seen the headless corpses before, brutalized by the creature Gascon had become. And such sights no longer caused him pain.

Blood clung to his sandals as he crossed to the coffin. A

yearning he had not felt for a long time filled his heart. A desire
to look at the lovely face again, to see the unlined brow, to kiss
the cold lips. To conjure in his mind the vision of Victoria
smiling, laughing. They might as well all be dead for the way
they existed without her gentle influence.

A single heavy candle burned at each corner of the coffin.
He lifted the lid and saw the dull gleam of the dagger, lying on
her black shirt.

*Now is the time*, he thought, fitting his fingers around the
jeweled hilt. His heart raced. Blood coursed through his veins,
but he felt no fear. Only love and the desperate desire for her to
rise once more even at the cost of his own blood spilled.

He knelt beside the coffin, pressed the point of the knife
into his throat, and closed his eyes. He had forgotten how to
pray. The seconds that followed filled an eternity. A cold hand
wrapped around his wrist, staying the motion that would have
ended the waste of both their lives.

Felix opened his eyes and saw a haggard creature lying in
the coffin. A thin hand clutched his wrist so tightly the dagger
clattered to the floor.

"Felix. Help me." Victoria struggled to sit upright.

He lifted her from the coffin and sat holding her.

She hid her face against his shoulder, unwilling for him to
see the creature she had become.

"Take what you need. I have nothing to offer but that which
will give you life." He leaned back against the coffin, exposing
his throat. The wrinkled cheek rested a moment against his
neck. Then cold lips sealed over the knife prick on his throat.
In one brief flash, his pain vanished and joy flowed over him as
she drank from the fountain of his youth. He thought he would
die from the sheer pleasure of giving her new life.

He sat for some minutes, cradling her in his arms, brushing
a strand of hair from her forehead, touching the soft unlined
face, before she spoke.

"Why were you going to kill yourself?" she asked. She held his hand to her cheek, feeling the hard callus, the rough nails.

"I had a dream. It was the only way to wake you."

"And Nikolai gave you the dagger with which to commit this act?"

"Yes."

"My dear Felix." She brought the hand to her lips and kissed the palm. "I have not been here to protect you and Nikolai has made you his pawn. It was never necessary to die to bring me back. The simple offer made of love was enough but that's an act Nikolai would never understand." She stood and pulled him up beside her.

"Where are we? What is this place?" She wrinkled her nose at the odor of rotting meat. "Where is Nikolai? And Gascon?" She walked several paces into the darkness.

Felix had grown used to the smell, but was made aware of it once more by the look on Victoria's face.

"Sweet Jesus! Felix! What is this?"

"It's—it's—Victoria, we must leave here. Right now, before the others wake." He tried to draw her away from the rotting body on the floor.

She moved further into the darkness, nearly stumbling over a cache of bones and partially decomposed bodies. The odor was unbearable.

"Felix, this place is an abomination. Please. No more, please!"

Shielding her from the slaughterhouse, Felix drew her into his arms.

"I—they tried so desperately to bring you back."

"No! No! I will not be the cause of this carnage. Don't tell me that! I refuse to believe it. How could this hideous—" She grew calm in his embrace. "You're right, Felix. We must leave, now. Hurry, it's almost dark. They will be rising soon and I will not be part of this inhuman conduct any more."

"We must take the coffin. Here, put this on." Felix handed her a bundle of black cloth lying on the floor. He stopped long enough to show her how to slip it over her head. The heavy woven garment fell all the way to the floor. He fastened the face covering in place, leaving nothing visible in the candlelight but her eyes.

"You look just like the women who walk the streets here. Follow a few steps behind me and it will look perfectly ordinary." He bent to lift the coffin.

"I'll help you."

"I can manage, Victoria. I'm not a little boy any more."

"Yes, Felix, I noticed. What is the year?"

He lifted the coffin to his back, bending under the weight. He thought for a moment, then said, "Sixteen hundred thirty-seven. You were asleep a long time. I've missed you."

Victoria looked at Felix standing near. She reached out and touched his face.

"All those years gone and only a grain of sand has fallen in the hourglass of my existence."

They moved out the cave-like entrance of the building into a shadowed alley. Never had the desolation of the street been so evident to Felix. The open sewer and scabrous one-legged beggar repulsed him. The level of existence he had sunk to made him sick. He led Victoria hurriedly away through the maze of streets, the single purpose in mind to put as much distance between them and the vampires as possible before complete nightfall.

The hour of moon-rise found them at a dead end. Felix knocked three times at the wall. A gate opened to reveal a woman dressed the same as Victoria. She invited them into a cool, fragrant garden.

The stones under Victoria's bare feet were smooth and soothing after the hot street. She watched as Felix set his burden to the side and moved to greet an elderly woman. She removed the burnoose he wore and touched his long dark hair as he bent to kiss her cheek. He spoke quietly into her ear. Victoria heard and the reply was surprising in its sincerity.

"Of course, both of you are welcome here. Haven't I told you many times to visit as often as you like." The old woman smiled at Victoria as Felix coaxed her toward them.

"You may show your face here, my dear. We are only old women, serving girls and occasionally this stalwart young man, to whom we are all indebted." She reached out and touched the veil, catching her breath audibly as the drape fell away, exposing the soft milky skin, full red lips.

"Felix," she admonished. "Do not lie to me. This child cannot be your sister. Who is she and how did you come about having her in your possession? A beauty such as this surely must belong to someone of much importance."

Victoria reached out and took the aged hand in both of hers, then spoke in French.

"Madame, I have run away. I cannot go back. Felix is not to blame. But you and I must protect him from the evil that will befall him when they find me gone." She knelt before the old woman, clutching at her hand.

The matron gently raised her. Lamplight gleamed dully from the single piece of jewelry Victoria wore. The Valfrey coat of arms. The old lady patted her hand gently and then pushed back the hood, releasing the mane of curly red hair.

"You are right, my dear. Our Felix will be in a world of trouble when they find you gone." She turned and drew the two of them inside, leaving the coffin to rest where it lay.


Outside, the moon covered the city with a soft sheen that white-washed the ancient buildings. Deep in the crumbling edifice that had sheltered the vampires since their arrival years before, Gascon rose and prepared for yet another sacrifice.

He straightened the filthy rags he wore and moved toward the candles flickering round Victoria's altar. A few steps across the way he stopped.

The coffin was gone!

"Victoria." Gascon spun around, searching the shadows for her presence. She was truly gone.

It took a moment for her absence to penetrate the chaos that had ruled his life for the last decade. He continued to turn around and around until he was sane enough to think.

"Nikolai," he whispered and staggered away to find him.

Through the maze of dark chambers he wandered, unsure of where to search, equally unsure of how much time was slipping away. Gascon set aside an impending sense of urgency to find Victoria and prove his devotion. Now he concentrated on locating Nikolai.

Gascon stood before the big coffin. Thick dust mottled the dark surface as though it had lain sealed for years.

"Nikolai. Victoria has risen."

He moved closer and swiped at the filth with both hands. "You must wake. We must go to her."

Gascon's words whispered around Nikolai. He lay in the coffin alone, lost in a wilderness that was at once a dream and a nightmare. His memory frozen on the child of light she had once been. He had taken that light from her—taken her into his night for his own purpose, that she might make his darkness brighter. His blood flowed in her veins but still she had found the strength to move beyond his control. To create Gascon.

And this oblivion. She did it to punish him for the painter whose name he could no longer even remember.

The coffin was full of noise, slamming doors, voices raised in anger. Rodrigo. Faithful friend. Gone. The pain of that loss was still a tangible thing. And just when he needed Victoria most—gone. But even now, alone here, he could feel her slight body lying across him. He could bear knowing she rose early only because it gave him an hour of pleasure knowing she shared this small death with him.

Now she was gone. Why didn't Gascon go away as well?

Near dawn the lid of the coffin rose. Nikolai emerged and sat in the dirt beside Gascon. "She has not awakened."

"She is gone, Nikolai."

"The coffin is gone. And Felix? Felix is gone also?"

"Yes." Gascon raised his head and looked at Nikolai.

"Then she is not awake. Felix has stolen her."

"What are you saying, Nikolai?"

"Only by sacrificing Felix could we bring her back."

"Why have you only told me this now? I would have cut his throat long ago."

"What a fool you are, Gascon. What a fool you have always been. Do you love Felix?"

"I—no."

"Neither do I. But Victoria loved Felix as he loves her. Love and blood, Gascon. We are all bound by love and blood. And the bond must be strong to call one back from oblivion."

Gascon scrambled to his feet and stood looking down on him. "You are insane. First to have caused this catastrophe. And now to think Felix would give up his life for her? Humans are pathetically weak but they cling to life like beggars cling to a crust of bread."

"Is that what you did, Gascon? Cling to life as she forced her divine gift on you?" Nikolai asked, his voice loud and mocking in an attempt to hide his jealousy.

Gascon stepped back, puzzled by the bitterness and envy he heard.

"No. No, I gave it freely, out of love—and desire—and need. I wanted to give her everything I was—"

"And you had to die to do it."

Nikolai continued to sit in the dirt. The silence stretched between them.

"Well, you are right on one cause, you and I have become the beggars. And Felix is our crust of bread. But instead of lying down to die for her, he has taken her away. Do not worry, we will find them."

The old woman remembered the way of young lovers so she hurried about, setting the servants to the horses and a small coach. By moon-set they were on their way from Algiers, bound for Cairo, the city of all worlds, determined to make the most of what they felt would be too short a time together.

Victoria and Felix traveled erratically, moving first along the coast, then inland, both sleeping by day and pushing the horses to the limits of endurance by night.

Neither spoke of the time in Algiers, eager to forget the waste of that portion of their lives. Occasionally they forgot the cause of their flight long enough to find pleasure in each other, but they never tarried long in one place.

After an absence of almost a century, Victoria's ability to see the future, and the past, returned with ruthless cruelty. In a surprising moment of understanding, she realized it had been there all along, merely suppressed by Nikolai's power. Now it reared an ugly head every time she touched Felix, plaguing her with visions of his participation in their madness and murder. But she touched him anyway, even when she repeatedly saw the part Nikolai had deemed he would play in her resurrection.

She gave in to his fierce demands, and reveled in the pleasure of his love, knowing in her mind that even his strong young body would quickly wither in the attempt to appease her needs. Just as she knew in her heart his despair was justified. And always, when she touched him, she felt the darkness that was Nikolai.

Felix drove for months, trying to escape the strong emanations of danger from the sea. Victoria's vision of their ultimate demise made him more certain than ever that they must not come within Nikolai's reach.

The roundabout journey eventually brought them to the outer reaches of the Sahara Desert. Felix set up camp in the shadow of the pyramids, too weary to travel further. The horses were beyond salvation, and but for the constant attention of Victoria, Felix would have given up long ago and succumbed to the mystery of the world where they now found themselves.

Felix watched Victoria, standing near the edge of a dark shadow that reached across the desert. The late autumn moon rose slowly behind the great pyramid, riming it with bloody radiance. A luminous prophecy of what they both knew awaited their arrival in Cairo.

He stepped up behind her, wrapping her in a warm embrace. She shuddered involuntarily, turning immediately to kiss him.

"Felix, my brave Felix. My champion. My bright knight. I have no armor to give you for protection. There is no victory in the coming duel for us."

He took her face in his hands and kissed her eyes, her lips, her cheeks. Fear shook her as she pressed closer.

The moon continued its relentless rise behind the eternal creation of mankind, its bloody existence fading to pure white light as the desert came to life around them.

"We must continue our journey without stopping in Cairo, if that is where danger lies," he said, not questioning her wisdom in those things he could not see.

Far away to the north, a wolf howled long at the full moon.

Her strong arms clung to Felix, passion and vampire strength threatening to crush him as she drew him down to the sand.

"Love me, Felix. Love me tonight. There will be few tomorrows."

The hot sand warmed her cold body, adding its fire to the heat of Felix's passion as the nocturnal goddess, Moon, rode her ever constant lover, darkness, across the sky. Dawn hesitated to break in the east, reluctant to cast its light on the thousand and one tales of Scheherazade. Stories of a lifetime relived in a few short hours in the existence of a mortal man and a woman as eternal and mysterious as Cheops.

Victoria held his naked body, listening to the fragile heartbeat, feeling his breath on her cheek as he slept. She fought down the blackness closing around her heart.

"I promise he will not hurt you, Felix," she whispered.

*But who will protect you, my sweet child?*

The voice came to Victoria from across the distance. She clutched Felix closer and stared at the woman walking toward her. The night was cold and still, yet the long flowing dress whipped around her legs. Her bare feet crushed heather where she stepped and the scent made Victoria close her eyes and smile.

"Mother."

*You cannot save him, Victoria. Even now the dark one destroys the other who gave you his life.*

"No!"

Victoria had hardly spared a thought for Gascon since her flight from Algiers. Now she couldn't escape. Her mother held her transfixed. Moonlight touched the flowing dress with silver and shadow. The wind off the moor swept dark hair back from her fine-boned face. But it was Gascon's face that smiled at Victoria.

Gascon, young and eager to share his knowledge. Gascon brave and filled with compassion for his fellow Frenchmen. Strong in his demand to belong only to her. Now that pledge was being broken forever. All she could do was cling to Felix while Nikolai punished her for giving Gascon life.

She could feel his anger so strongly it hurt. The wind blew fierce at his back, the white sails of a boat pale and ghostly in the moonlight as he approached. Gascon stood at his side, yelling to be heard over the crashing sea. Victoria heard their voices clearly, as though they stood as close as the vision.

"I tell you, Nikolai, she is alive!"

The silver sand pitched and tossed like the grey-green sea beneath the bow of the boat where Nikolai and Gascon stood.

"I would know if she were. My blood flows in her veins!" The dark cape cracked like a whip to emphasize his words.

"And *her* blood flows in mine! I tell you, she is alive!"

*Please, Gascon. Please, say no more.* Victoria wanted to scream. To tell him to seal his lips on the words that clearly inflamed Nikolai. But she could do nothing but watch the tragedy unfold.

"You could have chosen a more fortuitous time to remind me. I allowed it. I gave you to her. In a moment of weakness—and for reasons you could *never* understand."

Nikolai grasped Gascon by the shoulders and pulled him close. "I have come to regret my decision." The words were cold and deadly but Gascon was already captured, unable to escape—or defend himself. With slow willfulness Nikolai drew him close, lips lingering a moment against the flesh of his throat before sharp teeth ripped through the jugular and crushed the fragile tissue as he severed the spinal cord.

Victoria moaned, unable to do more than watch and whimper. She tried to look away, to close her eyes, anything to shut out the horror. But her mother held her enthralled.

Nikolai looked up from the bloody act of destruction as though he sensed her watching across the chasm of time and distance separating them. For an instant Victoria thought she saw remorse in his eyes. Then he lifted Gascon's body, heaved it into the turbulent waves, and turned his back to her.

Victoria heard her mother whisper through the thunder.

*You cannot defeat him now, Victoria.* The precious vision began to fade. *But the day will come* . . . .

"I promise he will not hurt you, Felix. I promise," Victoria whispered the words over and over as though saying them could make it true. She knew she could do little but surrender when the time came.


They lived on the brink of disaster, constantly running, hiding, always looking back for the approach of the darkness on the horizon that might announce Nikolai. The Nile swept them up in its display of feast and famine. Victoria regaled Felix with stories told to her from the memory of Nikolai and his early existence. The life and times of the warrior, dealing death on every hand, never tasting its horror, but savoring the sweetness of the draught of life.

Victoria fed only when it became crucial, hoping against hope the day would come when it was no longer necessary. Felix aged before her eyes, their fierce lovemaking draining him of life as she knew it would.

Victoria rose earlier than usual as they entered the Valley of the Kings. A stillness stole over them. The awe of the burial grounds filled the quiet afternoon. The wind ceased to blow. Not even an insect buzzed. Civilization as ancient as the evening that descended took away Victoria's fear. It filled her with a sense of amazement, of wonder, that centuries might pass and still those mortals entombed here would remain hidden from sight of man.

Hand in hand Victoria and Felix walked in the Valley. She ignored the present and used her gift to read the past. Pointing to the blank walls, naming those who resided within the hollows and mazes. All confined for eternity with the comforts of their earthly existence.

She stopped on a flat almost level plain.

"This one, Felix. This young one is the most important. This boy king with his treasures will be the one most searched for and the last to be found."

They turned and went back to camp. Without warning, Nikolai stepped from the darkness.

"My dear young friends, has your adventure been all you hoped for?" He was clearly back to his old charming self.

"Master. We have lived too long in fear of your shadow." Felix spoke, moving closer to Victoria.

Nikolai strode quickly to kneel before her. He took her hand and kissed the ring she wore. He rose, still holding her hand.

"It's time to go, my dear," he looked deep into her eyes, smiling to soften the command.

"She isn't going with you. Not ever again." Felix's voice trembled, destroying the bravery of his words.

Nikolai dropped her hand and spoke, still searching the depths of her eyes.

"I see you have experienced her sweet secret. The passion she brings to one such as you is something no mortal can long endure. Even now you decay before her eyes. Her love is a flame that will consume you as surely as she might drain your body of blood should she so choose."

He turned to look at Felix, a quiet smile on his face, cruel laughter in his voice.

"Tell him, Victoria. Tell him how he could never hope to hold your love. Tell him how his frail human flesh and heart cannot endure the passion our kind must have. It is as crucial to our existence as blood. Be kind and gentle if you must, but tell him now before my patience wears even thinner!" He disappeared into the darkness, leaving the sting of his words behind.

Victoria sank to the ground, relishing the pain as harsh gravel bit into tender flesh. She wrapped her arms around Felix's knees but she had no tears to wash away her betrayal.

"It's true, Felix. It's all true," she whispered. "I can see how my love destroys you but I cannot give you up anymore than I can give you life eternal."

Felix knelt beside her.

"I know. It could be no other way." He dug deep in the folds of the white cloak he wore. The hand that reached out to her held the jeweled dagger. "I know the end of this dream. This time with you has simply made it more bearable."

He pulled her down to lay beside him on the rough ground.

"Do it now, while I can think of nothing but you and the joy you give me." The knife flashed from hand to hand, making quick cuts across his forearms. He held both arms out to her.

Victoria took the dagger from his bloody hand, moved into his embrace and kissed him. He held her close. Blood soaked through the black garb she wore. She drew the thin dagger across his throat even as his lips moved against hers.

"I love you, Victoria."

The blood had begun to dry on her skin when she gathered him into her arms and retraced their steps of the early evening. Scrabbling in the gravel and rock, with torn and bleeding hands she unearthed the opening to the tomb of Tutankhamen and placed his body inside.

*A long time from now, the world will call you a grave robber, but this is a fitting monument to one I love.* She took the time to replace the stone exactly the way it had been, and with a deep sigh, gave herself up to the night.


Nikolai saw her walking toward him, covered in blood. Her own dripped from torn hands to trail darkly across the sand. The night wind blew at the black dress, freeing the dark hair. She lifted her face to the breeze and Nikolai stood before her, the reins of a black stallion held loosely in his hand. She allowed herself to be lifted into the saddle and Nikolai swung up behind. With a word to the small party, they moved swiftly across the desert, bringing the coach with them.

After an hour of hard riding, Victoria allowed herself the

comfort of leaning against Nikolai. Neither spoke, he simply drew her up against his chest and let his arms rest possessively around her. The lingering scent of Felix's blood washed over him, stirring him angrily.

*She cannot blame me for this death*, he thought and never spared a moment for her anguish.

They arrived at a large encampment, the men moving her coffin into a tent at Nikolai's command.

Victoria went to it without a word and shut out the world with its harsh reality.

The tent was bright with filtered sunlight when she rose. Fresh clothes lay on a cushion and a guard stood at the entrance. She must have made some slight noise for he turned, stepping inside. Bowing, he gestured with his hand from forehead to lips to heart and spoke in a language she did not know. He moved back to the entrance and clapped sharply. Women swathed in dark robes, faces draped against unwanted inspection, entered and moved around Victoria, fingering her red hair and touching her white skin.

Another woman entered and sent the girls scurrying away with a word. Within minutes they were back with a small basin of water and bottles of scented lotion. They cleaned her from head to toe with a minimum of water, one young girl moaning over her broken nails and torn fingers.

Victoria forced herself to think of Felix. Past the reality of his blood washing away along with the residue of the time in Algiers and their frantic journey to this place. Felix had indeed given back her life. Felix had opened her eyes to Nikolai, made her see what she had become. It wasn't pretty but she had no choice but live with it—and Nikolai.

The women dressed her in loose pants and a short jacket. The costume tied and draped all about with veils and gold fashioned into chains and coins. They dressed her hair loose and sweet smelling. One young woman slid a gold bracelet all the way up her arm past the elbow and another draped her face with a sheer veil that hid nothing.

The chatter hushed and Victoria turned to find a brown skinned man standing just inside the door. The white shirt he wore hung open to the waist, exposing bronzed skin. His loose white pants were tucked into tall boots and a curved sword hung from the belted waist. The women disappeared quickly. He looked at her a long time, not bothering to hide the hatred in his dark eyes.

"My Master awaits the pleasure of your company," he said, speaking in halting French. His lips twisted beneath the well-groomed mustache. He turned back to the entrance, showing his distaste for the errand but executing it as ordered.

Victoria moved out into the desert twilight, stopping to let the beauty of the multi-hued violet and pink sunset fill her with joy at being alive again. The escort touched her elbow, urging her forward.

Victoria entered the next tent, expecting to find an Arab sheik and found Nikolai. It all began to make sense. These were his people, his tribe and this young man had become more than his favorite. He had taken her place as a source of affection. If Nikolai sought to punish her for the transgression of Felix, so much the better. Perhaps it meant he would leave her alone for a time. She felt no need for his companionship or that of any other man and wondered if she ever would again.

Nikolai rose and pulled her to his side. He embraced her and innocently kissed her hand.

"Please. Join me. You are as beautiful as ever." He led the way to a large pile of cushions scattered on the floor and sat only after she was comfortable.

Her escort already lounged on another group of pillows to the right.

Nikolai waved a hand in the young man's direction. "Pay no mind to Hassan Saleh, our customs seem queer to him. He does not understand that looking at a beautiful woman makes the night pass so much more pleasantly." Nikolai spoke in French for the benefit of Hassan and Victoria was rewarded with a flash of hatred.

Victoria decided then to protect herself in whatever manner necessary when time for a showdown came. She shifted closer to Nikolai and spoke in English.

"And what of Gascon?" she asked, peering into his eyes and smiling, knowing full well what had transpired between them.

"Ah, Gascon," he said, reaching out to remove her veil. He threw it aside, ran his hand into her hair and pulled her close. His lips were almost on hers when he whispered. "Gone the way of all those who dare to disobey me."

She kept the smile on her lips as he crushed her mouth with his. Victoria could see the jealousy in Hassan Saleh's face as he hurriedly rose and left.

*This one will destroy himself if I allow it*, she thought, and gave over to the conquest Nikolai needed in order to trust her again.

Daybreak found them at the end of an old ritual and once again she lay in the coffin with Nikolai, now more for her own protection from Hassan than out of love.

## Chapter Fifteen

The years passed slowly, Nikolai seemingly content with their Nomadic way of life. They broke camp and traveled at night, always to another southern-most place, forever following the Nile.

The riches grew from time to time as Nikolai's young men formed raiding parties and attacked traveling caravans, robbing and killing. His male harem grew and still he spent most of his passion on her. Hassan finally destroyed himself in a fit of jealousy, riding into the desert to never return. Nikolai had not questioned why.

Victoria knew. She smiled. Only she could hear his agonizing pleas while the blazing sun ate the flesh from his bones. Such foolishness for the sake of one who had no compunctions about life and death, or the destruction of someone he professed to love held as much meaning as the wind that swept the ever-changing sand.

The desert changed to lush countryside and finally to jungle as the people became darker skinned and more hostile. Everything changed and still it remained the same. The passage of time was marked by the style of clothing they wore, the horses and camels they replaced. And the group traveled on. Its numbers swelled and diminished periodically as the years progressed, but Nikolai carefully surrounded himself with those of his own kind.

Victoria remained one beautiful white woman among the many dark-skinned natives. But it didn't matter. They never saw civilization as she had once known it. She was forced to dress as a man and to ride as a man, to join the raiding parties, to witness the bloody massacre of women and children. She withdrew into herself until none of it mattered at all.

Nikolai became a savage again, much in the same manner Felix had once described to her over a century ago. The black tribes of the region they passed through were constantly at war with each other and Nikolai enjoyed pitting his immortal warriors against the humans.

Sometimes the will to live in the humans was so strong, Nikolai's band would slink away decimated, licking their wounds before passing into another area to replenish the stock.

Victoria was never allowed to take part in the creation of vampires. She was constantly watched, never able to make close contact with anyone other than Nikolai. She could barely remember any other way of life. She learned to speak every new language they encountered and wrote a simple history of each part of the country they toured. She became a genius at planning strategy.

Nikolai slowly came to rely on her judgment though he always scouted out her plans before going in harms way.

They eventually found themselves in the desert again, fighting a band of small, hardy natives the other blacks referred to as Bushmen. Nikolai tried unsuccessfully to add several to his family, but some inner strength caused each one to die the true death rather than turn to the manner of existence that required them to drink the blood of another to survive.

Victoria could smell the salt of the ocean hundreds of miles away as they approached the southern edge of Africa.

Raiding a small camel caravan, they discovered a cache of diamonds among the booty and began to scout the source of such riches. Nikolai's trusted lieutenants returned with word of a place where black men picked up the rocks as they lay on the ground. In raid after raid, Nikolai amassed a fortune in the rough stones.

The year 1765 found Nikolai and Victoria once again pushed into the world of sophisticated humans. They rode into Cape Town, the capital for politics, religion and wealth of the

Cape Colony, and set up house. They were soon established as the couple to court for whatever the world at large could provide.

Nikolai found he could no longer control Victoria. She moved in circles of her own within the circles of domination he created. No one paid heed to their unconventional life style, the Count's extreme wealth allowed for a certain amount of eccentricity on his part and his wife could certainly do no more than adhere to his schedule.

Their lives became a constant round of entertainments, week after week, year after year, but there was no gaiety for Victoria. She played the part of the beautiful spoiled wife before those dignitaries Nikolai wished to impress but in private he was abusive, stopping just short of physical violence. The savagery of his feeding had not abated with their return to proper society.

The hour before sunset became the only time in Victoria's life that could be called her own. The inner clock they all functioned by had always allowed her to rise early, so that bittersweet time could be spent alone. The call of the sea drew her often away from the fine mansion with its tasteful furniture and fancy clothes. The dock was always crowded with ships, loading and unloading cargo. She would stand in the shadows and watch the black and white and yellow men, muscles straining under the tonnage of tea leaves and silk fabrics. Gangplanks bent and swayed with the rhythm of their steps to and from the waiting drays. The air was filled with the scents of the world; exotic spices from Cathay, honest sweat from the toiling men, cabbage cooking somewhere in the dark regions of nearby taverns. Time and again Victoria was hailed by sailors and workers, lauded for her beauty, only partially hidden by the dark hooded cape.

As the years passed she grew bolder. When the fog rolled in, obscuring the forbidding sun, she would don a provocative dress and strut the docks like the other whores, but no one ventured to tell of her conquest in the taverns. Those who sampled her wares were so smitten they lost all taste for food or wine or work and soon drove themselves to madness in their obsession to have her again. Most times Victoria contented herself with simply feeding the beast within. Her passion simmered unsatisfied, for Nikolai no longer gave her even that small gratification.

The political leaders and the faces of Cape Town changed constantly. Most were diplomats marking time, awaiting the next post up the ladder of protocol. They were happy to spend their time in Cape Town partying, growing rich at the expense of the few white natives and the many black ones. It never became necessary for Nikolai and Victoria to hide their constant youth from curious eyes as it had been during their long stay in Paris. Once gone from Cape Town, no memory of South Africa included the Count or his young wife.

One evening Victoria woke early as usual. She put on her favorite dress, a copy of an old style made up in dark green satin. The low-cut neckline bared most of her small firm breasts. Puffed sleeves fit the upper arm, leaving her shoulders bare. The three-tiered hoop skirt adorned with black ribbon bows complimented black elbow length gauntlets. She picked through several jewel cases before choosing an emerald set in a gaudy display of diamonds to slip on her finger. The maid dressed her hair and fussed over the folds of the dress.

For all the girl's devoted attention, Victoria knew she belonged to Nikolai and watched her every move. Victoria pined quietly for Chloe but that memory conjured the ghost of Gascon, his smiling face mocking her for her grief after more than a hundred years. With effort, she banished the memory to the dark recesses of her heart.

"Thank you, Ina. Please ask Jefar to come to me. I would have a word with him before the Count's guests arrive."

"Yes, madam." The girl curtsied impudently and moved slowly across the room, straightening the bed linens, gathering up the silk dressing gown.

"Ina! Jefar, please. Preferably before dinner." *The little spy*, Victoria thought as the girl finally departed.

Victoria stood on the balcony watching the sun plummet toward the sea when Jefar arrived. He shut the door softly and smiled as he crossed the room.

*There is still time*, she thought and reached for the cape. In less than a heartbeat, she stood on the dock, lifting the bulky skirt in order to move about more easily. A sudden, over-whelming sense of doom made her gag and retch. She stood very still and peered inward, visualizing the hold of the black ship anchored before her. She had never seen it before and sincerely hoped never to see it again.

The large cargo area was filled with a mass of teeming humanity; sick, starving human beings, chained and lying in filth. No air or light penetrated that dark place. Placing a hand over her mouth, she held back a cry of anguish. Victoria turned and rushed blindly away, cape billowing, fine dress forgotten in her anxiety, and stumbled into a man standing at the foot of the gangplank.

"Whoa, there. What's your hurry, ma'am?" He took in the fine clothes and jewelry in a glance and then she was gone, jerking out of his grip to disappear into the shadows.

Victoria watched from the growing darkness as her would-be rescuer was joined by another man and they walked away together. She shuddered and took a deep breath trying to contain her revulsion at the slave ship.

Her dark shadow moved away from the dock through the rapidly closing evening. Away from the horror of the waterfront and up the hill to what she thought was sanity. Victoria paused on the balcony, for once eager to be inside where the gleaming chandeliers and forced frivolity that always accompanied

Nikolai's entertainments might bring some relief to the suffering she had felt on the dock.

Inside, Jefar waited. More faithful to her than Nikolai, he never allowed his preferences to show out of fear for her safety. She swirled the cape off into his hand and continued across the room. She paused in her journey before a full length mirror. The image reflected there was of a beautiful young woman, the regal gown a bit disheveled. Victoria smoothed her dress and replaced a stray curl.

Jefar stood by the door, his silence cautioning her to be quiet. Downstairs Nikolai greeted his guests. Victoria knew his behavior would be unbearable if she were late. She squared her shoulders and shut her eyes for a moment. Then she smiled pleasantly at Jefar. He smiled back as he opened the door and bowed her into the wide hallway.

"Everything shall be as you wish, madam."

"Thank you, Jefar. You and Ina may go after dinner."

"Yes, madam."

Victoria moved haughtily down the wide staircase to where Nikolai waited.

The smile froze on her face as Nikolai spoke from the foyer, drawing her attention to his guests.

"Victoria, allow me to introduce Captain Emile Schmidt and Captain Jeremiah Stone."

The German, Schmidt, clicked his heels smartly and bowed. The sword at his side fascinated Victoria. Though nothing was visible, the smell of stale blood was nauseating.

"Madam," he said, looking up and reaching for her hand.

His hard face was curiously improved in appearance by a jagged scar running from the edge of his left eye halfway down the cheek. The German smiled cruelly, as though anticipating her reaction but Victoria had borne witness to far more hideous wounds. She tucked her arm through Nikolai's to avoid touching him and merely nodded in his direction.

The other man stood a head taller than the short, stout Capt. Schmidt. His evening dress was considerably out-of-date but the black jacket with gold braid on the collar suited him. Captain Stone looked far more impressive than the German, who wore his tailored uniform poorly. Sensitive gray eyes surrounded by a maze of tiny wrinkles looked at her in surprised recognition.

"Pleased to meet you, ma'am." The deep voice spoke of a land far away; of long, warm nights, of time slowed to the point of peaceful oblivion.

Victoria held tightly to Nikolai, more afraid of touching this man than the other.

"Good evening, gentlemen. Nikolai, perhaps our guests would like a drink before dinner," she said, leading them all into the drawing room.

Enthroned on a Louis XIV chair, Victoria drank her way through the early evening. She spoke only when spoken to and watched the anger grow behind Nikolai's blue eyes. Her own gaze dared him to reproach her for some imagined indiscretion.

They all sat at table, Capt. Schmidt and Capt. Stone both commenting on the pleasure of the well-prepared meal. The alcohol numbed Victoria until she was hardly aware of her surroundings, until Nikolai placed his hands on her bare shoulders.

"Captain Schmidt and I have some small amount of business to discuss, my dear. Would you mind entertaining Captain Stone?"

Nikolai held her chair as she rose, then she took her wine glass in hand and left the room without speaking. She could hear the Southern gentleman following close behind as she moved through the house toward the garden. The doors were flung wide to the evening and Victoria stepped out to the balustrade. The tangy breeze from the ocean cleared the alcohol fumes from her head.

Jeremiah Stone stood quietly at the edge of the light.

"Thank you, sir. For not speaking of our meeting at the dock," she said, without turning.

He stepped up to the heavy ornate rail, following her gaze to the open sea where an aging moon showered the water with splinters of light. Ships at anchor were rotting skeletons in the spectral trace.

"Your beauty rendered me speechless, just as it does now."

Victoria lifted the glass to trembling lips and drank. She turned to look at him.

"How can you associate with that monster?"

He looked at her, puzzled by the question.

"Captain Schmidt? Well, ma'am, I agree he isn't much to look at and Germans on a whole are not the most cordial folks, but I would hardly call him a monster."

He leaned against the wide handrail, watching her.

"The hold of that ship is overflowing with men, women, and children, chained together like animals. Forced to lie down with their dead brethren, in their own excrement. And you say the man is not a monster? The man is inhuman."

She tossed back the remainder of the wine and set the glass down so sharply it shattered. Turning her hand over slowly, she stared at the blood pooling darkly from tiny gashes in her fingers and palm.

The Captain stared, aghast at her violence and the force of her accusation.

"Countess? Are you saying Emile Schmidt is a slaver? Then, what manner of business is he conducting with your husband?" He made no move to aid her.

"Oh, it would be just like Nikolai to have a part in such misery."

He watched the beautiful face contort in rage and pain as she clenched the injured hand into a fist, forcing slivers of glass further into the wounds.

"Countess, you must excuse me for the rest of the evening." He started for the drawing room, then turned back at the door.

"I'm afraid there is nothing I can do about Captain Schmidt, I sail on the morning tide for New York." His quick steps echoed down the hallway, then she heard the front door slam.

"There is something I can do about my husband," she promised the night. Clutching her favorite dress with a bloody hand, she paced back and forth on the porch, allowing her fury to grow.

The moon no longer lingered on the sea when she heard the German take his leave. The soft clink of gold coins grated across her hearing, setting her teeth on edge.

Nikolai joined her in the darkness.

"Ah, here you are. Captain Stone left quite early. Did you enjoy yourself? I know how you are drawn to that type of man, my dear." He embraced her, and drew back at her trembling.

"What is this?"

"Nikolai, do you love me?" Victoria looked up into his eyes, probing with all her skill.

He looked away, his will challenged as never before.

"Love is far too simple a word for—what we share." He turned to walk away.

"Nikolai, give me one good reason to love you."

She hesitated, waiting for his answer and when he did not speak, she continued. "Keep your gold and send Captain Schmidt away."

He laughed—a mad cackling sound.

"So that's what this is about. Captain Schmidt has a product to sell and I wish to buy. Have pity on those poor creatures, Victoria, most will die before they reach their destination. I'm doing those I choose a favor."

"Please, Nikolai. Just this once. Let things be the way they used to be."

"I thought you would have learned by now, my dear. We

can never go back, only forward into the uncertainty that awaits us all, whether we be vampire or human." He stood with his back to the railing.

"I won't allow you to cause those poor souls more misery."

Her words were spoken quietly and in the next heartbeat, she struck him. Clenching the bleeding hand into a fist, she hit him again across the temple. Blood poured from a gash at the edge of his hairline made by the emerald ring.

The force of her attack surprised Nikolai. He staggered back and over the rail, crashing noisily into the dark garden below.

Victoria vaulted over behind him, with no thought for the cumbersome dress she wore until it caught on the balustrade and ripped half the skirt away.

Nikolai leaped upward and caught her in mid air. He wrapped her in a rough embrace, pinning both arms to her sides and, with a low growl, reached for her throat. He couldn't control her trashing but his teeth ripped open her cheek. Blood streamed down her pale face and neck.

Victoria slammed a knee into his groin and broke free, clambering awkwardly over the balcony rail.

Nikolai caught her from behind, burying both hands in her tumbled hair. They landed on the porch together, Victoria sprawled face down. Nikolai fell on her, his knee in the small of her back. Then he yanked her hair with both hands.

Victoria turned and twisted, trying to break free but her strength was no match for his. She heard the crack of her spine a heartbeat before numbness began to spread through her body.

Nikolai let her go and stood, his breath coming in harsh gasps. He staggered into the house, crashing into furniture as he made his way upstairs. Once in her room, he began throwing things out the french doors. Nikolai found the coffin, picked it up and hurled it out into the darkness.

He finished wrecking the room then ran to the balcony and with a single bound, changed in flight to a bat.

## Chapter Sixteen

Victoria held on to consciousness by sheer obstinacy. There was no pain, only an excruciating numbness that froze her to the stones. The coffin crashed somewhere in the rose garden.

A rush of wings swept past on the wind.

*He knows I am alive and he would still leave me. Bastard. How long must I lie here until the sunrise ends it all?*

*Not long, my sweet child. Not long.* The words whispered in Victoria's heart.

*Oh, mother, let it be done. Please. Let it be done now.* Victoria shut her eyes and her mother's face smiled at her from the ramparts of her long ago home in the Highlands.

*You can't give up now, Victoria. Duncan is so close. Close enough to keep his vow.*

*Duncan is dead, mother.*

*But he kept his word. Captain Stone commands the Sea Witch. Duncan sent her. To witch you away on the morning tide.*

*I am still Nikolai's prisoner.*

*He does* not *control your mind!*

Victoria turned her inner sight to the waterfront as the vision faded, taking her mother's face and words away. Jeremiah Stone tossed in his bed. Sweat drenched his naked body. In her mind, she lay beside him, quieting his turmoil, cooling the heat of his passion, giving the satisfaction he sought. His dream made it very clear he needed her. The words she wanted to hear filled her mind.

"I want you, Victoria. I need you. Come to me."

But she lay on the cold stones of the balcony unable to move, to even call his name. The effort of reaching out to him cost so much, too much, but she would not let go.

Jeremiah sat up abruptly, pistol in hand. "Who's there?"

The darkness of the cabin was overwhelming. He stared into it but the one brief image he had seen in his dream was not here. It was outside. A narrow section of grey stone, a wide balustrade, the scent of roses—and blood.

"Victoria." Jeremiah grabbed a pair of pants and jerked them on, tucking the pistol into the waistband. Pulling on a dark knit sweater, he hurried out and headed straight for the mansion overlooking the harbor.

From the outside, the house was dark but the front door stood open, a quiet invitation the Captain found deceiving. Drawing the pistol, he moved cautiously down the hall toward the pale glow of candles in the drawing room. He expected any moment to be set upon by the angry Count.

But no one appeared, not even a servant. He found Victoria on the porch where he had left her hours before. She lay face down, blood pooling wetly on the stones. He turned her over gently, the torn dress and bleeding face telling the whole story.

"I'll kill him," he said, through gritted teeth.

"No." The effort it took to speak caused Victoria's world to tilt. "Coffin," she whispered, concentrating on speaking the words as she thought them. "Garden."

The force of her words came through in Jeremiah's mind. He stumbled around in the garden until he found the ornate wooden chest. After a struggle, he managed to right it, then drag it toward the short flight of steps to the porch. Hurrying back to where she lay, he knelt beside her. From somewhere deep in his heart, he suddenly knew what she wanted. To be in the coffin.

As gently as he could, he gathered her up and started across the wide porch, stepping on the torn skirt, ripping it further. She moaned softly and opened her eyes when he laid her inside. He couldn't bear to shut the lid.

Turning away, he rose and paced around the small clearing.

Broken glass and small paintings littered the walkway and rose beds. Crazy bastard. All her beautiful possessions destroyed, like he had destroyed her beautiful face. Jeremiah looked back to where she lay like a shadow in the coffin. He had to have help to get her out of here. The long, elaborately chased casket was too clumsy to handle alone. He stood for a moment, the strength of her need demanding he do something, yet making him afraid to leave her.

Suddenly his indecision vanished and he started back to her, picking up a bright gold necklace and a wood-handled hair brush. Gathering up the torn dress, he stuffed the fabric inside, dropped the jewels and brush in then eased the lid down until it clicked shut.

He rushed through the deadly silent house. There had been no one to help her. He'd lay odds the Count was often abusive, driving the servants from the house at the first sign of violence.

Outside, the street curved away down the hill. Directly across the way, a man lounged against the fence. His clothes were much the same as Jeremiah's, marking him a sailor. Jeremiah studied him in the fading moonlight and for an instant wondered why he was there. Then he thanked the stars he'd found help so quickly.

"Yo, mate. Looking for a ship?"

"Ya."

"Give me a hand here. I sail with the morning tide."

The burly, fair-skinned sailor followed Jeremiah back through the house. Jeremiah picked up another necklace and stuffed it in his pocket. Once in the garden, he took up one end of the heavy box and the sailor grasped the other without a word.

After struggling for what seemed like hours, they reached the ship. The world was still shrouded in darkness but the Captain felt he had survived a week in a foreign land since first seeing the lovely, frightened woman on the dock at sunset.

Captain Stone kept his word, sending the sailor to find a bunk and get some rest before the tide turned. The Count appeared to be a man who would go to any lengths to keep what belonged to him and Jeremiah figured it would be best for the lady if no one in Cape Town knew where she'd gone.

Jeremiah opened the cabin door and maneuvered the coffin in as best he could.

"It's a good thing no one is awake to see this," he muttered as he lit a lamp. "Superstition may be dead and buried but someone would comment." Raising the lid, he knelt beside her. She looked dead but her chest rose and fell gently. He poured water into a basin and tried to clean her torn face.

"Why would anyone destroy such beauty?"

He cut away the ruined dress and the tight whalebone corset beneath, tossing the scraps in a corner. Her skin was pale and cold. He grabbed a quilt and covered her clumsily.

Victoria moaned but didn't open her eyes. He couldn't bring himself to shut the lid again.

Stretching out on the bunk, he fell asleep instantly. Only to be awakened moments later by sounds of the crew preparing to catch the morning tide. He jumped up and rushed out, returning quickly to lock the door. Jeremiah met the first mate coming down the passageway with a steaming cup of coffee.

"Must have been some party last night, Captain," he said, grinning wickedly. "I got a look at the friend you brought aboard."

Jeremiah swallowed a mouthful of scalding coffee and coughed harshly. He stared at the man who had made a hundred sea voyages at his elbow over the edge of the steaming mug.

"He was sleeping off a damned good drunk on deck, so I sent him below. Told him to take the dead watch tonight."

Captain Stone blew on his coffee in relief. The first mate meant the new crew member and not the woman lying in a coffin in his cabin.

"Well, I didn't know he was that drunk but we've been short a hand a while. This will be a rough trip and, God knows, we need all the help we can get."

The two of them made their way above deck. Lean, rugged men bustled about, each bent on his own task. Somewhere in the city a cock crowed, the sound just loud enough to intrude on Jeremiah's concentration. The deck was barely light enough to avoid confusion. The sudden rattle of anchor chains shipping broke the tension that knotted Jeremiah's neck.

*The sooner we put open water between the Sea Witch and Cape Town the less likely the Count will ever discover where his lady has gone*, he thought.

The tide carried the clipper away from shore and row upon row of cloud-like sails hoisted heavenward to billow and catch the northwesterly wind. The Sea Witch sprang forward like a pedigreed whippet. Its sleek black hull sliced through the swells with no pitch or roll. The sun finally rose over Cape Town but Jeremiah Stone never looked back. He stood on the main deck and prayed silently.

*Dear Lord, leave me this good wind today. 200 miles between us and Cape Town before the next turn of the tide is all I ask.*

"Put her full into the wind, Mr. Hamm, and leave her there for as long as it lasts. I'm going below for a while."


The black bat came to rest near the balustrade and Nikolai appeared. Darkening blood stained the porch where he'd left Victoria. She was gone. And the coffin. He'd done everything but rip her head off. It should have been impossible for her to get up and walk away but she was gone. He moved frantically through the house, searching. Across the street, the guard he had posted was gone, too. Somewhere in the distance a cock crowed. A final warning, the hour was late.

Where was she?

Nikolai rushed back to the porch and one ship leaving the harbor caught his eye. Clouds of white sails billowed skyward as it caught the wind and sped toward the edge of the world.

Deep in his heart, Nikolai knew. Victoria lived and this time she had made good her escape. He ran to the edge of the rail and shouted.

"You will never be free of me. My blood flows in your veins." He pounded a clenched fist on the rail and screamed. "You are mine forever."

The sun broke through the cloud cover, spreading radiance over the garden and porch, forcing the screaming Nikolai back into the house. Back to safety from the only enemy he had never been able to conquer.

## Chapter Seventeen

Jeremiah Stone sprawled across the bunk, exhausted. Ten days of good wind and hard work had almost swept his mind clear of those last hours in Cape Town.

He slept deep, lost in dreams cloaked in swirling mist. Through a thick fog he sailed, toward one glimmering patch in the distance. No wind filled the sails yet the ship moved through the gloom, ever pursuing that one beacon, its elusive brightness a siren song in the silence of his mind.

Captain Stone stood at the bow and peered into the fog, filled with a longing only the sight of her face could assuage.

*She's dead. I saw her broken body in the coffin.* A tear fell softly to the pillow he clutched like a lifeline.

The ocean whispered its comfort cool against the thin skin of the ship. The small room filled with haze. It swirled and moved, finally settling over his body to caress the fevered brow, to cool the hot throbbing in his groin. Jeremiah slept straight through the day.

Nightfall found him rested and eager for the evening. He took the case containing the astrolabe and went aft. The stars were so bright he could see almost as well as in daylight. They were still on course and the wind had freshened. At this rate they would make New York in another 60 days. A record trip even for the Sea Witch.

He placed the fine instrument back in the case and then he saw her. She stood barefoot at the rail, dressed in a pair of pants rolled up to the ankle. One of his shirts billowed away from her body. Loose hair became a tangled mass of curls in the wind. He was not surprised to see her alive and well.

Jeremiah stared at her watching the sea for a long while, then went to stand at her side.

"Do not come near me, sir."

"I won't harm you, Countess."

"Don't call me that! My name is Victoria." She gripped the rail with both hands.

Captain Stone took in the expanse of water with a glance.

"The ocean is as docile as a wife tonight." He turned a bit, for a better view of her profile. Starlight illuminated her pale skin. The wind whipped hair across her face, but she made no effort to contain it.

"Sometimes she's like a wild mistress. An untamed creature no amount of loving can soothe."

"Passion spent on such a temptress must be well worthwhile or men would not go to sea so often."

Jeremiah heard the tiniest bit of humor creep into her voice.

"I see you know a great deal about men."

She leaned forward against the rail.

"What does Mrs. Stone think of your love affair with the sea?"

"I have no wife," he said. "The call of the roaring tide seduced me at the age of eleven and until now I have never found a woman who could match her passion."

Victoria tossed her head, hair flying in the wind.

"I have loved many men in my life and my lust has doomed them all."

"Why, ma'am, you seem to have a caring, if not altogether gentle, nature."

"I am not what I seem, and if you come one step closer, I fear we are both lost."

Jeremiah placed a large hand on her frail shoulder, turning her to face him. The full force of her beauty struck him again, all signs of injury gone.

"I was doomed from the first moment I looked upon your face, even before I felt your cold kiss on my fevered brow and extinguished my fiery member in your cool liquid sea."

Victoria pulled away from his vivid remembrance of her dream but he would not release her.

"You cannot draw back now. There is no turning back for either of us."

Victoria leaned into the unexpected embrace, overcome by fear.

"You are my liberator. I would not harm you but the very act of my loving will destroy you."

He held her at arms length.

"I'm not so easy to defeat. Even that mad woman out there has tried and failed. See the gold ring in my ear?"

Victoria nodded, looking at the thin gold loop piercing his left earlobe.

"Only a few survive shipwreck and we all wear the gold ring. The men consider it good luck to sail with me. They say my good fortune rubs off on them." He took her hand and rubbed it against his face. "Stay with me and your luck will change, too."

"Such things might be possible in the real world, but I exist in the limbo of purgatory. Forever lost to paradise, held in thrall by my own private hell."

"We have many nights ahead, Victoria. I will hear every story of how you came to be what you are and I won't turn away from your need or your passion."

Jeremiah wrapped his arm around her shoulders and urged her back to the privacy of his cabin.

From high in the rigging, a lone sailor watched.

Jeremiah found the days busy and the nights magical. He listened with fascination to the tale of Victoria and Nikolai. Wept with her over the loss of twin brother, Duncan, the light side of her darkness. Saw in her the oracle that was her mother.

While the hours raced away like the wind that moved them closer to their destination, Victoria learned about the clipper. The legend of the Sea Witch sprang from her own homeland.

She stood at the bow with Jeremiah when he told her of the Scotsman, Donald MacKay, the designer. Duncan's voice thundered across the centuries, filling her heart and mind with words long forgotten.

*The bond we share will reach across time and distance and when you need me I will be there.*

With breaking heart, she told Jeremiah the tale of the night in the crypt. Of waking to the blood, waking to the need to feed the serpent even at the cost of those dearest to her. How Nikolai had provided this means of escape by denying her the blood of her brother.

Nikolai's voice echoed in her mind. *It must be my blood, Victoria. Only my blood can fulfill your destiny.*

Now this ship, designed by her brother's descendant flew through the night taking her further and further from the man whose love would destroy her.

The hour grew late and the pleasant silence between them stretched. He sat at the desk and plotted positions on the map. Victoria read from the journal he kept day by day. She deciphered his peculiar brand of abbreviations with little difficulty. "How long have you been at sea, Jeremiah?"

"Almost 12 months."

She laughed, then was suddenly serious. *And I left Scotland almost three hundred years ago.*

"I believe Duncan *did* truly send you to rescue me. The Sea Witch has followed my flight across the ages. Here," she pointed at one entry. "London." She flipped the pages. "Calais, Barcelona, Alexandria, Cape Town."

"Well, if he did, it certainly took a very long time. But that Scotsman puts his heart and soul into designing his ships. And even if I have trouble believing he created Sea Witch to be the fastest, most travel-worthy clipper ever made just for you, I knew the moment I walked on her deck I was destined to command her. And she did bring me to you."

"I can never thank you enough for all you've done," Victoria whispered. *Duncan, my dearest brother, my flesh and blood, my heart, my soul. I can never thank you enough.*

She continued to turn the pages slowly, reading silently until she reached the last entry.

"Why is there no mention of me here? I see where the bosun was ill and you found dead rats three days in a row."

He put his pencil down and rubbed the back of his neck.

"Oh, you're there," he said, getting up to look over her shoulder. Flipping back a few pages, he pointed to a small upside down v. The cuneiform appeared on random pages. Sometimes it had a vertical line drawn through it.

"I see. Then this must be you," she said, tracing the boldly stroked line with a narrow oval fingernail.

Jeremiah couldn't see her face but the smile in her voice pleased him. He placed both hands on her shoulders and pulled her back against his body.

"Tell me what the future will bring," he asked, caressing her neck.

She let his touch fill her mind with soft skies and warm night winds. "The future will bring us much closer together than this," she stated, unable to keep the laughter from her voice.

He let go and sat down across from her. He stretched both hands out on the table, palms up.

"I'm serious."

"So am I," she said, drawing their sign on his palm with a fingernail. Victoria looked at him for several moments and decided he really wanted to know. Smiling softly, she placed both hands over his and took a deep breath.

She was outside the cabin immediately. The sea had become choppy, white froth topping the waves. All the sails were furled but two and still the Sea Witch sliced through the turbulent sea. In the crows nest far above the deck, a lone sailor knelt, holding a large squirming rat. The crunch of bone and gristle drowned out the screech of the rising wind in bare rigging as he bit the rat's head off and gulped the token amount of blood.

Victoria jerked in the chair, causing Jeremiah to grasp her hands tightly.

"There's a storm on the way," she said.

He loosened the grip on her hands in relief. "Is that all?"

"There's another vampire on the ship." She looked at him across the table. "I don't know how he's hidden from me this long. The rats you found, they were decapitated?"

Jeremiah nodded.

"He's probably been spying on me for a long time and Nikolai warned him to be discreet. Only the young ones will resort to eating vermin when they cannot have human blood. He has every reason to fear Nikolai." Victoria continued to watch Jeremiah. "I must destroy him. Before we make port or he'll send word to Nikolai."

"Where is he? I'll go toss the bastard overboard." Jeremiah went to the desk and removed a heavy leather bludgeon, knotted at both ends and weighted with metal.

"It won't be easy. Vampires don't trust humans. I'll draw him out. Then you'll need something wooden. Heavy and sharp enough to pierce the heart. I'd do it myself, but I don't have the strength yet."

"Isn't there anything I can do alone? I don't want to involve you in murder."

"This is not murder, Jeremiah. This one creature could massacre every member of your crew if he needed to feed badly enough. Besides, according to human standards, he's already dead." Victoria stared at her hands to avoid looking at him. Fear that knowledge of the other would affect the way he thought of her hurt.

"What a turn of events. Here I thought we had escaped the

Count completely. You must think me very naive, but this is my first encounter with your world. Why can't they all be like you, then this problem wouldn't exist."

Victoria finally looked up. Jeremiah was smiling. It didn't matter a whit about Nikolai or this night sailor, all he cared about was her. A wave of relief lifted her spirits. The two of them could handle the situation.

"The storm is days away. We must take care of this by then."

They put their heads together and set about planning a course of action, each one concerned only with the safety of the other.

## Chapter Eighteen

Jeremiah Stone continued to live a life torn between light and darkness. If friends and crew noticed anything unusual, it was passed off as preoccupation with the record speed of their passage. Their destination loomed closer on the horizon and everyone knew the best prices would go to the first ship to make harbor. Tea and spices from the Orient were always in high demand in New York and the Sea Witch already had a reputation for being one of the fastest clippers ever built.

The falling barometer set the crew on edge. Nothing was visible in the sky but the lookout constantly scanned the horizon in all directions.

Jeremiah's sensitive ears ached. He wasn't sure if it was the approaching low front or constantly grinding his teeth in worry over the plan Victoria had concocted. He paced the upper deck and tried not to think about the past evening.

The cabin had been like a cage, but he remained there while Victoria sought out the night sailor. She had been curiously subdued when twilight brought her inside.

She went to the coffin and took several pieces of jewelry from her pocket.

"He's just a boy Nikolai sent to spy on me," she said, saddened by the fact she could not allow him to live.

"He gave you the rings he found in the garden. Does that mean he obeys you?"

"He serves Nikolai through the bond of blood. He respects me because we share that bond but Nikolai alone commands him."

"So we go ahead as planned?"

She lay down beside him. "Yes. And you must be strong for me." Dawn at last smoothed the crease between her brows.

Jeremiah wondered exactly what had passed between the two vampires. He was the outsider in this game. Would loyalty to her own kind win in the end? The encroaching storm heralded the final stage soon to be set.

The Sea Witch demanded attention but Jeremiah could read her moods. Rough seas reverberated through the sleek hull up to the deck under his feet. The clipper ship was in her element, slicing cleanly through the alternating swells and troughs with none of the wallowing of the older schooners.

The command to wait until the last moment to stow sails had the crew scurrying for positions. Lifelines were already strung for the safety of those needed on deck during the worse.

Overcast skies darkened to the north. Whitecaps whipped in the quickening wind. Jeremiah lashed the wheel in position. The wind shifted due south and still the clipper plowed through the sea under full sail. Spray washed over the deck, wetting everything, before Jeremiah finally gave the word to drop all but the two main storm sails.

The Captain stood with both feet planted on the deck as the fury of the gale increased all around him. The ship responded to the slackening sails, riding smoothly in spite of the high sea. Men and ship alike were already wet through by waves breaking over the rail when the first rain squall hit. Jeremiah sent all but a few crewmen below. Two sailors on the helm, four to watch the storm sails, all his best men. He made careful plans for the lady tonight because he would be busy elsewhere.

The excitement of the storm and the planned danger aroused Jeremiah until he could hardly stand the waiting. The electricity in the air communicated itself to everyone. He strode quickly past men busy at their tasks, some worried, some exhilarated like himself. He planted his feet deliberately in anticipation of every move the ship would make in the tossing elements.

Below deck he shed the wet oilskins and rushed to the

cabin. Victoria stood silhouetted against the windows, dressed in trousers, his shirt tied in a knot at her waist, hair slicked back into one long thick braid.

She rushed into his arms, kissing him hard.

"Are storms always like this?" she asked, breathless. She clung to his neck with one arm and wiped water from his curling hair with the other hand.

"Full of power. Yes. Excitement—and fear. Whatever it is, I love it." Jeremiah put his hands around her waist and lifted until he gazed into her face. Rain pelted the windows, deepening the darkness inside the noisy womb.

"Your eyes are the color of that endless stormy sea," she whispered.

Her words sounded like a poem he'd once heard but he couldn't quite remember where. He laughed. All the doubts about the coming battle disappeared. This was his woman and no man, human or vampire, would stand between them.

The Sea Witch had slowed considerably and the rain passed over. Jeremiah stood in the darkening room, holding her close, his breath ragged and fast. His body begged for release.

Victoria knew that feeling well and understood.

"First the hunt, then reward," she whispered, her lips moving against his wet beard.

Jeremiah lifted her higher and pressed his face into the open throat of her shirt.

"We must hurry," she spoke softly.

He set her down and tried to contain his feelings.

"I have everything ready. The short harpoon, the axe. Are you sure this is the only way?"

"I truly wish it were not."

They went to the door and looked out. The hall was clear. Victoria slipped past him and vanished into the shadowy recesses of the lower deck.

Jeremiah took the weapons and moved out into the elements

again. Stygian darkness melded ship and sea. He could make
out the helmsman only because of the nearness of the position.
Rain lashed the ship from all quarters but this section of deck
was an old friend. No surprises tonight. The wind died for a
moment and he caught a glimpse of Victoria near the aft rail.
She whirled around, revealing a tall man locked in what could
have been a lovers embrace. Spray surged over the deck and
sent them tumbling. Jeremiah rushed to help her as the rain
crashed down again.

"Victoria!" he screamed. The shrill whine of wind in the
rigging drowned out his voice.

Grabbing a lifeline, he turned round and round searching
the deck for the two struggling vampires. Then he saw them,
rolling toward the corner of the workshop, away from the open
drop to the water. The white of Victoria's shirt glowed wetly in
the dark night. She was on top when Jeremiah reached them.
He dropped the axe and grabbed her by the shoulder, tearing
her away from the grip of the male vampire. A look of surprise
registered on a handsome, clean-shaven face, the face of the
sailor that had helped bring the coffin aboard weeks ago.
Before he could move, Jeremiah drew back the short harpoon
and drove it into the vampire's heart.

The vampire screamed in fury and struggled to rise. Blood
spurted from the wound and was washed away by the lashing
rain. Victoria added her strength to Jeremiah's and the wooden
shaft of the harpoon plunged all the way through the vampire's
heart. Nailed to the deck by the metal spear, the body gave a
final shudder and lay still.

Victoria turned to Jeremiah and pressed her face to his
chest. He could feel her breath coming in greats gasps. The
storm wrapped them in a cocoon of fury where normal sight
and sound couldn't exist. She broke away and stumbled to the
axe.    Grabbing the double edged instrument of destruction
from her, Jeremiah braced both feet on the deck and brought

the axe down. The first awkward blow missed the vampire's neck and lodged in his shoulder. Jeremiah turned aside quickly, vomiting hot liquid as he lost his dinner.

Victoria broke the axe free and brought it down again and again until she severed the head. A cold wave broke over the rail, sweeping it into the angry sea. The dead vampire floated grotesquely in the rush of water. Victoria leaned against the harpoon anchoring it to the quarter-deck. The tempered steel broke with a snap and the body was consigned to the deep.

Hail battered down, forcing Victoria and Jeremiah together for protection. Jeremiah bolted for cover, dragging Victoria along. He caught a glimpse of the skeleton crew lowering the remaining sails, but he knew there would be damage. He turned into the storm to go below deck and a large hailstone struck him over the eye. He fell back unconscious, taking Victoria down beneath him.

She lifted and bodily carried him down the stairs. Once in the cabin, she placed him on the floor and quickly stripped off his wet clothes. Her own joined the same pile.

Jeremiah groaned and tried to sit up. He raised a hand to the knot on his forehead. Victoria briskly rubbed him with a quilt. A rush of blood surged through his cold limbs as lightning lit the room, silhouetting Victoria kneeling beside him. Her hair had come loose and curled in a tangled mass over her breasts. He buried both hands in the wet tresses and pulled her down, kissing her. Enlarged incisors dug painfully into his lips.

Victoria stiffened and tried to pull away.

"No! I need you!" he insisted

"It's the blood, Jeremiah. You're bleeding and I need to feed!" She tried to turn away, to hide from his prying eyes.

"Then do it, dammit, and for once we'll both be satisfied."

Victoria settled down over his body, accepting with great appetite all he freely offered.

The intensity of the storm diminished, unable to match the

passion contained in the small universe of the captain's cabin. Above decks the crew scurried about, raising sail, anxious to take full advantage of the wind. The dream of gold soothed the sting of hailstones and fear of high seas.

The weather grew cold and gray. New York loomed just over the horizon. The Sea Witch sailed into harbor at an full speed. The owner was waiting on dock, having been alerted to her arrival by the shore watch. They were no more ecstatic than the crew at making port three weeks ahead of schedule.

Jeremiah stood on the quarterdeck watching his men respond to the order to lower sail. It was a routine occurrence now, a drill the men practiced over and over during the long voyage so it could be done in a matter of seconds. The speed slacked off abruptly and the ship eased into the dock without even a bump.

The crew lined the rail as the owner and his wife came aboard. They joined Captain Stone on the quarterdeck and were met with a rousing cheer. Jeremiah's crew left the ship as quickly as the stevedores boarded. By the time he had packed a bag, the cargo was on its way to the warehouse.

Jeremiah usually stayed at a small boarding house for the short periods between voyages but now he wanted more. Something special for Victoria's comfort and pleasure so he ventured into the village. He needed to show her his New York, but he really wanted to show her off to the world. A trip to the Commonwealth Bank put cash in his pocket and a visit to Lord & Taylor's provided something more fashionable for evening wear than a ten-year-old dress uniform. He'd never been good at entertainments but now he welcomed his business partner's invitation to dinner. He smiled. It would be the beginning of all the pleasant time he could spend with Victoria. He wanted to show her the world and New York would be a good beginning.

He returned to the Sea Witch late in the afternoon, and waited for the hour before dusk when she would rise. It no longer bothered him to watch her step from her bed of death, her body young and firm, her exotic eyes bright with life. She smiled and slipped his shirt on, then perched on the edge of the bed beside him to brush her hair.

"Let me," he whispered.

Victoria handed him the wood-handled hairbrush he had rescued half a world away and they sat close as twilight shadows closed out the rest of the world. She still had not regained all of her strength. The damage to her back seemingly had numbed her perception as well, though she knew distance alone had weakened Nikolai's terrifying hold before. Fear and anger had also disappeared, giving her a sense of security she had not known since the early years.

Before Gascon.

The overwhelming grief for Gascon's love and loyalty had softened over the centuries. But not Nikolai's jealousy. Even after his demand for sacrifice had cost Gascon's existence, the suspicion and mistrust had not lessened.

Jeremiah's gentle strokes pulling the brush through her hair, the whisper of the sea beneath the Sea Witch as she rode at anchor in safe harbor, made Nikolai and all those centuries of struggle seem far removed from this time and place.

"I've taken rooms in town," Jeremiah said. "At the Prince George Hotel. It's quite the rage. You can eat, sleep and even have a hot bath right in the suite. But you can't just stroll into the lobby of the grandest hotel in town dressed in my shirt."

"So I must play the role of the Countess again?" she asked. Victoria stepped away from the bed, the collarless shirt changing as she pirouetted into the green gown she had worn that fate-filled night in Cape Town.

"No!" Jeremiah stood quickly.

His outburst chilled her and she banished the vision instantly under the sudden burden of tempting chance.

"How did you do that?" Jeremiah asked.

"It is an illusion," she whispered, her voice strangely disassociated in the near dark. "As I am an illusion. I can make you see what I want you to see. And it was but the last gown I remember wearing."

She read his mind and saw his alarm. "I'm sorry. I didn't mean to frighten you."

"I never want to see you like that again."

"So tell me what the women of New York are wearing."

Jeremiah shrugged. "I see them, but how can I ever notice what they wear when all I do is compare them to you."

From his thoughts she gleaned the image of a woman.

"What about Amy?"

"Walter's wife? Well, I did see her today."

His partner's wife had been at dockside, drab as the day in a grey wool skirt and jacket, pale hair pulled back in a severe knot beneath a hard brimmed hat. Victoria changed as he watched.

"It doesn't suit you," he said.

"It didn't suit her either," Victoria said. "Not enough color. And it needs a little decoration to make it less practical." The entire outfit transformed to navy blue with gold braid edging at the collar and wrist of the long sleeves. The hat disappeared and Victoria's hair softened around her face.

"I'm ready."

"I'm amazed. You do so much to improve a simple traveling suit." Jeremiah opened the door but Victoria turned quickly to the coffin.

Tearing open the lining, she scooped out two handfuls of fine, dry soil and slipped it into her skirt pockets.

"Now, we won't have to worry about moving the coffin."

"It's the soil that protects you?" Jeremiah asked. "Why can't you put it in your shoes and be safe all the time?"

"It might work, if the sun weren't too bright. But, Jeremiah, proper ladies do not sleep with their shoes on."

"Most husbands probably wouldn't notice."

She laughed at his shy humor. "So, shall we, sir?"

"We shall, madam."

He locked the door and followed her down the dark hall. The calm waters of harbor were misleading, making him stumble and he cursed quietly as they moved out into the night.

Outside, the thunder of wagons and mules had vanished with the setting sun that marked quitting time for the stevedores. Victoria paused at the bottom of the gangplank. The ripe odor of fresh fish mingled with the more earthy aroma of animal dung as the wood planking of the pier changed underfoot to cobblestone. Everything was coated with a slime that left Victoria a little queasy after months of the brisk wind through the clippers rigging.

Ships were docked as far down the pier as she could see.

"There are so many."

"New York Harbor is the busiest in the world," Jeremiah said.

They walked along South Street, where multi-storied warehouses lined one side of the thoroughfare and ships from all ports docked at the wharf. "There's the Cutty, just returned from another trip to San Francisco. Not a single ship here can beat her, except maybe Sea Witch."

His words filled Victoria with excitement that perhaps she had finally escaped Nikolai. In the time it took him to arrange passage, he might never know she had come here.

"Is the hotel close?"

"Actually, no. It's some miles away. But we can hire a hansom cab just around the corner."

"You don't keep a horse and carriage?"

"Whatever for? Public transportation is more convenient, and cheaper. Besides, I'm not usually in town very long."

South Street led them down into an open field bordered on one side by buildings under construction. Jeremiah was as surprised as Victoria to find it filling up from several directions with a noisy, bustling crowd.

He took her hand and drew her closer as they edged around the mass.

"Is it always so—" Victoria began to speak then stopped, unexpectedly overcome by the confounding mass of humanity assaulting her senses.

"Busy? No. Must be some kind of political rally. It's almost Election Day."

Paris and a distant century's political strife rose out of the darkness of Victoria's memory. But the devastating hostility she'd felt all those years ago that had led to dark and bloody death was not present here. She let the courage and strength of this crowd flow over her, and felt it warming her, welcoming her with some inherent value that touched a chord in her heart.

She and Jeremiah moved around the fringes, where the brick paving of the wide street made firmer footing. Light flooded the muddy open area from tall buildings on several sides and each intersection was marked with a street lamp.

Someone had pulled a wagon into the crossroads and a woman stood on it shouting for attention.

"Ladies! Ladies!" A hush shifted through those waiting. Victoria stared. Most of them were women. A few men accompanied some of the girls. She put a hand on Jeremiah's arm and they waited together as the woman began to speak.

"It's that Anthony woman. Preaching about suffrage again."

"Suffrage?" Victoria asked.

"She's practically inciting them to riot."

Victoria stared at him. "She is not! Look how organized and peaceful they are." Not at all like the men she had witnessed become murders and thieves in the name of what they believed was right. She could get to like this peaceful idealism. America's democracy was so much better than the angry revolution of Gascon's Paris.

"Give it fifteen minutes." He pulled her reluctantly away from the crowd, but the woman's words followed her all the way to the corner and beyond.

They walked another few blocks without finding the cab Jeremiah looked for so they caught the first trolley that passed heading in the right direction.

Victoria sat in the covered carriage and marveled at the sophistication of New York. The hour was far past sunset, yet people strolled the streets, the women draped in furs and the men wrapped in long coats and scarves. Gas lamps on every corner gave the night a festive glow.

"Where do all these people go? Is it a party?"

"Oh, yes. New York has an abundance of night life, as Walter puts it. There's a new opera house on Broadway. I'm not sure who's performing but we'll go. And there's the symphony."

"I love music. And it has been a long time since I had the pleasure of such entertainment." And even Paris, with its arousing boudoir soirees, had never presented the possibility of so many diversions. If only—if only it were not necessary to endure the dark side of her nature. For once, the animal was quiet, but it would return. At least here, she could spare Jeremiah that maltreatment. She could feel his gaze lingering on her face, soft as a lover's caress, needy as a beggar starving for bread. She had to stop feeding from him. Soon.


Jeremiah's idea of putting her soil in her shoes proved interesting as she ventured out more and more into the cold overcast winter days of New York. He introduced her to Lord

& Taylors, and it proved a place of constant amazement, providing all the accouterments to accompany the high neck dresses with their soft lace bodices, tiered skirts and finger length tight-waisted jackets that suited her small figure well.

Dinner with Jeremiah's partner, Walter and his wife, Amy, turned into a somber affair, with Victoria being spirited away upstairs before dinner by two tiny children. She had responded to their sweet goodnights of breathy little French phrases in kind and they immediately insisted she talk to their new governess. The girl, recently arrived from France was homesick and fell tearfully on Victoria as she cried out her misery.

The bleak childhood rode to Victoria on a swell of darkness that threatened the confidence she had so recently found. It brought painful memories of her dear sweet Chloe. Victoria had not been able to help Chloe. But she could help this girl. And she promised she would.

After dinner, while the men enjoyed their cigars and brandy, Victoria toured the surprisingly pleasant Sutton house with her hostess. The combination of mellow wood-paneling, soft sand-colored marble and the simple graceful form of the Louis XVI furniture filling most of the downstairs rooms pleased her.

"Your home is very lovely," Victoria said.

"Thank you. Walter allowed me to do all the decorating. You and Jeremiah are our first guests." The young woman was far more attractive tonight, the ever-changing illumination of gas lights shimmering through the blonde hair and elegant brocade gown.

The fumes still bothered Victoria, who longed to throw open the wide windows flanking the many fireplaces.

"Only the first of many who will enjoy your lovely choices." She led the way out of the library. "I hope you will not object but I've invited Genevieve to a meeting tomorrow evening. It will, of course, be after the children are asleep."

"What sort of meeting?"

"She wants to become a citizen of this country and I will introduce her to a lady who can give her special instruction."

"And who might that be?"

Victoria ignored her pointed question. "You are welcome to attend. I'll bring a coach at eight for your convenience."

"I'll speak to Walter and if he thinks it's acceptable, we'll be ready when you arrive."

"Thank you. I believe you will enjoy the meeting. Although in a very different way from Ginnie."

They joined the men in the parlor and Jeremiah and Victoria said their goodbyes. In the cab she told Jeremiah of her plans.

"You're taking Amy to a Suffragette meeting?"

"She doesn't know yet."

"Oh my god, Walter will be furious. Come to think of it, I should be furious with you for suggesting it. But I'm not."

"Because my desire influences you. And Walter isn't going to know until it's too late. Support from the Amy Sutton's of this city is what Miss Anthony needs if she's going to be successful here. And I certainly hope she will. The entire world needs to treat women better."

"Can't you see what will happen?" Jeremiah asked.

"There are some things only history can judge. I fear Miss Anthony's crusade will be one of those things. Its resolution is so far removed that even my mother's gift cannot bring it into the present. Don't you think the children are pretty? And smart?" Victoria asked, in an effort to lighten the conversation.

"Yes. And thank goodness they look like their mother and think like their father." He watched her with a hunger in his gaze so bold it made her turn away.

Victoria stared out at the passing parade as the coach traveled through the city, using her vampire power to hold Jeremiah at bay. Amy's comment earlier that the silver strands at his temples made him look very distinguished told Victoria a far more destructive story. She was determined not to feed from him again while she had other choices.

The following evening Amy and Genevieve were both ready when Victoria arrived a few minutes before eight.

"Walter thinks offering classes in citizenship is quite an idea. He says I should get more information and perhaps organize a school where those who want to can go and study."

Amy was dressed grandly, fitting her position as a successful merchants wife but Victoria had chosen a pristine white shirtwaist and dark skirt and cape in deference to the French girls simple wardrobe. Her hair was dressed in one long braid coiled around her head in a manner almost like Genevieves. The now constant craving for blood made her teeth ache. Her hands trembled ever so slightly. Despite Victoria's control, once in the coach the serving girl grasped her hand and spoke rapidly, the language of love soft as she was drawn to Victoria's need.

"What is she saying, Countess?"

"Please. Do not use that word. Here I am Victoria. Nothing more." Victoria shushed the girl with a smile, bidding her to sit quietly. "She thanks us both for helping her. And the cook is teaching her to speak better English."

The promise of snow in the air had forced the meeting inside, so the three of them crowded into the back of the wide lobby of the *New York Evening Post* building. Tonight there were almost as many men in the room as women.

*She's gathering strength*, Victoria thought, then she concentrated on the charismatic voice of the speaker.

"'—Some may think it too soon to expect any action from the convention. Many facts lead us to think that public opinion is more advanced on this question than is generally supposed. Besides, there can be no time so proper to call public attention to a radical change in our civil polity as now, when the whole framework of our government is to be subjected to examination and discussion. It is never too early to begin the discussion of any desired change. To urge our claim on the convention is to bring our question before the proper tribunal and secure at the same time the immediate attention of the general public.'"

The lecture came to an end all too quickly with a loud round of applause and the assembly scattered into the night. Their conversations lingered at the edges of Victoria's sensitive hearing.

"Come with me," she said, leading her companions into the company surrounding the table at the front of the long room. So great was her resolve that the crowd parted before her, allowing them easy access to the three people answering questions.

"Miss Anthony? How do you do? I'm Victoria MacKay and I am very pleased at last to meet you."

The woman in the middle acknowledged her greeting.

"I'm very pleased to meet you, Victoria. And your friends?"

"Mrs. Walter Sutton," Victoria introduced Amy and waited as she shook hands with the pioneer of female equality, "and Miss Genevieve Orman."

They all smiled as Ginnie gushed over Miss Anthony in French.

"Ginnie would like to become a citizen of the United States and I told her you would be the perfect person to educate her."

"I'm very flattered, Miss MacKay. If you'll help Miss Orman give her name and address to Elizabeth, we can have someone come round to visit her in a day or two. Meanwhile, perhaps Mr. Bryant and I might have a word with Mrs. Sutton."

"I would like that very much, Miss Anthony," Amy said.

*Heaven help Walter when she gets home*, Victoria thought.

Victoria and Ginnie followed the older woman up stairs to an office where all the vital information was set down in a ledger. There was no way to avoid the hand the woman offered in friendship. Victoria grasped it tentatively, then more firmly as it became clear the words the woman downstairs spoke to charge her followers came from the passion of this woman's heart and mind. The two of them had formed an impressive partnership.

The night slipped away swiftly. Victoria hurried Ginnie into the street and hailed a cab. Once safely inside, hidden from the world, she stopped fighting her need. The familiar fog filled the coach, tinging the close universe red around the edges, and she invited the girl to sleep on her shoulder. Searching her mind for some pleasant thought to fill her dreams, Victoria found only loneliness and despair, so she swept the girl away on her own dreams of home and happiness, of Duncan and a time when the world was light, before her choices took her down this dark path that had led her so far astray.

She loosened the buttons at the front of Ginnie's shirtwaist, exposing the juncture of soft shoulder and throat. Enlarged incisors slipped easily into the tender flesh and Victoria drank, the sweet blood of youth filling her with such a sense of sorrow she could hardly breathe.

Victoria woke Ginnie when the cab pulled around to the rear entrance of the house. She watched the girl enter the kitchen then gave the order to return for Amy. Victoria found her having coffee with Miss Anthony and Mr. Bryant, whom Amy introduced as the editor of the *New York Evening Post*.

They hurried out to the waiting cab.

"Oh my, it is late. Where's Ginnie?" Amy asked.

"I took her home earlier. She was very excited. And tired. I told her to go straight to bed."

"You're so thoughtful. I can see why Jeremiah is attracted to you. Though you're not his usual choice."

"You seem to know very much what he likes."

The driver dismounted to help Victoria into the coach, but she set him aside with a tilt of her head, deferring him to Amy.

When she was settled inside, Victoria sat across from her, knowing the darkness would serve as a shield against scrutiny while she could watch Amy's face when they talked.

"I know the sea is his only love, his wife, his mistress."
Amy's voice dropped to a whisper. "He will never marry you."

"I know. Even more than you. I have stood watch beside
him, seen the sea at her worse—and best—and knew there
would never be a cure for the enchantment which binds his
heart to her. He also knows I can never marry him—for more
practical reasons. I already have a husband."

"I see."

The look on Amy's face told Victoria she did indeed see,
though only the part intended.

"You must tell him about the child."

Amy didn't seem surprised at Victoria's knowledge.

"I cannot. Walter would never understand."

Victoria reached across the way and touched her cheek. "I
can promise you Walter will never know. Jeremiah will not
marry, for reasons you can't be expected to understand. But he
will always think of you with fondness. Please. Tell him."

They rode the rest of the way in silence, Victoria very much
aware of the turbulence she had stirred in her companion.


They had been in New York barely a month when Jeremiah
rushed in and found Victoria dressed in lace trimmed camisole
and pantaloons.

"I'm glad you're here," she greeted him, turning her back
and grabbing the bedpost. "Help me."

He looked at her. One lace strap trailed off her shoulder. His
gaze traveled down to a waist so small he could have spanned
it with his hands. Shapely hips filled out the fancy underwear
ending in a ruffle at black stockinged calves.

"What in heaven's name am I to help you with?"

"The corset. Pull the cords."

He tossed his hat on the bed and fingered the satin ribbons.
"Why?"

"So my waist will be small enough to fit into that dress." She nodded toward the bed where a mauve silk moire gown lay across the ivory crocheted spread.

He took the strings and tugged gently.

"Tighter," she demanded.

After a moment she said, "I can see why Amy has two maids. This could be endless bother."

She reached for the skirt.

"I have tickets for the symphony tonight. And I'd like you to wear the green gown. It did, in fact, bring you to me and for that I am forever grateful. And tonight I want to be the envy of every man in this city."

"Then the Marie Antoinette dress it shall be." Victoria agreed to his demand, a vague disquiet hiding his underlying reason. She didn't press further, suddenly unwilling to know what the evening might bring. Her frank conversation with Amy Sutton had produced nothing and it saddened her to think Jeremiah would never know his daughter, even vicariously. So she let his enthusiasm sweep her away. She watched his face as she created the vision he wanted, complete with upswept hair cascading into curls over one shoulder. A glance at her hands told her the illusion was true, right down to the gaudy emerald ring on her finger.

Everything he wanted from the evening came to pass, though maintaining the illusion even for a short period of time sapped her strength. The crowd parted in awe as the wide skirts of her dress swept majestically toward the stairs and a private box near the orchestra.

The works of Beethoven dominated the evening, the miracle of his music reaching into the core of Victoria's being. The New York Philharmonic Orchestra performed with such grace and talent she was only one of many overwhelmed. Even twenty years after the German composers death, the everlasting beauty of his gift lifted her above the pain of her own existence, to a place where she felt she might find hope and joy.

Jeremiah had reserved a private table at Berlini's for after the performance. The odor of the gas lamps Victoria usually found so harsh was camouflaged by the delicious smell of herbs and garlic of the Italian cuisine that made the restaurant one of the most popular with the theater crowd.

"Walter wants me to go to California. The market for commodities in San Francisco has been enormous since the discovery of gold a few years ago. I'll take the Sea Witch round the Horn with supplies and we'll make a fortune with just one trip. You'll go with me?" he asked hopefully.

This was clearly the reason for his elaborate plans for the evening. And while his request was much more a demand than a question, Victoria sensed there was more.

"Where is California?" she asked. "And San Francisco?"

He leaned across the table, anticipation tinging his voice with impatience. "Thousands of miles from here. Overland, the journey takes forever. By sea, three months will see us there, round Cape Horn. It could be dangerous."

And there lay the darkness she envisioned. Danger. Jeremiah thrived on it, especially when it came from the sea and he wanted her to share his thrill.

"It could be another record voyage for the Sea Witch," he added.

"Then we really have reason to celebrate." Victoria raised her glass of wine. "When do we leave?"

"Tomorrow on the evening tide. The cargo is being loaded now."

She set the glass down without drinking. "That doesn't leave me much time. I want to enjoy this voyage. Be prepared, with proper clothing and such."

"I think you look fine in my trousers and shirt." He leaned close and took her hand. "I want you to make me a vampire."

She was wrong! The darkness here was not the danger of

the trip around the Horn but the danger of his passion. His words startled her. The casual way he said them made her hesitate to look up. She couldn't tear her gaze away from his fingers gently caressing the back of her hand. He was serious. A gentle reaching out with her mind allowed her to see just how serious.

She fought the impulse to jerk her hand away and run from the room. Instead she swept the intimate restaurant, and when she was confident no one paid attention to their conversation, she spoke to him.

"You do not know me well enough to ask such a thing."

She let her hand lie quietly in his, as though touching her might give him some insight into the brutality of her long existence. Instead, she felt his determination to control the situation.

"I know you've had a harsh and lonely life until now. I don't want you to go through anything like that again. Let me join you and we will make our own happiness from today forward."

She jerked her hand from his grasp.

*Sweet Jesus*, she thought. *Those are the same words I used to convince Nikolai of my desire three hundred years ago.*

"Jeremiah, I never meant to make you a vampire. You are my lover, but you are above all else my hero, my friend. I would never wish for you the way I am forced to live."

"I only want what is best for you."

"Allow me to be the judge of what I need," Victoria said, her voice quiet but forceful. She smiled. He rose and held her chair as she left the table. The rustle of her gown was loud, too loud as she crossed the carpeted room. She paused at the outer door to sweep a dark cape round her shoulders and looked back. Jeremiah sat at the table, accepting a bottle of champagne from the wine steward. She gently suggested he finish it before leaving, then disappeared through the double doors.

A moment later she stood on the front stoop at Sutton House. The maid welcomed her in, showing her to the parlor where Walter folded his paper and Amy set aside a slim volume of poetry.

"Please forgive me," Victoria began, "the lateness of the hour—"

"Walter, will you allow us a moment for some girl talk?"

He spoke around his pipe stem. "Of course, my dear. I'll look in on the children then retire. Good evening, Victoria."

"Walter, thank you."

Amy closed the wide doors behind her husband and motioned Victoria to sit, but she went to the fireplace and tried to burn away the chill the evening had brought.

"The Sea Witch sails tomorrow for San Francisco."

"I know," Amy said.

"I fear he will not return if you do not tell him."

"I did. I *did*! He refused to listen and spoke only of you. Of loving you. Of being with you forever! What does he mean?"

"It means nothing. He knows it can never be. I sail with him but I cannot protect him from dangers only he can foresee."

"The Horn. Walter lost a ship there last year." She came to stand beside Victoria. "I don't want to think about that happening to Jeremiah—or you."

Victoria grasped her arm.

"What else can I do?" Amy pleaded.

"I do not know. I see nothing beyond this night. My gift has deserted me when I need it most." She dropped to her knees before the dying fire, pulling Amy down beside her. She stared into the gray ash prickled with fiery embers and tried comprehend the cold fog that filled her heart and mind.

She released her hold on Amy, but she continued to kneel beside her, putting an arm around her shoulders.

"I will finish what we've begun here. Ginnie will have her citizenship, Miss Anthony will have her bank account. And I will do *everything* possible to make Jeremiah understand why I made the choices I did about Sarah."

Victoria took a deep breath, somehow surer now than she had been a moment before that they all stood some chance of surviving. Victoria slipped her arm around Amy and returned her embrace. "You are an extraordinary woman, Amy Sutton."

She laughed, the sound soft and light in the midst of Victoria's confusion.

"Oh no I'm not. I'm just human, full of flawed judgement, making mistakes I can only hope time will correct."

"But that is exactly what I mean. I can never be like you. No matter how I long for it."

They helped each other up, Amy disentangling herself from Victoria's hoop skirt.

"You're all dressed up. Where is Jeremiah?"

"He took me to the symphony. I left him at Berlini's consuming a magnum of champagne."

"Oh my, then I suppose I'll find him at the hotel in the morning sleeping off a little headache."

"Yes. Please. I have many things to do before we leave."

"Walter and I will be at Pier 10 before you sail."

Amy walked her to the front door. "Where's your cab?"

"I sent him to make sure Jeremiah got back to the hotel. Don't worry, I'll catch another at the corner."

Snow fell in big soft flakes. Victoria shifted the cape over her hair and hurried down the steps. At the end of the block, she changed into a small mongrel dog like those roaming the streets of New York and raced into the shadowy night.

The dock was all alight with flickering lamps that pitched long shadows among the ships and workers. The animal Victoria had become slipped easily aboard. Once inside, she went directly to the coffin. The constant shuffle and thud of men working on deck and in the hold told her she would not be disturbed. So she lifted the one thing that was truly the center of her world and moved it to the empty cabin next to Jeremiah's. Tomorrow there would be time for moving her other things from the hotel. Now all she wanted was the small death and the accompanying oblivion sunrise always brought.

Rising early the next day, Victoria dressed in heavy gray wool and high top shoes with a layer of soil inside. The weeks on shore had passed quickly and she'd taken no time to get a gift for Jeremiah. Removing several pieces of jewelry from the coffin, she left the cabin and ventured out into mid-afternoon New York. The streets were crowded with Christmas shoppers flitting about, packages piled high. She found the place she was looking for on the main thoroughfare. TIFFANY, the modest sign over the door announced.

Victoria entered the small showroom. A young man came from the back to greet her.

"How may I help you, ma'am?" He looked far too inexperienced to know the value of gemstones but she told him what she wanted.

"I'd like to sell some jewelry. It's quite old and I'm not sure of the present value." She followed him to the display case.

Opening her reticule, Victoria removed the first ring and placed it on a scrap of black velvet. The opal, set in platinum and surrounded by two rows of diamonds, glowed with an inner fire. She took out another, an unpretentious but perfect canary diamond set in gold with double rows of baguettes the same incredible color on each side. The stones warmed with a life of their own when struck by the gas light. The clerk made a small sound deep in his throat as Victoria placed it on the black velvet cushion.

She placed the last ring beside the others. The clerk stared at it fully half-a-minute then adjusted the *loupe* and critically examined the four carat square cut emerald framed by a full carat of brilliant white diamonds shot through with green fire.

"This piece is superb. But it's damaged. Several diamonds are missing and there's blood crusted on most of the stones."

He removed the eyepiece but continued to hold the ring.

"Yes, Mr. Tiffany. Blood. The history of that ring would turn your hair white. I know it will be difficult to replace the missing stones because of the quality and brilliance but I will take less for it because of the damage. Perhaps you could break it up. Create a fresh new design from the pieces."

"I can give you two hundred dollars."

"Perhaps you would like to confer with someone else before making such a commitment." Victoria had not thought any of the rings would be so valuable. It would be more than enough money for her needs.

"There is no one else. Someday I hope my young son will join me, but many years must pass before that day arrives."

Victoria glanced around the small showroom.

"I would really like to make an exchange. Something for a gentleman."

"For your husband, Mrs . . . ."

"No, but no less loved because of our situation." She smiled as she spoke. A flush crept up the neck of the young man as he turned away to hide the direction his thoughts were taking.

"When was your son born?" Victoria asked to distract him.

He cleared his throat and spoke.

"Only a few years ago." He placed a simple pearl stickpin on another display cloth in front of her.

"Not a pearl," she said quickly. "Nothing from the sea. Something meant to stand the test of time. Something he can place great personal value on, above the fact I gave it to him."

"I think I have just the item. Pardon me a moment." He hurried away and returned almost immediately, placed a small square box on the counter, and removed the lid. Inside lay a watch. He lifted it, rubbing his thumb over the fine engraving.

"I made this on commission last year. The gentleman was the captain of a clipper that sailed to San Francisco. I didn't quite have it completed before he left. He caught the gold fever and never returned."

Victoria removed her glove and he placed the watch in her hand. The intricate detail of the ship on the faceplate might have been modeled from the Sea Witch. The sails billowed full and the sea broke angrily along the bow. The jeweler touched a finger to the stem and the case opened.

Years flashed by in a jumbled multitude of beautiful things. Victoria's vision suddenly clarified into a lamp, purple glass grapes cascading from green glass vines. Victoria raised her eyes from the watch to meet the young man's direct gaze.

"The watch is not worth two hundred dollars. Perhaps we could exchange for one of the pieces other than the emerald. I'll add the fob and chain, too, if you like."

Victoria shut the watch and held it close in her hand.

"Take the emerald, Mr. Tiffany. I insist. I would also like you to engrave a few words for me while I wait."

"Absolutely. What shall I inscribe?"

"Forever is an endless stormy sea. And no signature please."

He left her alone for a short while and returned, the task completed. He handed her the watch, open for inspection.

She smiled at the words engraved in a script that flowed smooth and tranquil belying the turmoil of the words. She put the watch in the box on the counter and put it in her handbag.

He took three small pouches from his pocket and placed a ring in each, keeping his newest acquisition separate and handing her the others.

"Thank you." Victoria started for the door and turned back. "Mr. Tiffany? Your young son, his name is Louis? Louis Comfort?"

He nodded.

"He will create such beautiful things, the likes of which you have never dreamed. Some day the name Tiffany will be known throughout the world for much more than fine jewelry."

She opened the door, stepped out into a rush of falling snow and was gone before he could call out. He stood searching the street for her, one gray kid glove in his hand.

She reappeared on the dock a few feet from the gangplank, pausing to watch Jeremiah as he issued first one command and then another in preparation to leave. Victoria sensed the confidence the men had in him and his anticipation of being at sea again. He raised his arm and waved, moving down the deck to meet her.

"Where have you been? It's snowing and you don't even have on a coat." He looked lovingly at her face, cheeks and lips red with the cold, snowflakes clinging to her long lashes and the close brim of her hat. "Walter was here. And Amy. But they couldn't wait."

"I'm sorry I missed them. I had to have one last look around before we left. I love New York."

"We'll be back." He walked beside her toward the quarterdeck.

Victoria closed her eyes and knew in an instant of sadness she would never return. She turned her face up to Jeremiah's and smiled.

"Of course we will."

## Chapter Nineteen

After a week of routine sailing, Victoria found Jeremiah breaking out a keg of rum to go with the Christmas dinner laid out for the crew. She'd met all hands by now and they knew she was the Captain's lady. The men treated her with respect and if they had any thoughts about her curious behavior, it was explained away by her being a foreigner. Most of the men were regulars on the Sea Witch crew and seemed pleased the Captain had brought his woman on this journey.

It was hard to tell which the crew enjoyed more, the rum or the Captain's gift of a twenty dollar gold piece each. He toasted them to another successful trip, and they toasted his continued good luck. Everyone toasted Victoria's beauty.

Victoria tilted her glass as often as did the men and they cheered her time and again for it. She had already drunk a couple of young men under the table by the time the party wound down.

Jeremiah escorted her from the galley as the drunk boys were carried down the hall by rowdy bunkmates. She cringed at the discomfort tomorrow would heap on them. Her own would be none too sweet but alcohol sometimes numbed her to a world that threatened to close in.

Jeremiah had seemed distant since leaving port. But if he sensed some inner meaning to her having moved out of his cabin, he kept it to himself. Tonight he lingered at her door.

Rum softened her uncanny hearing until a hundred heart-beats slurred into a soft thrum. The gentle buzz in her head turned the breathing of the crew into a sibilant whisper that joined the sound of the sea caressing the skin of the ship. She could feel the flush of warmth from the alcohol suffusing her cold body. So when he finally spoke, she responded graciously.

"I have something for you. May I come in?"

"Please do. I have a small gift for you, too."

He opened the door and she led the way inside. A single lamp swung from the rafter, bathing the small cabin in an amber glow. She took the square white box from under her pillow and turned. He, too, held a velvet jeweler's box. They exchanged packages and both spoke at the same time.

"You first—" each laughed uneasily. Victoria moved closer to the lamp and Jeremiah sat on the edge of the bed.

Inside the small black box was an elaborate carved ring. Highly detailed, the figure of a woman wrapped gracefully around, creating the band. Long hair flowed, legs bent in a semblance of flight extended from a short slip, and caught in her hand was a shank of horses tail. The ornate carving was accented by small brilliant stones and delineated with dark contrast against the polished silver.

"Sea Witch," she whispered.

From the abyss of Victoria's long forgotten past came a childhood memory of the legend of Tam O'Shanter. He rode like a madman down the edge of the ocean while the Sea Witch, scantily clad in a short slip called a Cutty Sark, chased after him. In the end he escaped her pleasure but not before she had come close enough to tear away his horse's tail.

She heard the delicate click of the watch when Jeremiah opened it. The silence of the room became unbearable and she turned to look at him.

"I gather your answer is still no." He sat with bowed head, looking at the words engraved inside the watch.

"The answer to that question will always be no. I cannot accept your ring either, much as I would like."

"Can't or won't?" Jeremiah stood up, the watch in his hand.

"It's silver."

"I see. Not as good as gold? The stones aren't impressive enough for the Countess?"

"You don't understand. Silver has an impurity in it that changes when it's processed. I can't wear it against my skin."

"Oh, I understand well enough. Next you're going to say you're not like me—"

"Sweet Jesus, Jeremiah! I'm *not* like you. I'm almost four hundred years old. I'm not a sweet young matron bored with a bookish husband, ready for a romp in bed with a rogue of a sea captain."

His eyes widened in surprise at her knowledge of his situation with Amy. Before he could speak, she continued.

"Don't you *see* what I am?" Her voice rose in anger. "More lovers have died by my hand than you will ever know. I drink their *blood* so I may continue this wretched existence because it is all I have. I will *not* condemn you to this life of darkness. And silver causes me a *vast* amount of pain."

Victoria tilted the jewelry box over her hand and gave it a shake. The ring fell face down into her palm.

As Jeremiah watched, tendrils of dark smoke and flame rose around the ring. He stood, frozen in place while the smell of searing flesh filled the small room. He saw her fingers curl over the heavy ring, smothering the flame and forcing the smoke to flow from her fist. The sound of her agony drew to an end with a hiss, drawing Jeremiah's intense gaze to her face. She stared at the hand as though it belonged to someone else. A sound of shock exploded from his lips and she raised her head to look up at him. Eyes blazed red and lips stretched back from fangs as pain contorted her face.

Victoria shrieked in pain as he reached out and slapped her hand, knocking the ring across the room. She clutched the injured palm to her breast. Jeremiah tried to hold her but she jerked away, leaning against the wall.

"I'm sorry. I'm so sorry." He repeated the words over and over. The sound of her pain tore at his heart. He kept seeing her flesh burning around the ring. His stomach churned.

Victoria knew the damage was severe but she stretched her hand open and looked. In the middle of the swollen, charred flesh, the imprint of the ring was clear. A brand of the Sea Witch seared across the delicate lines in her palm.

Victoria called on the fierce strength she had been trained to as a warrior centuries before and forced down the desire to destroy everything within reach of her power. When the red rage finally faded and she could think clearly again, she spoke.

"Go away, Jeremiah. This wound will be slow to heal without blood." She turned away from the wall and glared at him, the pain in her eyes tinged with a hunger he had never seen before.

"Can you ever forgive me?" He pleaded. "I begin to see I really know very little about you and your situation. I never meant to hurt you." He back slowly away, closing the door softly as he left.

Victoria heard him move down the hall and make his way above deck as he took up a lonely vigil at the helm. She tried to remove her dress but neither hand functioned properly. She lost patience with herself, finally ripping the dark blue satin from her body, throwing the pieces into a corner. Layer after layer of clothing followed until at last she lay down in the coffin as naked as she had come into the world.

The crew clearly blamed the Captain for the screams they had all plainly heard coming from her cabin. But by his conduct day and night they became more and more puzzled by her absence. He suffered greatly for whatever injustice he had committed and waited for some sign from her that all was forgiven. Several of the younger men wanted to burst into her room to reassure themselves she was all right, but Mr. Hamm told them in no uncertain terms to mind their own business.

A week passed while she slept and woke and kept to herself in the small cabin. The charred flesh fell away, leaving a tender red scar as the only reminder of Christmas evening.

On New Year's Eve, Jeremiah could stand being away from her no longer. He could hear her moving around in her cabin and decided he had to act. He knocked and after a moment, she opened the door.

The room was dark but he could see she wore a plain white wrap. Disheveled hair and heavy circles under the eyes gave her the appearance of being ill. She did not speak.

"I've had a bath drawn in my cabin. It will make you feel better."

"I can't manage a bath, much as I would like one. I can't do my hair or clothes, either."

"I'll help, if you will allow me." He moved aside and she took the few short steps to his cabin.

The only illumination in the room came from a small coal fire contained in a closed brazier. A long wooden tub stood nearby, wisps of steam rising in the dim light. The loose white dressing gown slipped from Victoria's shoulders as she moved toward the bath. She stepped into the tub and sat, easing her knees down into the warm water.

Jeremiah lifted her heavy hair clear as she leaned back. He took his brush and began to untangle the mass of curls, drawing the harsh bristles through the soft hair again and again. He stopped long enough to add hot water from the kettle on the fire to the cooling tub.

Her sigh was barely audible in the quiet room. Coal popped in the stove. Water rumbled in the kettle.

Jeremiah finished his task and twisted her hair together in a rough braid. Victoria stood in the tub while he lathered her all over with sweet smelling soap. Water ran from the cloth down his arms, soaking the rolled up sleeves and shirt front as he sluiced the suds away. He reached into the dark shadows around the room, took a quilt from the bunk and wrapped her, lifting and carrying her to the bed. He started to move away when she opened the quilt with her good hand. It was all the invitation he needed to shed the wet shirt and lay, half naked beside her. He felt the puckered scar of her hand on his back for an instant before her teeth sank into the skin at his throat. Pain shattered outward from the ivory daggers, filling him with her need until her darkness overwhelmed his very soul with visions of despair without end.

Victoria drank deeply, and so great was her need that she set aside any thought of Jeremiah. But at the last moment, she relented and let him rise above the grim future that was all she could see for herself. She rose and disappeared as he spiraled slowly down into the pleasure she always bestowed for his devotion.

The Sea Witch and all hands moved smoothly out of the cold weather into warm regions as they approached the Equator. Victoria took to spending some small amount of time above decks during the rain showers that fell every day. She envied the bronze skin the half-naked crew displayed.

With the heat came a stillness that held the ship in thrall for days on end as they barely moved through calm waters. At Jeremiah's order the crew changed the heavy canvas for a lighter sail more suited to the tropical climes. He became the Captain once again and she merely a passenger while his attention was needed everywhere. He spent day and night on the quarterdeck. Most times he never took his clothes off even when he lay down to rest.

Victoria became well acquainted with the nocturnal ocean. She had listened and learned much on the trip to New York. The ocean was much like the woman Jeremiah professed her to be. She reflected the mood of the sky, dressed herself in a sparkling raiment of stars; darkened when the heavens clouded over and brightened in full moonlight. She responded to the wind just as a mortal woman might. Gentle breezes ruffled her with a soft touch, a stiff wind excited her and storms roused in her a passion that could not be fought, only surrendered to.

The old woman sea was married to the wind, and he made a most capricious and undependable husband. It was never more noticeable than when the Sea Witch crossed the Tropic of Cancer.

Victoria delighted in the sight of the huge tropical moon. She stood at the rail, hair piled high in a mass of curls, shoulders and neck bared by a light summer dress and remembered meeting Jeremiah in Nikolai's fine house in Cape Town. This was just the scene she had divined from his future—and hers. She knew now that all her fears that night had been justified.

Everything was still and quiet. She could feel Jeremiah watching from the quarterdeck. The below watch moved about their duties in a hush. She closed her eyes to the sight of moonlight creating an illusion of icy caps on the waves. The soft murmur of command carried to her as Jeremiah gave over his watch to the mate. It was the first time in a week he had even approached her. His calloused hand was rough against her bare shoulder.

"It's just as well you are a creature of the night. Moonlight becomes you." He gathered her into his arms, oblivious of the men moving to and fro.

Victoria let herself dream for a moment of what eternity would be like held in his strong arms. The vision was so strong, she could tell he felt it, too. She welcomed his crushing embrace. His kiss bruised her mouth and moved down her neck as though to drink from the vein pulsing against his lips.

"Make me a vampire," he murmured. "You want it, I know you do. Just as much as I want it."

She pushed him away, resisting his efforts to hold her close. "Will you lie down and die because I say you must?"

The shadow of the captain's visor was sharp against his illuminated cheek. She looked into the darkness and saw the answer in his eyes.

"I thought not. Even I fought death without realizing I had no choice. Nikolai had already decided I was to be his bride and nothing else would suffice. I sought to destroy him and in the end only hastened my own defeat. I will not make you a vampire because I love you." She raised a hand to his face, her fingers gently brushing the silver hair at his temple. With a single thought in mind, she concentrated and pushed his desire aside, burying it deep in his brain, wrapped in a black void even she could not penetrate.

*You will forget. My love is strong enough for both of us. I will make you forget you ever wanted to be a vampire.*

Jeremiah took her hand and kissed the palm. Not even the thinnest scar remained from the incident of the ring. He held her hand and they stood at the rail admiring the sea.

"This is the perfect setting for you, Victoria. Moonlight becomes you." He drew her to his side, wrapping his arm protectively about her bare shoulders.

Victoria smiled sadly at his words. She had succeeded in making him forget the plea to become a vampire. The easy part was over. The next step would be much harder.

How would she ever survive being alone again?

The days lengthened and the ship sweltered. The muggy calm affected everyone. The below watch stood about in what shade they could find. Victoria stood in the open door and looked out from beneath the quarterdeck. Pitch melted and bubbled in the seams between the planks. The vile smell turned her stomach. It had been so long since she'd fed. The sea had a brassy cast from a sun setting overhead too long.

Every bone in Victoria's body ached. Even her skin seem to be on fire. The need for nourishment intensified her discomfort. The fickle wind played its mischievous tricks, puffing the sails with a weary breath just enough to push the clipper across the water for a mile or two then die again. The crew sweated, working on deck in the sweltering heat, but Jeremiah kept strict discipline, knowing it would be better for the men. He cut the watch to four hours in an effort to give his crew some ease.

The red fireball tracked hesitantly toward the horizon, painting the western span of ocean the color of blood. The still sea formed a mirror reflecting skyward the dying day as though reluctant to have such misery come to an end.

Victoria stood on deck bathed in the wine-colored afterglow of sunset and gave thanks for the oblivion that had spared her this distress on the journey to New York. The evening darkened and stars appeared in the sky so big you could almost reach out and touch them. Not to be outdone, the ocean gave forth its own ballet. Phosphorescent shapes darted through the water, trailing glimmers of light in their wake. As quickly as they appeared, they were gone and the night exploded as great beasts of the sea leaped out of the deep in pursuit of unknown prey.

Jeremiah joined her at the rail, his nearness fueling the sense of panic growing within her. But he simply stared at the ocean, no thought in his mind but the beauty of the moment.

The next two days Victoria spent in her cabin, locked away from the sun in the dark comfort of her coffin.

Just after noon on the third day of doldrums, Victoria was roused from her stupor by shouts and cheers as the Sea Witch caught the wind and romped away toward Rio de Janeiro. The wind invigorated the ship and crew. A late afternoon squall obscured the sun and Victoria walked the deck once more.

The sound of drums and pipes drew her forward. The ship seemed deserted but for the whistle and thrum of the simple instruments. On the bow deck the crew danced. Jeremiah sat on a makeshift throne, draped in a scrap of white sail, a crown of rope circling his brow as he held court. Everyone wore some sort of costume. One young man wore a high hat and a scarf tied round his neck but very little more.

Jeremiah saw her standing in the shadow of the mainsail and called to her. "Victoria. Join us."

Mr. Hamm, the first mate, bowed her into the circle. The growing need to feed held her curiously aloof, beyond the absolute abandon of their merriment, as though she watched from afar. The music swept her away and the red-haired gypsy girl swirled and danced barefoot among them as they paid homage to the sea.

The one new member of the Sea Witch crew was baptized as they crossed from light to dark at the place King Neptune decreed to be the Equator. Victoria lent her strength to the rope as they hauled buckets of water out of the sea and drenched him repeatedly. Young and strong, he vaulted to the rail and made to jump. Victoria snatched him away and he grabbed her, romping across the deck. Saltwater flowed from his hair, splashing her face, drenching her clothes until she was wet through. When the music died, she stood facing Jeremiah.

The men passed quietly to their posts, one by one, and Jeremiah led her to the rail.

"You must pay tribute. For the promise of safe passage."

Victoria gripped his hands and forcing her need aside, looked into his eyes.

"What shall I sacrifice, Jeremiah?" *What will the old woman accept? Love that lasts forever? An eternity of pain? 300 years of darkness?*

"She will take anything you dare to give."

Victoria shut her mind to the flash of darkness that was the only part of his future she could see and allowed him a kiss.

"You choose, Jeremiah." *I'm so weary of the struggle.*

"The pearl choker you were wearing Christmas Eve."

"Yes. A thing of beauty, borrowed for a time, now to be returned." How she wished to return to what she had once been—but neither her mother's gift nor Nikolai's dark power could take her anywhere but forward.

Forward into a century of nights—alone.

For one brief moment she considered Jeremiah's request. Her constant awareness told her that even now, in this close embrace, he no longer thought of those demands. His affection fell into more human realms as the image of the two of them lying in a big brass bed in the city by the bay flitted through her mind. Moonlight flooded through wide windows, bathing the bed and its occupants in ripples of silver and shadow.

And from nowhere, the darkness that was uniquely Nikolai.

Victoria wrenched free from Jeremiah's grasp.

"I must go. For the pearls." She hurried away, letting fear cleanse her mind as though not to think of Nikolai would hold him at bay.

When she returned, all but the four o'clock watch had gone below. She stood at the bow like the figurehead, the speed of the Sea Witch's passage cooling her growing fever with biting spray, hair curling wildly in the wet. She grasped the triple strands of perfect pearls in both hands and broke the strings, scattering them back into the deep.

"Dear mother," she whispered. "Where are you? Tell me, what am I to do now?"

She waited until almost dawn but there was no answer.


Standing watch on the forecastle, Victoria could smell Rio for two nights before they made landfall. She stayed in the cabin out of the scramble and rush of docking, following Jeremiah as he moved fore and aft supervising the freshening of the ship's stores. Even connected to firm land, she could hear the shrill wind in the rigging. Heavy swells from a storm somewhere far beyond her aggravated perception lifted the Sea Witch rhythmically and dropped her in the troughs.

Victoria paced the confined quarters, alternately reaching out into the waning night and searching her inner self. For a sign, for anything that would give her a reason to leave or stay.

Lost in a sea of longing, she fought the wild energy burning in her veins. She clawed at her forearms. The starched white shirtwaist shredded along with her flesh and she roared in pain. Both bloody hands went to her face to stifle her loathing.

"Nikolai." Why now, this persisting invasion. Because his blood flooding her heart fed her need? It always had, but never so vehemently.

Raking her hands downwards, she ripped the high collar loose but still she could not breathe. She had to get away. She threw open the door.

The first mate turned, concern etching his weathered face into planes and shadows in the dim light. He started toward her and she threw up her hands to ward him off.

"Do not enter this lair!"

"Countess, let me help you."

"No, Mr. Hamm. Never! Never! No!"

She pushed past him in a blur and rushed out, the long gray skirt twisting around her legs as she ran. On deck the wind caught her, sending her stumbling forward. She hit the gangplank with both hands and, changing into a sleek black panther, leaped over the side.

Half way down the wharf she slowed. The rats alley she raced was deserted, intensely black and seething with monsters that rode the wind. She sidled along, her inner perceptions warring with the fierce desire to hunt and a lingering humanity that warned 'don't go'.

The fever dream led her farther from the Sea Witch, farther from those she called friend and lover, but no nearer anyone who could provide the substance for which she hungered. Not a single heartbeat called to her. She hesitated, then suddenly the night became more giving. She veered off the main track into a jumble of huts lining a narrow street and followed the rapid heartbeat echoing down the red corridor of her reasoning.

A shriek of terror filled the night. Victoria stopped and tested the air. The young girl was near death when she found her. Only those who hunted the night like herself would have killed in such a way. She approached cautiously. The precious treasure of life still dripped from a multitude of bites on the neck and legs. The panther dropped to its haunches beside the girl and Victoria appeared.

"My sweet child, what have they done to you?" She gathered the limp body into her arms. There was nothing she could do to repair the damage. Pressing her lips gently against the torn artery, she tried to give what comfort she could but tasted only the incredible aching loneliness of death as she laid her own demon to rest for one more day.

*My sweet child, what have they done to you*? Her mother's whispered warning penetrated the darkness filling her heart almost too late.

Three vampires fell on her out of the sky.

She rose to her feet, throwing off the one gripping her hair and shoulder. She faced a man—and a girl, hardly older than the one lying dead on the garbage heap. Young and clumsy, their lack of skill left them seriously handicapped. But the other—his silent instruction marked him as the leader. She whirled. A wicked curved scimitar hung from the waistband of the loose pants he wore. But she knew he wouldn't use it. The other two wanted only to kill, but this one had his orders.

Take her alive.

They would never succeed. They'd made a critical mistake in allowing her to feed. To regain her strength.

And Victoria had nothing to lose. Even the true death was preferable to the life she was living, especially if that life forced her to embrace Nikolai again. She rushed her enemy as though it were Nikolai himself standing before her.

He raised an arm to protect his throat as he went down under the force of her strike. Victoria had more deadly intent.

She swept up the sword. And turned, whirling it overhead the way she had learned all those centuries ago. The first vampire fell before the blur of cold steel, his head tilting grotesquely backwards while his body fell forward. Nikolai's blood flowing in the creature's veins gushed over her. The scarlet flood drenched her face and clothes. Gasping for breath, the memory of this blood shared in passion almost made her falter but it was not truly Nikolai's blood, only a poor substitute diluted many times over.

Victoria's pleasure cooled instantly. The girl disappeared into the night. Behind her waited the true servant. She turned slowly, the wicked curve of the sword dripping red.

"Where is your Master?" she demanded, speaking in the language easy enough to read from his thoughts.

He almost hesitated.

"I am Master here."

"Not any more."

It was no real battle to bend his will to hers. With deliberate cruelty she forced him to kneel. The scimitar swept down, the grace of its descent part of the deadly masquerade that chopped off his head. Throwing the sword down, Victoria stood for the few moments necessary to render the body back to dust.

All the old horror came screaming back. She had allowed her hatred for Nikolai to pull her down to his level. To pull her back into the savagery of the time in Algiers. No wonder she had not been able to see the future. The force of his power was everywhere here. So great even the connection to her mother was diminished. As it had been before.

She could not stay. Not here. He would be back.

Around her the night lightened, twilight heralding day soon to break. She had to get back to the Sea Witch. But first she must finish what she had begun.

The girl was easy to find. Hovering beside her, in a filthy shack not far from the waterfront, were two other children who would never age. Victoria silently petitioned all the old gods of earth and water and fire to forgive her. She broke the skin of one wrist and gathered them close, offering each a swallow of her blood. The younger two quickly fell under her command and slept but the other girl resisted.

"Shhh! My sweet sister. Do not fear me. I bring you peace. Forever." She overwhelmed the frenzied mind with darkness, using her own command to end the control afforded by Nikolai's diluted blood.

When all three had succumbed to her oblivion, Victoria walked away. Not even Nikolai could raise them from this small death.

She rose into the air, circled once and made straight for the pier. The Sea Witch waited on the swell of the morning tide and far out over the ocean, the sun edged over the rim of the world.

## Chapter Twenty

For the space of a heartbeat, Victoria panicked. Then logic told her Jeremiah would not leave without her. But she couldn't waste a moment. She spared one last thought for the children far below, asleep in the oblivion of her making until she called them forth—or the end of mankind, whichever came first.

Then she caught the morning wind off the mountain and was gone, flying high. The sound of her wings on the wind thrummed in her ears as she raced out to sea. High in the sky, the ever persistent tilt of the horizon brought a sliver of the sun into view. The shrieking gull folded wings and plummeted toward the water.

She skimmed the surface until she reached the deep shadows surrounding the Sea Witch and fluttered to the rail. The deck was bustling with activity. She had to get below before the sun rose completely.

At the far edge of her vision Jeremiah stood on the forecastle. The wind freshened, ruffling her feathers and still he did not give the order to weigh anchor. He knew she was gone. And waited for some sign of her return.

*Go below*, she urged silently. *And check one more time.*

He moved tiredly down the steps and the moment he opened the door, the gull flashed through. The bird disappeared and Victoria stood before him.

Relief at seeing her eased the lines around his eyes, then turned to concern.

"What has happened? Are you hurt?" he asked.

She was still wearing the torn and bloody shirtwaist.

"I'm fine, Jeremiah. Now."

He stared at her. "I was worried. I thought you had left me."

The old hunger flared in his eyes for an instant then

vanished, replaced by sadness—and fear. He stood close enough for her to feel his breath on her face.

"Captain?"

Jeremiah answered without turning away from Victoria. "Yes, Mr. Hamm?"

"The tide, sir? Shall I give the order?"

"Yes, Mr. Hamm. Give the order."

He continued to hold her gaze and Victoria would not let it go.

"I would never go without telling you goodbye, Jeremiah. I promise."

He took her hand and raised it to his lips.

"Thank you—for not lying to me." He turned and moved slowly away, back to his ship, back to the sea.


Sea Witch and all hands plus passenger swept down the southern Atlantic toward the Horn at an unbelievable rate of speed. They hit the first cold weather two days out of Rio and the easy sailing ended. Jeremiah had the crew begin overhauling the running gear. As the clipper approached the tip of the Horn, everything was in good order. Gone were the light sails, replaced days before with storm canvas. The crew trusted the Captain's experience and obeyed orders without question. They were sailing toward fog, adverse currents, sudden storms and doubtful positions. The wind strengthened steadily from the east.

Although the lookout had been doubled for the past 500 miles, Victoria was the first to sound the alarm. The small amount of nourishment won in Rio had long been spent and her sense of impending danger proved misleading. She shrugged it off at first as irritation with herself for not being able to control the beast within better.

Night had fallen. The darkness had an impenetrable depth.

Victoria stood on the quarterdeck, unwilling to venture further from what she considered safety. Out of the darkness loomed a shapeless bulk only a shade lighter than the night.

"Sweet Jesus, what is that? Off to the left."

Jeremiah turned to follow her gaze just as the lookout yelled.

"Iceberg! To port!"

The bosun set off a flare before the Captain gave the order. The bright cold light revealed the peak of a mountain less than half mile off. Everyone but Victoria knew this part was only one-tenth of the true hazard. The deadly ledges might reach out a mile undersea–and in any direction.

"Run! To starboard!" came the command from Jeremiah and the men ditched some sail and raised others.

Sea Witch had barely gathered speed when she grated, lifted and trembled all over. She sat over ice. A groan ran through the fine lady. The shiver under Jeremiah's feet chilled his soul. She scraped again.

The words "Cut sheets!" had barely escaped his lips before the crew let go all sails. Sea Witch ground to a stop. The threat still remained but a few voices rose in prayers of thanks.

Soundings to larboard told Jeremiah the berg was still under them. It was also moving fast.

"Four fathoms," came the call from the bow.

"Four." The call repeated from amidships.

"Here three," reported the watch from the quarterdeck.

Victoria clung to the rail and watched Jeremiah giving his all for the Sea Witch. His bravery and knowledge assured her he did exactly the right thing. He shouted for sail. Once more the ice scraped. Now at the stern. Then the Sea Witch caught the wind and moved ahead of the danger. They crept on into the night, not daring full speed lest the sea be filled with more of the iceberg's unseen mass.

When she sensed deep blue lay under them once again,

Victoria released her hold on the rail. Jeremiah drew her close in an effort to still her trembling.

"I have never been so frightened. Next time I shall go overland."

He pulled her cape close and smoothed her hair with a grim laugh.

"What? And risk losing this beautiful hair to Indians? This is far safer, I assure you."

The rest of the night passed in freshening wind but rather than risk further disaster of running aground, they hove-to under little sail.

If the drift ice weren't bad enough, early morning brought a mist thick enough to eat. Victoria stood at the bow, still as a figurehead. A vague sense of disquiet whispered 'danger ahead' but land was close enough for her to divine no real immediate peril. True jeopardy had to lie around the Horn where adverse currents churned in conflict, where hell raged in icy waters.

The fog burned away toward mid-morning and the wind freshened. All sails were up and drawing. Sea Witch gathered headway for the run around the Horn. The sky cleared and the southeast wind in the rigging made sweet music in Victoria's ears.

She lay down to sleep, weary to the bones of the sea, tired of battling the need to feed. Her own music of oblivion mixed with the love song the wind sang to the sea. It filled her with a longing to forget, a desperate need to forget that would not be satisfied. She tossed on the bed and dreamed of a future too shrouded in rain and mist to comprehend. Rousing a body drained of everything but a heinous demand to find blood was easier than trying to remain below. Victoria reached for the black cape with hands she hardly recognized. The fingers were no longer straight, the nails long and contorted. She moved to the small mirror on the wall. Reflected there was a deathly pale face with red-rimmed eyes. Her hands shook as she lifted the hood, partially obscuring the expression of evil emanating from within. Without conscious thought she turned toward the door and disappeared, reappearing a moment later on deck.

The lookout cried, "Cape Horn!"

Victoria turned to the southwest. The horizon had misted over. A cloud of birds flew about, cape pigeons wheeling and diving in confusion. Victoria shuddered at the high screech and whistle of their calling voices. The rock ahead disappeared before her very eyes. Then reappeared again, farther away. She blinked and once again it was gone. No wonder sailors were superstitious. If you couldn't believe your own eyes, what were you to think.

"Mr. Hamm tells me the first sighting is always a mirage, ma'am." A lone sailor stood nearby.

Victoria pulled the cape closer about her face.

They sailed into the thin mist, gear clattering as a desultory wind blew through the rigging.

The young mariner moved toward her. She recognized the sun bleached hair and dark face. Blue eyes gazed landward.

"There." He pointed as the true rock came into view. As they approached, the promontory raised its black head like the tombstone to lost ships and dead men that it was as he shared his new found knowledge with her. The mild wind and strong current carried Sea Witch on. Westward they sailed, past the twin peaks her guide called the Cloven Hoof. He laughed at the reference to the Devil but Victoria knew evil wore Nikolai's face when it walked in the world. She turned away from his inspection lest he see the devil she had become. He stayed near doing first one small task, then another while the Horn sat on the horizon in haughty repose before sliding forever into the misty sea. He moved away as quietly as he had appeared.

The day finally died with little more than a peep of sunset on the horizon. The wind was fast becoming a driving force and Jeremiah put forth all sail, coaxing every measure of speed possible from the clipper. The ship plowed through rough seas. Jeremiah drove the crew relentlessly in an effort to leave behind a part of the world where to tarry most often meant disaster. Already cross currents hammered at the ship.

The watch had changed. Off-duty crewmen huddled about the stove. Victoria stood in the corner invisible to wandering eyes and watched the blond sailor. Muscles rippled under his shirt and in his thighs when he stood and moved away from the table where he played cards with the others. He started toward where she stood, a part of the darkness. So great was her need, she drew him like a magnet. At the last moment, discretion got the upper hand and she disappeared, leaving the young man standing in the dark corner, dazed and confused.

Victoria materialized in her own cabin. She locked the door against human intrusion before throwing off the cape. It wasn't necessary to look in the mirror to track the changes she felt.

"Mother! Help me," she prayed. With arms folded tight across her stomach, she doubled over. "Make it stop." Her voice became hoarse until finally the room was filled with harsh, guttural howling. The scratch of paws scrabbling for purchase on the wooden floor was loud in the small room. She ran in circles, somehow containing the fury of the animal she had become within the four flimsy walls.

Outside the storm raged as the old woman gave the old man the full measure of her wrath for his indiscretions. The Sea Witch, caught between heaven and hell, struggled to survive.

Exhausted, Victoria lay in the coffin. Once again simply a woman, still held prisoner by her own disgust and desire.

The storm worsened and continued through the night while Victoria lay in a stupor. She slept, caught in a purgatory filled with dreams of Nikolai and a needless cruelty that whetted the appetite of the beast she sought to control.

Above decks the men endured their own hellish nightmare. They were stranded in a pit filled with water that wetted everything and turned immediately to ice. The ship suffered as much as the men. All sails had been hauled in but one fore storm sail being used to steady her on the raging sea. Men worked with broken fingers too numb to even know they were injured. Clothing froze on their backs and still the storm worsened. One man slipped on an icy deck, missed a grab at the lifeline and was caught by a green sea just washing aboard. The surge raced across the deck, throwing him into another lifeline where he held on for all he was worth.

Victoria gave over to the torment of her nightmare and endured, the same as Jeremiah and his crew. For three days and nights they struggled with their own peculiar demons. Some time during the afternoon of the fourth day, Sea Witch sailed clear of the storm. The coast of *Terra del Fuego* lay behind them. Jeremiah unfurled maximum sail and all but a skeleton crew went below for a much needed rest.

Smooth seas roused Victoria from an exhaustion bordering on oblivion. All those below decks slept deeply. Jeremiah snored heavily in the next cabin. She unlocked the door to her cabin, ignoring deep scratches in the heavy wood. She combed wild hair with twisted fingers. Shutting her eyes, her mind roamed the confines of the sleeping quarters. The siren song of her lust overlaid the sound of sighing wind and rushing sea.

A few men stirred restlessly in their hammocks. Others dreamed more deeply. Of blue skies and brown skinned women playing in a clear lagoon, their naked breasts gleaming wetly in the bright, hot sun.

Victoria searched until she found one mind that dreamed differently. The young sailor stood once more on the deck beside her, patchy fog rolling in thickly as he moved closer.

She stepped away from the door and spoke softly.

"Come to me. Let me grant your every wish."

The sailor left his bed without disturbing his sleeping companions. Bare feet made no noise moving through the hall.

The door opened soundlessly and once again he stood on the deck near the black caped woman. He reached out for her hand and moved closer. He touched the hood, freeing the heavy red hair. Dense fog closed around them. For one moment he considered the fact that she was the Captain's woman and decided it made no difference. He had lived his entire life for this one act. Her hands moved across his chest, brushing the nipples to send waves of excitement coursing through his trembling body. Somewhere in the distance the sound of drums lingered in the air, the rhythmic beat fading to return louder as he held her close and kissed her. He felt her cold lips against his face and neck. For one brief second he glimpsed a red-eyed monster standing before him. He barely felt fangs sink into his neck as the skirl of a bagpipe joined the sound of drums and he was lost forever, roaming a verdant meadow with a red-haired gypsy girl.

Jeremiah stood in the open doorway, numbed to the core of his soul. He had responded to Victoria's call, sleepwalking in the same manner as his crewman. Eager as always to submit to her needs, whatever they might be. But the bright dream dissolved from his mind before its fruition. He opened his eyes to see Victoria and one of his crew wrapped in a thin mist.

The familiar ritual drew to its usual conclusion. The sailor shuddered and sank slowly to his knees as passion receded.

"No," Jeremiah moaned.

Victoria turned to face him, lips drawn back from fangs still dripping blood. She tried to speak but the words would not come. Swirling her cape round her head, she sank to the floor to cover her victim. Jeremiah turned and stumbled away. He stopped abruptly halfway down the hall and stood, once more sleepwalking, caught in a nightmare that he couldn't escape.

Victoria sat on the deck, cradling the head of her fallen hero in her lap. And cried. One real tear streaked with blood. A healing tear for the young man whose name she did not know.

She wiped it from her cheek with a straight, slender finger and soothed the deep puncture wounds. He stirred at her touch. The edges of the injury closed over and within moments all signs of bruising disappeared. She left him sleeping, knowing he would wake with the dawn and remember nothing.

Then she went to Jeremiah whose memory of her act of betrayal would be as simple to take away but much harder to bear.

## Chapter Twenty-One

Victoria stood alone on the deck, one shadow among many, night after night as the Sea Witch roared up the latitudes. Using her vampire power to hide from Jeremiah and crew, she spent her new found strength isolating their memories of her every word and deed and replaced them with their own pleasant dreams. Days and nights voyaged into weeks as the sea and wind forgave each other and once more acted like perfectly suited mates.

Sea Witch sailed into San Francisco harbor on the evening tide. The scene confronting Jeremiah was like nothing he'd ever seen in all his days of sailing. Dozens of ships were anchored three deep along a non-existent dock. The gentle ebb and flow of the tide caused the empty masts to sway restlessly.

The area appeared deserted. Jeremiah dropped anchor in the Bay and decided to wait for morning to off-load his cargo, hoping San Francisco would be more encouraging by daylight. The sound of gunfire in the darkness prompted him to post guards and inform the crew there would be no going ashore until further notice.

Victoria stood in the darkness and surveyed the desolation that the new city presented. She felt none of the cloying darkness she had in Rio. Nothing of Nikolai. None of her own kind. Only a bleak miasma of human frailty.

There could be no return to New York for her. Her future was here regardless of her wants or needs. But if Jeremiah's crew weren't loyal enough to withstand the lure of the golden goddess, he too might be stranded in a place she could already feel was a quagmire of misery.

She added a gentle admonition to the lie that kept her presence a secret in each sailor's mind. *The only gold in San*

*Francisco is that which you will receive from the sale of your cargo*. She felt each man's thoughts turn from the fantasy of the biggest nugget to wash from Sutters Mill to how much a twenty pound sack of flour would fetch across the counter of the local General Store.

She waited until the midnight hour had come and gone before calling the strong young sailor.

*Now is the time*. He rose and accompanied her down the hall as though he heard her command. With a short motion, she indicated the coffin now lying on the floor in plain sight. He lifted it easily and waited.

She left him where he stood motionless and went into Jeremiah's cabin. He sat at the desk, writing in his personal log. Victoria read as his pen scratched on the page.

Arrived San Francisco. Another record voyage. At first view seems a strange, desolate place. A malady of madness surrounds the harbor area. Perhaps sanity rules further into the city. Tomorrow will tell. Tonight must cope with incredible sense of loss.

She reached out to touch him and hesitated. He stopped writing, pen poised just above the paper and looked away from the page. She could see his reflection in the dark window and knew he could no longer see her standing behind him. Victoria leaned down and kissed his temple.

"Goodbye, Jeremiah," she whispered, sighing as she turned back to the hall and her willing servant.

A small boat was already in the water waiting to transport them to shore. They were soon lost in the colony of ships crowding the dock. Most were so close, she might have simply walked from ship to ship until reaching shore.

Heavy fog muffled the slap of oars in the water. Victoria crouched near the coffin while the sailor rowed through the maze. They slipped through the last layer of derelicts and glided under the wharf. Water lapped against the pilings, creating a world of darkness filled with constant sound. They continued inland under buildings actually constructed over the water until Victoria pinpointed the reason for her search. A dim glow penetrated the gloom where a trapdoor hung open beneath one of the buildings.

The boat bumped against a pier large as a mainmast and was tied off. The sailor stood and pulled up into the opening. Victoria raised the coffin on end and it disappeared into the hole. Then she followed, unsure of where this path led but eager to go. Anywhere would be better than surrounded by those she loved but could not acknowledge. Jeremiah's loneliness cut her to the bone. Her own heartache would be long in subsiding.

Her aide followed with the coffin. The two of them moved through several levels of storerooms, finally leaving the water behind. They descended into a cellar and then into a sub-cellar beneath a general store. A lack of stock gave it the appearance of being deserted. It took less than a minute to set the coffin in one corner. Victoria produced candle and match but the feeble flame did little to illuminate the cell. The nearness of four earthen walls enclosed her in comforting silence.

She turned to her helpmate. He dropped to his knees before her and wrapped strong arms around her waist.

"You must go," she whispered, freeing herself of his embrace. "Back the way you came and think no more of me."

She stooped and kissed his forehead. The pleading look left his eyes and he stared blankly ahead. He turned and moved away and she watched until he was gone. Without thought she opened the coffin. It was filled with all her worldly goods so she set about to make herself a home.

Victoria lay down at last. Wrapped in the comforting closeness of earth gave a semblance of peace she had not known for years. Her last thought before sinking into the void was of San Francisco and a fearful future she could not see.

## Chapter Twenty-Two

San Francisco was not New York. The wind off the bay was not the cruel, cutting knife that sliced through a body on the East Coast. It brought the fog and rain. Rain turned the streets of the young city to rivers of mud. No one seemed to care. The gold seekers were used to being up to the knees in muck.

For the miners a trip to town was a treat. It meant hot food, a hot bath and a hot time in the saloon. A little mud was no hardship in view of the potential rewards. They were free with their newly found riches, too, so it didn't matter that a meal and bed with sheets cost the world.

Victoria roamed the streets for weeks, a watcher, a non-participant in the bizarre brand of living going on in this old-new barbaric land. She watched the whores ply their trade, taking the miners for all they were worth. A good whore could booze, bed and roll her way to more gold in one night than a man could wash out of Sutters Mill in a month.

She saw husbands leave wives, mothers abandon children. The men lost all reason in the frantic search for gold while their wives became whores and stole from other miners, gathering more of the precious substance than their men. The children were the real victims, suffering continually from exposure to the weather and lack of proper nourishment.

The men may have been single minded in their mission but the women were the most greedy—everyone had to have gold. The children were too pathetic for words.

Victoria hated San Francisco. She hated the weather, she hated the men and women, but most of all she hated the gold.

One night she allowed herself to be picked up on the street. He was a rough man with a beard and his gray eyes reminded her of Jeremiah. When she drank his blood, her heart broke a little out of loneliness and she only took a little of his gold.

Once was all it took for her to realize she couldn't be a whore. There were too many broken dreams and too much despair in the touch of others. So she dressed in the mauve colored gown and walked boldly into the Silver Slipper, the poshest saloon on High Street. She sat at a table near the back and observed. It took less than an hour to figure out the games and the scams.

The card game, Faro, was by far the most complicated but also the fairest. She couldn't really see a way to cheat, either on the part of the dealer or the player. It took a lot of discipline to remember who was dealt what and where the cards were and which ones remained in the boot.

Victoria rose and moved through the noisy crowd. The men, though well dressed and far less rowdy than their brothers down the street were still miners by choice and gamblers by nature. She drew admiring glances from all sides as she headed toward a table slightly removed from the others. Victoria knew without error that her target was the man in the gray suit, Winston du Champe. The crowd parted before her, giving over a wide path for her skirt as it swept the wooden floor.

A gentle seeking prod with her mind and the non-descript man turned to watch her approach. Victoria felt chilled. Cold, almost colorless eyes glanced from side to side taking in those who deferred to her without question. Thin, white hair combed straight back from a high brow gave him a look of strained intelligence. Greed hung round his table as thick as the cloud of pungent cigar smoke. The two men seated with him rose as she stopped in front of the table.

Victoria fed his greed with a vision of increased profits and he rose as she told him what she wanted. A soft brogue took most of the sting from her demand.

"Mr. du Champe, I want that man's job. The Faro dealer."

One corner of his mouth turned up sardonically. He looked

over at the nearly deserted gaming table. The dealer stood woodenly shuffling cards from the boot, full sleeves of his white shirt caught up in garnet and black lace gaiters.

Then in his mind du Champe saw Victoria standing in the dealer's place, a dark-blue velvet dress with tight fitting bodice and sweetheart neckline attracting a crowd to the usually lean table. Bare arms hid nothing as she dealt cards deftly to the increased number of players. He looked back to where she stood, waiting for his answer.

"Can you start tomorrow?"

"Yes."

The entire exchange took no more than a few seconds. He never questioned how she knew his name and only now thought to ask hers.

"Who the hell are you, lady?"

"You may call me Victoria, the rest is unimportant."

Cold eyes appraised the prim hairstyle and fine dress, still sure he was making a very good decision.

"See Lily for something to wear," he said, nodding at a buxom blonde at the bar.

"I shall return tomorrow. At sunset." Victoria turned and walked away, leaving him feeling very satisfied. The three men sat and resumed their discussion of the evenings take spiced with a vision of future earnings.

On close scrutiny, Victoria could tell Lily was older than she looked. The blonde hair had faded and the seams in her fancy dress were stretched almost to bursting. Tiny blue veins around her nose and across the cheeks were not quite masked by powder dusted heavily on her face and neck.

Victoria watched her down a glass of amber liquid. She didn't seem to be attached to any of the men standing nearby. Victoria approached and called her name. "Lily?"

"What do you want?" She picked up the glass the bartender had refilled.

"I'm Victoria. I'll be working the Faro table beginning tomorrow night."

The older woman laughed and began coughing. When she finally got the spasm under control, she said, "You won't last a week, honey. Those hardtacks will chew you up and spit you out." She ended with another harsh cough and quickly tossed back the contents of her glass.

Victoria looked her in the eye and spoke softly.

"It's better than the street."

Lily reached for the glass again, bringing it more slowly to her lips this time. Victoria forced her to look at her and made sure she saw a young woman's pale, flawless skin, a fine chiseled nose with a sprinkle of tiny freckles. She looked deep into sad brown eyes shadowed by long, dark lashes. The glass paused on its journey.

"I cannot take away the cause of your pain but I can offer more ease than that poison allows."

"What can you know of my pain—" Lily began, then her hand went to her side. Her mind filled with pictures of a verdant meadow. The delicate smell of flowers just beginning to bloom filled her nose while the mild spring sun eased her aching body. The pain was gone, blown away by a soft breeze that ruffled her dress and fluffed her hair.

"Think on these things and your pain will be gone for a while. I'll help you if you only give me what small aid I seek."

Lily was very much aware of her surroundings, the men drinking at the bar, the shuffle of cards at the blackjack table, the click of the ball on the roulette wheel but the pain she had lived with for over two years was gone.

The young woman standing before her had just become an angel. She knew instinctively not to touch her. Angels had a way of vanishing when you tried to see if they were real.

"I need a suitable dress. Can you help me?"

"Let's go upstairs and see, honey. I was never so slim in all my born days but maybe I can find something that will do."

Lily glanced around the room, checking on the other girls. Each was occupied with at least one man and several were entertaining two. She reached out for the full glass sitting on the bar and changed her mind.

Victoria followed her up the stairs set to one side of the saloon, very much aware of the heads that turned to watch her ascent. Sounds of intimate revelry rushed through the thin wooden walls as they passed on to the end of the open balcony.

Lily pushed open a door to reveal a room dominated by a large brass bed. The floor was bare, the part that could be seen through the clothing strewn everywhere.

The older woman dug in the chaos, tossing garments aside to reveal a large trunk.

"This belonged to a pretty little green-eyed blonde. She was sickly when she arrived and didn't last long in the damp. Must have been TB or something worse. Died following a damned good for nothing gambler. I tried to get her to go home but she wouldn't have none of it." Lily stopped picking up clothes and looked at Victoria. "Ain't you got a young man somewhere who wants to marry you and give you a houseful of kids?"

"There is no one and I prefer it that way. All I want to do is be someone else for a while, Lily, and I need your help."

"Well, I ain't never been asked to take a fine lady and turn her into a saloon girl before. Most times it's the other way round." She sat on the edge of the rumpled bed. "Funny how the pain always kept me going. Now it's gone, all I wanna do is sleep." Lily's words began to slur together as the alcohol took over.

"I'll be here. Go ahead and rest for awhile." Victoria moved to the bedside and pulled a shabby quilt up to cover her. The heavy breathing turned to snores before Victoria returned to sorting through the small trunk.

Several hours later, she had found many things to wear. One

very beautiful dress with thin straps in a peculiar shade of gold only certain blondes and a rare few redheads could wear and not look hideous in. She decided it would be just the thing for the first night on the job. Its fairly short length decreed a need for the pair of fancy black shoes and sheer hose also contained in the trunk. The next hour she spent dressing in the new attire.

Victoria glanced now and again at the slumbering figure on the bed. She had just finished re-doing her hair when a soft but urgent knock sounded at the door. Light from the room flooded the now semi-dark hall when she opened the door a crack.

"Where's Lily?" A young woman stood outside, a short robe thrown hurriedly over her shoulders. She held one hand to her nose and blood dripped between her fingers.

"Sleeping. I'm Victoria. What's wrong?"

"Drunk son-of-a-bitch hit me and then passed out. I need to get rid of him."

"I'll go. Show me where." The two women went down the hallway together.

"Messed my face up. Won't be able to work for a week."

The darkened hall hid Victoria's agitation. The smell of fresh blood both intoxicated and aggravated. She shuddered and brought her mind back to the immediate problem. How to get rid of a drunk without relying on vampire strength. They pushed through a half-open door. The man sprawled across the bed on his stomach, trousers bunched around his boots. Victoria knelt and went through his pockets. Finding a small bag of gold, she gave two nuggets to the injured girl.

"Since you won't be able to work for a while, it's only fair he should pay extra for his pleasure." She put the pouch back into his pocket and hitched his pants up as best she could.

"He couldn't even get it up. That's what made him so damned mad." The injured girl had found a handkerchief and dabbed at her nose while she cleaned her hand. "Rose is my name, honey, and we still got to get him out of here."

"If you take his other arm and lead the way, we'll dump him down the back stairs and trust he won't remember anything when he wakes up."

Victoria pulled one arm across her shoulder and lifted him bodily from the bed. Rose took the other and they dragged him away between them. The stairs were very narrow with a turn halfway down, so they leaned him over his knees and Rose gave him a not-too-tender shove with a foot. Victoria heard him snoring as he bumped against the steps on the way down.

"Welcome to the Silver Slipper, honey. It don't get no better than this," Rose said, once again dabbing at her nose.

Victoria fought down the urge to feed and welcomed the harsh darkness threatening to stifle her as Rose put an arm across her shoulders. The two young women walked back the way they had come.

The nights passed quickly, seasons changed but the rain and fog remained constant. The city grew. The miners lost their gold to the gamblers. The saloon girls entertained the customers and went to bed with those who could pay.

All but Victoria.

The Silver Slipper was always full and her Faro table had become the most profitable game in town. Winston approached her again and again with sexual overtures only to be put down each time by some innocent darkness that always left him wondering why he would want her at all.

Each of those who worked for Winston regarded her differently. She stood up for the girls, protecting them when possible from the pain and degradation that was often heaped upon them. They in turn shielded her from customers who felt they could sleep with no one but her.

Lily grew sicker with each passing week, until in the end Victoria could no longer camouflage her pain. So she sat on the rumpled bed, holding Lily's hand and reliving the nightmares along with the pleasant memories as her life passed away.

The dying woman spoke often of her young son, left to live with a family on a farm near the outskirts of town. When she became too ill to visit the boy, Victoria took it on herself to go and see to his welfare. She found the farmhouse in ruins, gutted by fire, the family gone. A few nights of searching in the city and Victoria found him. Alone, cold and wet, wandering the streets half-starved. He caught on quickly when she took the time to show him how to find shelter from the rain under stairs and between buildings. Since that time Victoria had given him gold for food and seen to his welfare in one way or another. He never saw his mother alive again. Victoria stood by his side on the cold, fog bound day they put Lily in the ground. No one else at the Silver Slipper had ever known of his existence.

"Take care of my Billy," had been Lily's words to Victoria as she closed her eyes, the pain completely gone at last.

Victoria adopted the name of Honey, since they all insisted on calling her that anyway. None of the girls used their real names for one reason or another. Every morning just before dawn, she would put on her cape and disappear quietly from the front door of the saloon. Thick fog rolling in from the Bay veiled her retreat, hiding even the sound of her footsteps from those who sometimes followed.

The refuge she sought by day was far removed from the street on which she worked by night. The sub-basement of the store near dockside was a place so dark and damp even the owner had forgotten it existed. She fed often enough to curb the craving of the beast within but never gave over completely to her passion. Or the need to assuage the desperate loneliness by creating another of her kind.

Victoria thought often of Felix and Jeremiah, the two human lovers she had sought to live with for a time and how both relationships had ended badly.

Most of the time it was Gascon who came to mind. Gascon, the vampire of her own creation, with his love and devotion.

Gascon with his greed and cruelty she could not control, once he came to know the power of the position she had given him.

She forced all thought of Nikolai from her mind, as though to think of him would call attention to her whereabouts. She knew he searched for her as surely as the sinking of the sun in the west brought forth the night with all its evil.

She would venture from her lair shortly before sunset, make her way into the Silver Slipper unnoticed and change clothes upstairs in Lily's old room. Winston continuously entreated her to move into the saloon for her own protection but she always refused. Evening found her the center of attention in the casino.

"Place your bets, gentlemen," the soft lilting brogue spoke to each man. Everyone standing round the table eagerly awaited the smile accompanying the whispered "thank you" addressed to each individual as he offered his chips.

Red-gold highlights played over the cluster of curls falling across one almost bare white shoulder. The emerald green velvet dress with its black trimmed neckline dipped to a modest V in front. Black crinolines held the skirt full to show off shapely calves and ankles. High heeled shoes and the black feather caught in her hair made her appear taller. It was an illusion she loved. When Victoria's life as a vampire began she had been tall for a woman but as humanity blundered forever forward in its constant effort to better the world, she found herself shorter than most women.

Always determined to be different from the other girls, tonight she wore a gaiter to match her dress on one bare upper arm. She could tell from the initial reaction that each man's eyes were drawn to it and stayed there. She wore no jewelry but Nikolai's marriage ring on the index finger of her left hand.

Winston thought she used these tricks to cheat the players, but the real reason for the increase in profits from her table lay in her ability to give the men enough distraction that they didn't care if they won or lost. No one ever left her table unhappy.

Most were so drawn to her they would put gold nuggets in her bodice just for the thrill of touching her.

Occasionally she would glimpse something in a man's future that made her shy away but most of the time all she saw was the futility of their search. The broken dreams always made her sad, but she had lived with shattered hopes for centuries.

The hour was late and the crowd around her table had diminished when the door to the saloon opened. A young man entered. He wore a round brimmed hat and a black shirt with no collar. Blue eyes burned in his sun-browned face with a fevered glaze as he glanced around the room. In his hand he held a black book. His gaze stopped at Victoria. She watched him approach, as taken with his guise as were the men at her table.

"Repent, sister. Repent and ask God to forgive your sins." He held out his Bible.

Victoria looked at the book and spoke.

"There is nothing to forgive. I am not a whore. I earn my living by my wits." The men around the table laughed heartily.

"By God, that's telling him, Honey."

"Come away from this evil place with me now, sister. I will show you how to atone for your sins." The blue eyed fanatic railed away at her.

The men continued to laugh.

"Dammit, brother, don't you know we all beg her like that every night. And the answer is always no."

Even Winston, drawn by the commotion to her table, defended Victoria. He grabbed the man by the collar, breaking his focus.

"Preach to anyone else here if you must, but not her."

The slender, well groomed young man roamed through the sparse crowd, passing out pamphlets and occasionally speaking to one of the other girls. Victoria sensed his movements away from her as she resumed the interrupted game. He left the saloon without further preaching.

In the slow hours toward morning, she sat at the table with Winston and several other men. They played poker and, as usual, Victoria won. The game broke up finally as she claimed her gold and rose to leave.

"I wish you would move in here like the other girls, Honey. That fanatic might be hanging around outside waiting for you to leave. You never know with those Brother's of Gideon. They're a strange lot. I could walk you home, if you like."

"I'll be fine. Even Brother Gideon doesn't frighten me. And if I lived here, I might really become just another one of the girls." She smiled to soften her tone, hoping he would understand that she could never be like the others.

He helped her with the floor length cloak she always wore, no matter what the weather. She couldn't allow anyone to walk her home. It wouldn't do for them to see how she spent her well-earned cash—or her days. She hefted the small bag of nuggets as the door swung to behind her, then disappeared in a swirl of fog very much aware the strange young man watched from the building across the way. Victoria made her one daily stop but did not tarry long before continuing to the welcome darkness of her resting place.

Brother Gideon became a regular at the Silver Slipper. He would slip in, berate her for the sins of everyday living and be thrown out before he finished. Sometimes the blue eyes would burn with an intensity that astonished even Victoria. He always attempted to follow her home and always failed.

Victoria saw through his fanaticism right away. Men were always drawn to her in one way or another. This young man was no different, even if desire for her aroused in him the passion of his religion. Worship was all he knew and he tried to draw her into his fervor for God in an attempt to seduce her.

Summer passed and autumn became the wet, foggy winter typical of San Francisco. The brightly lighted saloon couldn't allay the loneliness Victoria found unbearable this time of year.

Christmas had come and gone with no celebration on her part. Brother Gideon had preached at her for a moment about the birth of baby Jesus before being dumped unceremoniously into the wet, muddy street. His tirade only served to remind her of the plight of the poor abandoned children of the city.

She left the Silver Slipper as usual, wrapped in her black cloak. The rain had stopped earlier and the fog rolled in from the bay thicker than ever. It swirled and eddied about in the street obscuring the buildings along the way. She knew he was there. Could feel his thoughts as he moved to where she had just stood. She reappeared momentarily so he might orient himself to follow. The fog was an old friend, both bright and dark as she moved through it, not quite on foot, but never quite disappearing.

Victoria rounded the corner and the waiting children gathered close. Not one uttered a sound as they crowded near for the comfort she offered. Five children, boys and girls ranging in age from thirteen to four, reached out to touch her. Eager for the escape she brought to their arduous lives. The eldest girl held the youngest. Victoria forgot Brother Gideon as she gathered up the limp child. They all moved to the fire.

The preacher came slowly around the corner. He stopped and peered through the inconsistent fog. He saw her sitting on a stool, caped and hooded like a dark Madonna, a golden-haired tousled-headed babe cradled in her arms. The fire created a halo in the fog around her and the children gathered to her side in adoration.

She spoke without looking up as he approached.

"See how I atone for my sins, Brother Gideon?"

"God has forgiven your sins, sister. He is a loving God." He knelt before her.

"Does your God love little children? Where is He when they need him? Where was He when this angel was abandoned to the street by her mother? Look at this child!"

The cold fury in her voice forced him to look at the pitiful little girl she held.

"Where are the dimpled knees and pudgy fingers clutching at her mother's skirt? Where is the gentle hand to dress her hair and soothe away her fears in the night?"

The child's thin legs were covered in rat bites. Fever raged in the tiny face. Blue eyes had already begun to glaze in death.

"She will not live to see the dawn. How can your loving God allow this?"

The older children drew close. The fire blazed, filling the tableau with shadows. The young preacher rose from the mud. He stood close enough to see the clean, dry hem of her cloak.

"Go away, Brother Gideon. Leave me with my children. There is no one to mourn them but me."

He turned and walked hesitantly away. At the corner he looked back but they were gone. Swallowed up by the fog his mind said, but his heart told another story.

Victoria left her gold with the living and carried the dead child away. The mist enveloped her tenderly in a shroud as she held the small burden beneath her cloak until she reached her resting place. The odor of wet earth was not offensive as Victoria lay the little girl aside and dug a small, shallow grave with her hands. Somewhere far above, fog became drizzle and then rain. She buried the baby in the damp earthen-floored crypt and mourned for them all.

"Sweet Mother Earth, in whom we abide for all eternity, I beseech thee take pity on this thy innocent daughter. Take her to thy breast for sweet repose. Give unto her the peace I am denied. Have mercy as I make my way through the darkness."

Victoria lay down in her coffin, repeating the litany like a catechism. The words finally faded into silence as her own small death crept in like a welcome friend.

## Chapter Twenty-Three

Nightfall roused Victoria. She lay in the dark coffin and felt the monster's craving. For once in her long existence she actually wanted it. Ached to slake her thirst from the throats of all those who offended her. Yearned to punish them for abandoning their children. Hungered for the devastation her desire could create. Victoria gave over to the demon and burst from the coffin like a mad woman.

Outside, she was immediately engulfed by the black rainy night. She leaned against a rail balanced atop the shoddily constructed building just as the frantic search of the preacher brought him into view below. A sudden downpour of rain forced him to seek shelter between the saloon and the hotel that shared the alleyway. Halfway up the open stairs to the second floor landing he sank to the step.

Victoria watched him lean tiredly forward and rest his head on his knees. Desire to begin her revenge with the pompous young man in black sitting across the way stoked the fire raging within her. The cape flapped in the cold windswept rain but the near freezing temperature could not cool the inferno threatening to explode.

Without conscious thought, she stood at the bottom of the stairs in front of him. The scant light from surrounding buildings could not compete in the contest between night and rain, leaving the alley barely illuminated. She could see the frayed cuffs of the threadbare coat he wore. Almost a year had passed since he had first entered the Silver Slipper. The tall thin body had become gaunt.

She read his poor guileless mind without sympathy. His money was gone. Tomorrow he would be thrown out of the dismal room he once shared with others of his calling. They were already gone. Seduced by the corrupting influence of gold. The last three letters from the Elders lay on his bureau. Come away, they said. Now. Away from the iniquity of the City. How would he ever explain his loss of faith to an evil as old as the Bible itself. He was so close to the truth with his assessment of Eve and the serpent. But San Francisco was no Garden of Eden.

Victoria stepped closer. The rain had slowed to a drizzle.

"Thomas."

He looked up at the sound of his name.

She approached slowly.

"I have failed to do my duty," he said. "I am a missionary and should be without sin."

"All men born of this world are sinners." She sat down, sweeping her cape around to cover his shoulders. He shivered uncontrollably before leaning into the fever heat of her body.

"I'm sorry the baby died," he whispered, not looking at her.

"It wasn't your fault. It has been a long winter and there is no protection on the street."

"Don't they live with you?"

"I have no home."

"Then you should get one," he said matter of factly, as though it would be the easiest task in the world.

"It would take a lot of gold to make a home for all the orphans in this wicked city. My children don't have much time." She placed a hand on his knee and felt him tremble at her touch.

"Will you help me, Thomas?"

"I don't know how to do anything except preach."

"Just say yes and I'll teach you all you need to know." Her quiet soothing tone had the calming effect she wanted. He turned to look at her. For a moment uncertainty clouded his brilliant blue eyes, then he smiled. It was the first time she had ever seen him smile. A constant serious demeanor gave him the look of a much older man. Now appeared much younger.

"Yes," he said. "I will help you any way I can."

He continued to smile as she wrapped him in the cape and drew him close. Her free hand moved to the back of his head. She grasped a handful of shaggy hair and drew back, displaying his long neck with a prominent adams-apple. Her mind filled with visions of fangs ripping and tearing into the pale flesh, blood gushing from the wound. Her heart pounded with rage, with anticipation. Then she looked at his face. The smile froze on his lips as her vision filled the bright blue eyes with terror.

Suddenly she was back in Africa, overcome by the madness of Nikolai. Filled with contempt and loathing for his actions. And the insanity of her own impending deed overwhelmed the desire for revenge. Never. Never would she allow herself to become as deranged as Nikolai. She took a deep breath to still her racing heart and searched through Thomas' memory.

Victoria drew him close and pressed her lips to his neck. He became a man of God again, presenting a humble offering to the saint he envisioned her to be. She felt his arms surround her in a chaste embrace and drank his blood while dreaming of tomorrow and the house they would build together. A place of warmth and security not only for her children, but all those with need.

## Chapter Twenty-Four

The next night the Silver Slipper rollicked with laughter and music. Victoria had appeared with nightfall, to the approval of Winston and the regular patrons. The girls were so glad to see her, too. They all but ignored the customers. Winston passed out cigars and Randall, the house gambler who cheated unsuspecting miners for a percentage of the take, set up drinks for everyone not once but twice.

The house was so full no one noticed the well-dressed young man who joined in the merriment. He helped himself to a drink and toasted Victoria along with the others. Then he settled down, lighted cigar and all, at the table where Winston and Randall were playing poker with a select group of mine owners. He fit in well with the moneyed crowd. Caramel colored tight fitting pants were tucked into rich brown boots at mid calf. The tailored brown jacket matched his boots and a cream colored shirt hid his thinness. Months of dirt had been washed from his shaggy hair, lightening it to a golden brown. Only the preacher's blue eyes remained the same but now Thomas avoided looking at the object of his obsession.

Victoria stood across the room at the Faro table, once more the center of attention in a slim-fitting burnt-orange dress. Puffed sleeves rested high on her upper arms, leaving the shoulder and neckline bare. On that perfect stage was displayed an elaborate necklace. A dozen dark yellow topaz graced gold filigree buckles from which a large tearshaped Oriental sapphire hung to nestle in the slight cleavage of her breasts.

She smiled, treating the customers to her most expansive manner and dealt the cards the same easy way she always did. In the back of her mind she read the poker table. The excitement of the evening ran high. Everyone laughed a lot and the cards floated round the table again and again. She passed information along to Thomas with instructions on when to fold and when to up the ante. Far into the early morning he gracefully lost his second hand of the evening and left.

Victoria ignored the advances of her last customer and took a vacant chair at the poker table just as the group called it a night. Winston dealt her in.

"What did you think about the dude, Honey?" He squinted at her through a cloud of smoke from the cigar stub held tightly in his teeth.

"Nice dresser. How did he handle the cards?" She glanced at her hand and put chips on the table.

"Like a tenderfoot." Randall laughed and matched her bet.

"Probably straight off the boat but he had a streak of luck after a slow start." Winston took one look at his own cards and folded them together. "For some reason I can't concentrate this evening."

Victoria looked up and laughed. "How much *did* he win?"

Winston glared, daring her to laugh again. "Enough."

"More than enough." Randall tossed his cards aside and finished his drink.

"First man I ever saw come through that door and not head straight for your table." Winston leaned back in his chair and really looked at Victoria. "Might be a dandy as well as a tenderfoot."

"Even the virgins hang around you like lovesick puppies," Randall added. He reached over and touched the necklace. "Fine piece of jewelry. I've never seen you wear anything like that before. A gift from some rich old man?" His hand rested a moment too long on her breast.

"Watch yourself, Randall." Pale eyes glittered as Winston called Randall's attention to the glowing stub of cigar held just above the hand resting on the table.

Randall jerked both hands back at the same time.

"It's none of our business, but we were worried about you last night." Winston turned back to Victoria.

"I am sorry. There was no way I could be here. I spent the evening with a sick friend." Victoria looked across the table at Winston.

"I hope he's better." The sarcasm rang clear.

"She was four years old and she died." Victoria was out of the chair and halfway to the door before Winston caught her.

"Was she your—" he hesitated.

"No. But I was the only person who cared if she lived or died."

"Stay here tonight, Honey. Lily's room is still yours to use."

"I really am all right, Winston." She stopped to get her cape and allowed him to pull it snug around her shoulders. Victoria looked into his eyes and read his thoughts. *Who are you, Honey? Where do you come from and where are you going? What man has hurt you so badly you won't allow another to get close?*

She sighed.

"The necklace has been in my family for generations. It's one of the few good pieces I have left. There is no place here to sell it or it would already be gone." She drew the hood up over her hair. "My hatred is all that keeps me sane, Winston. Without its focus I would be lost. Someday I shall seek him out but not now, not soon for I am not strong enough yet to bring about his destruction."

She pulled the door with its stained glass window closed as she left. The rain had stopped and she stepped out into a fog that reflected a sparkle of rainbow hues around each lighted lamp. She could barely make out Thomas' window from the street but his eager anticipation of her arrival was perfectly clear. The children were nearby. Silently bidding Thomas to join them, she hurried down the alley to where they waited.

Billy moved away from the fire to make a place for her.

"I got a job at the store, Victoria. It ain't much, but now I can help out with food for the others." He nodded around the fire. The group had grown in her one night of absence. "That there's Johnny and his little sister, Alice."

Betsy, the thirteen-year-old mother to them all held a filthy little girl on her hip. The blonde haired baby had already been replaced. Only Victoria still mourned her passing.

"I have good news, too." She crowded them into the make-shift shelter under the stairs where it was relatively dry. "In a few minutes I'm going to bring someone for you to meet. His name is Thomas and from now on all the gold we get goes to him. He's going to build us a house. A home where we can all be safe and warm and it won't matter how many boys and girls join us. Everyone will be welcome."

They all stared at her. Betsy spoke first.

"A real house? With a kitchen? And a bed for everyone?" Alice got down from Betsy's lap and stood in front of Victoria.

"I used to live in a house. It had a porch and flowers in the yard."

"She's right," Johnny added. "Ma used to make me water 'em from the well in the summer and I hated toting that bucket worsen anything. I sure wouldn't mind watering flowers now, if me and Alice could just live in a house again." Victoria smiled gently at the boy squatted on one knee at her side. The sleeves of his coat and pants were two inches too short. Long shaggy black hair hung over his collar and the shadow of a mustache already adorned his upper lip.

"You'll all have chores to do in this house." She looked away into the darkness. "But here's Thomas now. Don't be frightened." Victoria raised her hand and beckoned him into the ring of light. He had changed back into his old clothes, and in doing so had taken on the visage of a stern preacher again. Alice pressed closer to Victoria as Thomas dropped to one knee and drew her hand to his lips.

"You've done well, Thomas. Thank you." She patted the bench and he sat beside her. "I thought perhaps you might remember. Gambling is an interesting sport. It takes a quick-witted person to be successful over a long period of time."

"I won a lot of money. It's a good start for our home."

"First you must find a piece of property to build on. Away from the city. Far enough away so day to day life can be carried on without the constant reminder of what these children have left behind. Everyone has to forget the hardships of the street. There will be other burdens to bear before we are finished."

"I know a place. There's a barn but the house burned down," Billy said. "I can show Thomas tomorrow." He got up and stood beside the preacher.

"Good. If there's a barn, we can get a cow for milk and maybe have chickens." Thomas said softly. "I grew up on a farm. We can use the barn for shelter until the house is done."

"See, you can do more than preach." Victoria added her small bag of gold to his winnings.

"Don't buy anything you can steal," she said. "Go to the docks and take things from abandoned ships. Most have been cannibalized to the point they will never sail again. The boys can help." She leaned closer and whispered to Thomas. "Please get Johnny some larger clothes. And starting tonight we all pray for an early spring."

The two adults said goodnight to the children with promises of an end to their suffering soon and left together. They walked along, heads close, speaking softly for all the world like lovers.

"The hardest thing I have ever had to do was not go to you tonight. Being in the same room and not being able to even speak was intolerable. How will I ever manage?"

"Next time you must go to another saloon. If you come back to the Silver Slipper too soon Winston will suspect. The clothes really do change you. No one even suspected the gambler might be the preacher."

"It isn't the clothes. The change in me is you. When I gamble, you give me confidence in myself."

"No, Thomas. You find your own strength to accomplish what you can. I could never make you do anything against your wishes."

"As long as you are with me, I can do anything."

"Is that not what your God says? Abide in me and I shall give you strength for any task? You are a strong man, Thomas, even standing alone."

She turned and walked away, leaving him standing in the fog.

The light spatter of pebbles on the window woke Thomas. Apparently the fog had burned off hours ago for the dingy room was bright with sunshine. Gravel hit the glass again so he rose and threw up the sash. Billy stood below in the alley.

"Thomas. Come see what I found."

Thomas stepped into threadbare pants and put his arms into both shirt and jacket sleeves. By the time he reached the stairs the shirt was buttoned and tucked into his pants. It took longer to put on the boots but he was completely dressed when he left the building and stepped round the corner where Billy waited.

The red haired, freckle-faced boy held a short piece of rope in his hand. The other end was fashioned into a halter and securely attached to a small animal.

"Where did you get that—thing, Billy?" Thomas cautiously approached the beast and looked it over.

"Gee, Thomas, don't ya know a burro when ya see one?"

"Of course I do. Only it's a little puly looking even for a burro. Did you steal it?"

"Naw. The poor guy that owned it just got shanghaied so I figured to do him a favor and watch it while he was gone. Takes a long time to sail to China, I hear."

Thomas stepped up and reached out a hand. Billy tightened his hold on the halter.

"If you set much store in having five fingers on that hand you won't touch him. He's got a nasty set of teeth."

"Incredibly stubborn creatures, too, from what I hear. Well, what shall we do with him?"

"Get on. You and me are gonna ride out to see the Reeves place. It's too far to walk." Billy held the mule's head firmly between both hands.

"I can't ride this animal. It's not big enough."

"It don't matter. He's used to carrying bigger loads."

Thomas moved cautiously around to the side and threw a leg over its broad back. Billy handed him the makeshift reins.

"Kick him if he tries to bite." The burro stared straight ahead.

Billy swung easily up behind Thomas and kicked the animal sharply in the sides with his heels. The burro started forward with a jerk and stopped after four steps.

"Giddyap," said Thomas, slapping the rope against the animal's neck. The creature stood still as a statue.

Billy kicked him again, harder. The burro reached around, snapped at the nearest object, and bit Thomas above the knee.

"Damn you, creature of Satan," Thomas screeched, and grabbed at his injured leg.

The burro tore out of the alley at a fast trot. Thomas yelled and swore halfway down the street while Billy held on the best way he could.

"Are we going the right direction, Billy?" Thomas asked, once he calmed down. The pack animal slowed to a placid gait.

"Yeah. You ok?"

"I'll probably never walk again. From this moment on this creature shall be Beelzebub. Not only is he surely a demon from hell, he is also the lord of flies." Thomas swatted at a small cloud of insects swarming around them.

Man and boy continued on their journey at a pace scarcely faster than walking. Thomas's feet dragged the ground if he relaxed for a single moment and their arrival at the burned-out shell of a house happened none too soon.

"Jesus surely had the temperament of a saint to have ridden on such a beast." Beelzebub, apparently having endured enough punishment for a while, stopped in the shade of a huge oak tree a hundred yards short of the barn.

Neither Thomas nor Billy had the courage to hobble the burro so they left him standing meek as a kitten and began their tour of the homestead. The barn roof and walls were intact and well made. Everything inside was dry and being out of the wind made it seem warm. The attached corral was small but all the posts were upright. The only rail missing lay on the ground a few feet away.

"We can use this building for our home beginning today. It's better shelter than any of us have in the city." Thomas kicked at the hay spread about in several stalls. "It's as dry and warm as a blanket. When we get back, start bringing the younger children out. Betsy can stay with them while you and Johnny and I round up the things we need to build the house."

"Thomas, how will you and us kids ever fix the kind of place Victoria hopes for?"

The question made Thomas stop and wonder about all the difficulties they would face.

"It won't be easy. But it'll be a fine place when we're done. A place we can all be proud of." Thomas hobbled outside, half leaning on Billy.

Double chimneys still stood with the burned out remains of a comfortable sized house scattered in between. They kicked around in the ashes and were rewarded with nothing for their trouble but sooty shoes.

"Billy, look." Thomas pointed back down the hillside. The house had apparently stood at the top of a small rise and several miles away, directly down the hill, huddled San Francisco. Only a few ragtag tents still stood scattered among the multitude of wooden structures. A glut of ships in various stages of disrepair cluttered the bay. Far out over the water sunlight danced on choppy waves stirred by the chill wind.

"Victoria is gonna love this place. It's so quiet and pretty." Billy looked around at the rolling hill and big tree in the yard.

The harsh braying of Beelzebub disturbed the peace.

"Let's get back and start gathering supplies." Thomas's leg had finally stopped throbbing but he gladly mounted behind Billy for the ride back to town.

"Have you known Victoria long," Billy asked as the burro plodded along.

"I didn't know Victoria at all until yesterday. For almost a year I thought she was someone named Honey who worked in a saloon. I still don't know who she really is."

"My Ma worked in the Silver Slipper. She left me out here to live with the Reeves. I was here when the place burned. It used to be real nice, Thomas, but a couple of the kids died in the fire and Missus Reeves made her husband take her back east some place. By that time Ma was sick and didn't come to see me no more anyway. Victoria found me on the streets. She was a friend of Ma's. By the time Ma died Victoria had already been looking after me for a while, bringing me money. I'd have starved to death or been shot for stealing food by now if she hadn't helped me. Pretty soon a whole bunch of kids were hanging around with me cause I always had something to eat."

"That's an awful story, Billy, but mine's worse. I can't bear to even tell it yet, but someday I will. Someday when I've learned to live with my guilt. Someday when I begin to repay my debt to Victoria."

Thomas spent his nights gambling. It didn't take long to

learn the ropes. He could feel Victoria's influence when he concentrated but somewhere along the way her commands changed to gentle humor as he won more through his own wits.

Victoria remained sequestered in town. Protected by day in her earthen grave, she sought always to conceal her true identity from the children.

Once bitten by the serpent, Thomas continued to gamble in earnest, living his dual life with ease and confidence. He rolled up his sleeves and tended the children and the farm by day. By night he dressed in his fine clothes and wiled away the hours smoking and drinking and dealing cards.

Victoria and Thomas met each morning in the early hours before dawn, laughing and carrying on like a couple of children who had successfully pulled the wool over the eyes of their elders one more time. The house went up quickly. Victoria's simple design worked as well in reality as it did on paper.

The children fell into a comfortable routine of rising early and taking care of their chores so Victoria saw them less and less. Occasionally Billy would wait up and relate all the wonderful things they had accomplished. Betsy had the girls working a small garden and here and there a few flowers grew. He grimaced when he told her Thomas insisted they all spend some time each day learning to read and write. Thomas's strict rule also included a weekly bath and haircut.

As the summer progressed they became more and more self-sufficient. San Francisco continued to grow, with more tent buildings filling the spaces and spreading outward. With the boom in population came an increase in pollution and an explosion of disease. Victoria was glad the children were safe away from the contaminated drinking water when a coughing sickness ran through the City, making many sick.

She rose early, dressed in the now sadly out of fashion mauve gown and disappeared into the fog rolling in from the bay. The children were sitting down to dinner when she stepped

up on the porch. Thomas had already dressed for his foray into
town and sat at the head of the table. She could hear him saying
grace and waited to knock until a chorus of "Amen's" went
around the table. Alice opened the door and crushed the full
skirted gown in an attempt to hug her.

"Victoria's here," Alice called, skipping merrily down the
long hall.

Everyone jumped up from the table, including Thomas. The
children crowded around, even those who did not know her,
laughing and calling her name. She smiled at Thomas over their
heads. Good food and a few comforts had filled in the hollow
spaces of his body and face. Sun bleached hair a shade darker
than his hands and face gleamed in the light from the lamp in
the hallway. His thoughts spoke eloquently to her. *See how they
love you. See how I love you.*

They made a place for her at the end of the table and the
evening meal was spent with each child competing for a
moment of her time. Afterwards, the older children put the little
ones to bed while those in the middle cleared the table and
cleaned up the kitchen. She spent a few minutes with Johnny,
Betsy and Billy, listening to them read, talking about their plans
for the future. Betsy wanted to be a teacher like Thomas. Billy
and Johnny were planning to hire some Chinese and open a
laundry. She laughed at their attempts to explain how much
money they could earn for the orphanage by taking in washing
from the city. By midnight they were all practically asleep on
their feet so she kissed them goodnight and promised to return
the next evening.

Thomas stood on the porch, smoking a cigar and looking
out over the bay. Fog lay in a solid sheet over the water while
high above, light from a full moon washed the hills surrounding
the basin. Victoria joined him, leaning into his embrace as his
arm went around her shoulders.

"Give it up. Come and live here. With us. You can see how

the children want it." He leaned over and kissed the hair at her temple.

"You know I cannot bring my darkness into this house of love. No more than you can give up the gambling." She felt him laugh silently at her reference to his addiction. "The city is full of sickness. No one must come into town for a while."

"I knew something was wrong. I could almost read it in your thoughts." He took a deep draw on the cigar. The glowing tip lit the night briefly before turning to ash. He dropped it into the flowerbed as he exhaled.

Victoria turned to face him, holding herself away as he tried to draw her closer.

"I can see I have been too thorough with your education. Is there nothing I can hide from you anymore?" She searched his face a moment then leaned her cheek against his chest. The steady beat of his heart soothed even as it excited her.

"No. Sometimes I see you in that dark place where your spirit sleeps by day and I want to be there with you. Then I'm distracted by one of the children asking about some task or another and I know my place is here with them, always. If only for your sake and what it would mean if I were to leave." Thomas leaned his cheek against the top of her head. "The children have a name for our home. They call it 'Victoria's Hope'."

The two of them stood on the porch for a long time. The sounds of sleep covered Victoria like a favored quilt, filling her with a sense of arriving home safely after a long tiring journey.

"Stay with me tonight," Thomas whispered against her soft hair. "I would feel your body close for a while."

Victoria drew away and took his hand. They stepped off the porch and walked together toward the barn.

## Chapter Twenty-Five

The traveller had not had a bath, nor apparently a meal, in weeks. He sat in the kitchen, stinking dirty, and devoured two plates of eggs and biscuits. The children left to do their chores, leaving Thomas to sit across from the starving man and listen to him ramble.

"I know exactly the area you're talking about. I traveled that route when I came to San Francisco. Once I got here I could barely afford to eat but I certainly didn't starve along the way. It didn't take that long," Thomas said, not quite believing the young man's story.

"That's just my point," Eugene Gordon said, around a mouthful of biscuit. He paused to wash it down with a swallow from his third glass of milk. "It's not many miles but the scenery was so breathtaking I lost track of time. I wandered for days." He reached for his pack and took out several small leather cases, one of which he handed to Thomas.

The first opened to reveal a natural pool of water surrounded with rocks. Scattered here and there were trees already barren of leaves. Thomas laid it to one side as the photographer opened another larger case. Inside, captured in poignant copper tones were three men of different ages. One was clean shaven. The other two had grizzled whiskers. The look on all three faces made them ageless. The hunger recorded in their eyes was for more than food. A starvation for riches, for love. A yearning for dreams that each one doubted would ever come true. Thomas shut the jacket gently.

"I can see how you got distracted. Your treatment of such different subject matter is truly remarkable. I've seen this type of thing before but never so finely detailed."

"It's because I'm a professional. I'm going to set up shop in

San Francisco. If and when I ever get there." The photographist leaned back and patted his stomach.

"It's just a short walk from here. The city gets closer every-day. It'll soon be on our doorstep."

Eugene sat up straight, Thomas had his complete attention. "You mean if I had continued walking in the dark last night, I might have gone right past San Francisco?"

"Dropped into the bay would be more likely."

He jumped up and started collecting his belongings. "I must go. I have to see this wonder for myself."

"Come. I'll show you the city." Thomas rose and went down the hall to the front door, his guest close behind.

Thomas opened the door and stood to the side as his guest stepped out. He heard the startled gasp as the photographer took in the view. The early morning fog had lifted from the bay and blue water sparkled in the sunlight. The graveyard of ships seemed to have taken root and sprouted from the dark landfall.

"I have to get my camera. I must preserve this moment," he said, excitement making him hurry.

"Don't worry. The view is always spectacular from our porch." Thomas leaned against the rail.

"Oh, but never quite the same from one moment to the next. Please, let me stay. I must capture this. I have no money but I'll make it worth your effort if I can make this my base until I have a chance to look for a place in the city."

"Will you make daguerreotypes of the children?"

"And you and your home and whatever else you want. Deal?" Thomas smiled and held out his hand .

"It's a deal." They shook on it, then Eugene Gordon of Boston brushed past Billy in his hurry to get his equipment.

"I figured he would stay once he saw the view." Thomas said as Billy came out on the porch.

"Why's that, Thomas?"

"The man is an artist. Watch him close, Billy. We're seeing

the beginning of a new art form, one that may just last forever."

"Would it make a better business than a Chinese laundry?" Billy asked.

Thomas laughed and put his arm around Billy's shoulders. The boy grew so fast these days.

"Nothing will ever replace the need for clean clothes, but it would undoubtedly be a more interesting profession. I'll write a note to Victoria. You can take it into town and bring back any supplies our guest needs." The man and the boy walked into the house together.

The daylight hours passed in a flurry of excitement. Eugene set up the box camera on a tripod in the front yard, away from the shade of the oak tree. He took shots of the city to the west as the morning sun progressed toward noon. After lunch, the children gathered round while he took various pictures of the house and the barn. Once again he had forgotten to eat and would have continued working except for Billy. On returning from town, he stood nearby and watched the photographer for a while. He moved closer and the smell of dirty clothes and body odor forced him to comment.

"Thomas doesn't allow us at the supper table till we've all washed and changed clothes. I know it's not Saturday, but I think you could use a bath and a haircut."

Eugene paused and decided not to prepare another plate.

"Can't have supper till I've washed. Sounds like Thomas runs a strict house. Well, I do have a crick in my back. Help me dismantle the equipment." He showed Billy how to pack up the camera in its special box.

The tripod folded together compactly. The box with the unexposed plates simply closed and locked. The new work fit snugly into another box to await packaging. Billy was surprised when everything fit together, making it easy to carry.

It was Eugene's turn to be surprised when he saw the bath house. Being attached to the south side of the house made it nice and warm. Steaming kettles of water waited on a slatted bench beside a narrow, high-backed tub. Some ingenious mind had placed a pump at the shallow end. Eugene dumped the boiling water in, primed the pump, added just enough cold, clear water to make it bearable then stepped gratefully into the tub.

"Ah–Ah–Ah, that's so good."

Eugene sucked in short breaths of air. Then he leaned back and relaxed. It had been a long time since he had bathed in anything near this luxury. In his own bathroom. In his father's house. Clothes laid out by the valet. Dressing for dinner. The scent of his mother's perfume mingling with the aromas rising from serving platters being passed around by a graceful maid. The clink of silver against fine china.

All the grand times in the grand old place were overlaid by the last hellacious argument. His father's office looked out over the shipyard. Eugene had stared out the window at the latest clipper under construction because he couldn't bear to see the disappointment in his father's face as the tirade blasted through the large office. Surely the whole world heard the words "You are no son of mine. Get out and never come back."

He'd grown up in that shipyard, knew all the men by their Christian names just as they all knew he would someday be their boss. All lost because of his sister's gift of a camera. She'd been to school in Paris. It had been the latest rage there, to have ones likeness captured on the little piece of metal.

The past two years had been hard but Eugene accomplished his goal. He had become a dammed good photographer. The water in the tub cooled and smells of supper grew stronger so he picked up the bar of lye soap and scrubbed so hard and fast his skin turned red. The rumbling in his stomach forced him to hurry. A mirror above the basin showed blue-black hair curling tightly in spite of its length. His thin face was dominated by big blue eyes and a nose that turned under a little more than he cared. He looked all around but his dirty clothes were gone.

"What have you done with my clothes," he called through the closed door.

"Burned them," a female voice replied from the kitchen. "Thomas left you something to wear. On the bench. Call when you're ready for a haircut." The voice moved away from the door and then grew stronger.

"Who's going to be the barber?" Eugene asked timidly, stepping into a clean set of long johns.

"Thomas, of course."

The older girl must have been supervising the younger children as they set the table for supper. He was amazed the children took care of their particular chores without complaint. But this territory was far removed from the pampered life he'd led in genteel Boston.

"Well, tell him to hurry. I'm starving. Supper smells good." Someone knocked on door, taking him by surprise.

"Are you decent?" Thomas asked.

Eugene grabbed the dark trousers, hurriedly put them on and opened the door.

Thomas peered intently at him.

"You're Jewish."

Eugene ran a thumb and forefinger down his nose.

"It's a little difficult to hide but I assure you it's in looks only. My father hasn't spoken to me since the day I took up my new profession. He wanted me to take over the family business. I doubt he would be very pleased to see me now."

He sat down on the bench and Thomas took the scissors to his clean wet hair and beard. Dark ringlets fell to the floor.

"Some folks here might be offensive. I've tasted a bit of their prejudice. I came here as a priest with a religious sect known as the Brothers of Gideon and spent my first year in the city preaching. This last year I've devoted all my free time to gambling. Not a lot of the good folks here give consideration to the fact it was to raise money to build the orphanage. Victoria and I were determined to make a home for the children." Thomas clipped and cut until Eugene's hair was fairly short and even. Then he picked up the strait razor.

Eugene jumped up from the bench. "I'll do that myself, if you don't mind."

Thomas handed the razor over and started for the door. He watched as Eugene applied lather to what was left of the ragged beard and stropped the blade.

"Who's Victoria?" Eugene asked, without looking up from the mirror. "The children were talking about her this morning."

"There's not much I can tell you about Victoria. She's a woman each man must worship in his own way." Thomas opened the door and left, leaving his guest to finish shaving.

Victoria took the note from Winston.

"Where did you get this?"

"A red-haired boy gave it to me early in the day. He asked very nicely would I hand it to the pretty lady. I swear your admirers get younger every day."

Victoria slipped the small piece of folded paper into her neckline, tucking it completely under the dark-blue satin bodice. She smiled at Winston as he watched.

"Aren't you going to read it? It could be important." Winston walked around the empty table. Tuesday nights were usually slow and the evening had yet to begin. "Do you want the night off?"

"If you're going to pester me all evening, Winston, you might as well play." Victoria had the game set up.

He backed away from the table. "You know I haven't the vaguest idea how. It's beyond me how anyone ever wins at Faro." He stuck a half-smoked cigar in his mouth, turned and walked away.

Victoria didn't need to read the note to know what it said. She could smell the clean scent of Billy's hand on the paper. Could see the mischievous grin on Thomas's face as he wrote the words. 'Cannot come to town tonight. Meet me early tomorrow. At home.' No signature was needed but the short message intrigued her. What was he planning now?

The weeks when the coughing sickness ran through the city had passed pleasantly in spite of the quarantine. She went to the children every night instead of the saloon. Victoria could almost believe it might be possible to live at the farm. Thoughts of such an arrangement strayed into her mind more often these days. But she'd never quite figured out how to hide her true self from the children. Thomas knew, of course, and certainly didn't hold it against her. But children could sometimes be cruelest to those who loved them most. Telling them was simply out of the question.

The city was in the throes of another growth spurt and the end of the recent outbreak of disease had coincided with the destruction of a large tent city within San Francisco proper. The rat population had been gigantic, overflowing into the streets where they were clubbed to death. The streets were finally cleaned of debris and scrapped level by horse drawn crossties, the excess heaved into the harbor. The layer of ships nearest the dock quickly became part of the new landmass. The city spread out over the water almost as fast as it expanded to swallow up the hills surrounding the bay.

Victoria had watched fortunes won and lost on the turn of a card. The *nouveau riche* built mansions high on the hills looking down on the city. Some changed ownership before the construction was finished. *Victoria's Hope* still stood alone on its high summit, enticing her to visit more often and when there, the pleasant surroundings created by Thomas and the children entreated her to stay.

She smiled as her mind sorted through a jumble of

incoherent ideas she perceived from Thomas even at this distance. He whistled tunelessly as he milled about in the kitchen. Victoria felt the presence of Betsy, probably at the stove tending some aromatic pot. Another adult was there with them and she sensed an easy camaraderie.

The house always attracted strangers moving from some place or another to San Francisco. Once an entire novitiate of nuns stayed a week under its roof while searching for a place to establish their own home and school. They praised Thomas for his good work and prayed for his continued success.

Victoria finally gave up trying to fathom Thomas' thoughts and turned her smile to the few customers willing to play Faro. The evening promised to be slow and since Thomas would not be coming to town, she reconciled herself to a solitary evening.


The box camera sat atop the tripod, its tent of canvas sheeting reaching to the ground. Before its intent gaze the children stood formally arranged in rows, the four taller boys across the back with the other girls and boys surrounding Thomas according to size.

Cloaked and hooded against the suns slowly diminishing threat, Victoria stood in the shadow of the oak tree. A layer of soil in the flimsy shoes she wore would have been laughable. It had been weeks since she last fed and she felt the indomitable force of the sun all the more for lack of nourishment. She watched Thomas standing motionless among the children, his dark suit and shirt making a harsh statement beside the bright colors and white pinafores.

So this was his surprise.

She had seen itinerant photographers in San Francisco before. They chronicled the growth of the City from month to month.

"All done," came the call from beneath the canvas shroud.

Everyone relaxed. The kids chattered excitedly with one another. Billy and Johnny moved toward the camera and its still unseen operator.

"Just one more minute."

Thomas moved away from the group, having seen her at last.

"I'm so glad you're here." He stood and gazed at her. "It seems like weeks since you came to see us."

"I know, Thomas." She truly did know how long it had been. But time moved at a different pace for her and even as she hated the slow passage of her existence, she lived in horror of the fast passing days that robbed her children of their childhood and Thomas of his youthful enthusiasm.

"Come," he said. "I want you to meet Eugene Gordon. He's truly an artist." Thomas turned to the man standing with Billy. "Gene. Gene. Victoria is here."

"Ah yes. The wonderful, the marvelous—" he turned to face her, "Victoria." The last word was spoken quietly. "I have traveled to the end of the world. And found incredible beauty."

Victoria laughed. "I assure you, Mr. Gordon, there are other lands beyond the ocean."

The sound of her laughter hung in the air, soft as the morning fog. Her words rolled with a soft brogue, inviting him to see those exotic ports—through her eyes. But he had no desire to go further, indeed, he now wondered why it had taken him so long to get here.

He stepped closer and loosed the hood of her cloak. Sunset fire streaked hair so tightly braided it looked black. Her skin, pale as porcelain, shimmered like a silken veil in the summer twilight. He moved around her slowly. She was like no other woman he had ever known.

Thomas smiled at him and unfastened her cloak. Eugene slipped it from her shoulders, draping it over his arm.

A slight tremor shivered across her bare back and arms. He

felt it in his hands, as though he touched her instead of just wanting to—needing to. His lips ached to kiss the silken grace of breast just visible above the dark-green satin bodice.

Victoria stood very still as he considered her with an artists eye, and was suddenly taken aback. Long ago and far, far away. And another dark-haired artist with a sinners vision of good and evil. But this smiling face did not belong to Dominie the Greek. Oh, no. She had had to teach *El Greco* a thing or two about love but Eugene Gordon's thoughts washed over her in a rush of blatant sexual craving. The hot smell of his sweat mingled with the slightly acrid odor of chemicals. His gaze scorched her flesh, sending rivulets of quicksilver spilling over her breasts to leave her breathless. She felt his hands on her face before he touched her.

Thomas' thoughts intruded. *He's in love with you already. Even as I was from the moment I saw you in the Silver Slipper.*

The gentle flood of his affection became an anchor in the storm of passion aroused by the photographer. Thomas smiled at her. *He is so much wiser than I could ever be, because he will tell you so eloquently. His pictures will worship you far better than I ever could.*

*Oh, Thomas*, she thought. *You are right. I will love this man but never to your disfavor.* All the while, the photographers desire threatened to override her restraint. He stopped circling and stood behind Thomas and suddenly she knew she had to remain in control. She allowed Thomas a fleeting glimpse of the other man's desire. He had the grace to blush, then his eyes met hers and they both laughed at Eugene's unabashed display.

"What?" Eugene Gordon looked first at Victoria then at Thomas. "Did I say something funny?" he asked. The look on his face reflected their amusement.

"I'm very pleased to meet you, too, Mr. Gordon."

The children gathered round, laughing and speaking at the same time.

"Take Victoria's picture, please."

"We want a picture of Victoria."

"I intend to do just that," Eugene said. "Right away. Now, before the light is completely gone."

They were pushed into position and Eugene entered the tent to work his magic. The camera recorded a simple family scene; a tall man dressed in black, hat in hand. Close at his side stood a beautiful woman, dressed in a handsome though vulgar manner that did not detract from her charm. Her left hand rested lovingly on the shoulder of the child standing in front of her. Even from a distance, the camera recorded the detail of the heavy, ornately carved gold ring on her index finger. It was a style not seen for centuries and the coat of arms entwined round the Germanic V belonged to neither Thomas nor Victoria.

# Chapter Twenty-Six

Eugene lifted his end of an eight-foot length of ten-by-twelve and held it while Thomas nailed the other end in place.

"Thomas, if you don't get Betsy to teach that Chinaman how to fix fried chicken, I'm—" Hammer blows punctuated his words. When the noise stopped, he continued.

"—going to eat in the City from now on."

"Hold that beam steady, will you." The hammering began again. When it ended, Eugene groaned.

"Thomas, this chapel will never be finished—"

One more time the pounding cut him off.

"Dammit! Thomas, we need help!"

"Don't curse in front of the children, Gene. You're the one who suggested building a church."

"Well, thank God, you *can* still hear. And if you were listening you'd know everyone has deserted but us."

Thomas brought the ladder around and climbed high to put two nails in the heavy beam. Then he climbed down and sat beside his friend.

"I hear you complaining a lot, Gene. But I don't hear what you're really trying to say."

Raising both arms, Eugene surveyed the large area they were framing.

"Me and you working in our spare time is going to take forever to build this chapel. That Chinaman in your kitchen would do a better job out here cutting lumber and we need ten more just like him to finish in time."

"In time for what?" Thomas asked.

"I sent to Boston for a piano. My sister telegraphed that she shipped it out three weeks ago. It'll be here in a couple of months."

The hammer landed on the floor with a clomp. "Well, I'm glad you finally confessed. I was beginning to think you'd done something really unforgivable."

"Not yet. But only because she won't have me."

"Angels rush in where you fear to tread."

"Don't preach to me, Thomas. I know you're not the self-righteous bastard folks around here believe. I've seen you all decked out, raking in the gold across a poker table."

"That's true enough. I'm no angel. But Victoria and I—it's not what you think."

"Don't tell me what I think. Dammit, Thomas! I don't know *what* I think. But believe me, you never enter into the picture when I think about her."

"It wouldn't matter if I did. Every man must worship her in his own way, Eugene. I have mine. You have to find yours. And if we expect to have a roof over our new piano when it arrives, we both better settle in and do some serious gambling. Starting tonight."

Eugene stood and offered Thomas a hand up. "I was going into the City anyway."

"Why doesn't that surprise me?" Thomas asked.

"I can't stay away. I don't know how you do it, going for weeks without seeing her."

The two young men walked toward the house together. Thomas picked at a blister on his palm. "All I have to do is shut my eyes and I see her."

"So where is she? Tell me, Thomas. Tell me how she spends her days."

The blister broke and he raised the wound to his lips for a moment and sucked at the clear liquid. "Sleeping. She's sleeping."

"Where?"

Thomas didn't have to shut his eyes to go to that dark place where she lay. He felt the afternoon sun warm on his back while the odor of damp earth surrounded him, making him sick at heart, but she would not come here and chance this bright world might intrude on her small death. He had tried often enough to persuade her but he was, after all, only here to serve her needs. And she needed him here as much as she needed to be there.

"Some place down by the docks," he finally said.

"Dammit, Thomas! That's no answer." Eugene strode angrily away. He had primed the outdoor pump and was soaking his head under the fount of cold water when Thomas reached him.

"So, has Winston thrown you out of the Silver Slipper yet?"

"No, but I'm not nearly as obnoxious as you were." Eugene's words still carried a note of exasperation.

Thomas laughed. "She told you. Well, I was pretty serious about myself in those days."

Eugene worked the pump for him.

"Did you ever—I mean, in the beginning—"

"Didn't I just tell you it's not what you think? Our relationship—it's never been carnal. Victoria and I share a bond that—"

"Transcends the flesh? Like priest and nun?"

Thomas combed sun-streaked brown hair with his fingers before he spoke.

"It's even different than that. You see how she is with the children. She gives them much more than I ever could, even with the home, and my simple attempts at education. She's their inspiration to hope—and dream. That's what I see when I love her. She is my—Madonna of the dark."

"Dammit, Thomas. You're too good for this world. And I'm an evil fool. When I'm with her I only see what I want to see. Us—she and I—together, in a way you can't even imagine."

"Oh, I can imagine. And if it helps, she sees it that way, too."

"Then why won't she let me get close enough to show her how I feel?"

"It's all very complicated. My best advice is if you want it badly enough don't give up."

"Dammit, Thomas! That makes me feel a hell of a lot better! Like my father just gave me permission to fuck my sister!"

"Don't talk like that in front of the children, Gene. Please."

"Don't worry. I've imposed on your hospitality too long already. I'll stay in the City until I find a place for the shop."

"You don't have to do that."

"It'll be easier, at least on me." *Easier to live with my guilt,* he thought, *if I don't see you every day.* Less of a betrayal of friendship and never-ending generosity. Maybe put an end to the anger and frustration at being so close and yet unable to touch her. Maybe it would murder the green-eyed monster that made him so jealous of what Thomas and Victoria had and he couldn't share. "Besides I can't spend any more of my time being a carpenter. I came to San Francisco to take pictures."

"I understand. But you'll have to explain it to her." Thomas left him standing by the pump and walked away.

Eugene watched him move quickly across the yard to where she stood, a dark shadow in the heavy shade of the massive oak tree. Then he turned and went into the house alone.

Upstairs, he put on a shirt and pulled a valise from under the bed. He was throwing clothes into the bag when she appeared.

"Were you going to say goodbye?" she asked.

"I'm moving into the City. So I can see you more often."

"We see each other every night."

He turned and faced her. "It's not enough." Then he went back to his packing. "I can't stay here knowing how much you love Thomas."

"Moving out will not change how I feel about either of you.

Thomas will always be with us. And as much as I want to love you, I can't."

Something in her voice made him turn. She stood with her back to the closed door, looking young and vulnerable in a simple white shirt buttoned to the throat and a pair of men's blue jeans. Dark hair framed her pale face in soft waves. He left the valise on the bed and went to her.

"Nothing you say can change the way I feel." He wanted to touch her so badly his fingers ached. She looked up at him and her magical eyes held such promise he hardly dared think. But still he could not touch her as he felt her conjure the ghost of some long ago heartache to stand between them.

"If you have the power to deny my desire," he whispered hoarsely, "then please—use it to take away my need."

Suddenly the barrier between them was gone. He virtually fell on her, his fingers threading through her hair, his body pressing her back against the door. His mouth found hers and he thought he would drown in the hot sweet consent his tongue discovered there. Her hands pressed against his chest, burning his flesh with lust's perfect promise. Her darkness whispered around him, perfumed secrets of hot sand cooled by night and abruptly they were in bed. An enormous bed with satin sheets that tangled beneath him. Moonlight flooded the room with brightness and her hair trailed across his naked body, tracing dark fire that pained him with such intense pleasure he barely noticed Victoria struggled in his embrace. Then she was gone, leaving him leaning against the door, his anger and frustration soothed but still no more sure of where he fell in her affection.


Victoria climbed the back stairs at the Silver Slipper slowly. When she reached Lily's old room, she sat on the bed and tried to convince herself what she'd seen wasn't true. It was the same vision she had seen on the Sea Witch but then it had been

Jeremiah. Tonight it was Eugene, sharing her life, her passion, her blood—because he had been like her. A vampire. And somewhere in the vast darkness of the future, that same frightening sense of Nikolai.

"Mother. Help me. I'm so alone. Am I seeing the future I want to see because I need it so badly?"

The noise from downstairs swelled in a storm of conflicting emotions that only heightened her sense of isolation. When he walked through the front doors, his heartbeat became an anchor in her turmoil. He made his way to the bar and with a gentle reaching out, she made sure the bartender told him which room she was in. He climbed the stairs deliberately, like a man with a calling he would not be turned from easily. She opened the door before he knocked and stepped toward him. His arms closed around her as he kicked the door shut. Lifting her, he carried her to the bed and sat, cradling her like a child.

"Why are you doing this?" Thomas asked.

She hid her face against his jacket and let his peace wash over her.

"I can't give you everything you need. You've told me that from the beginning. So why can't you accept what Gene has offered? He's strong. And full of that fierce passion I feel in you. It's time you thought of yourself again and I don't want to lose my good friend. So why don't you make him part of this family?"

"Thomas, you don't know what you're saying."

"I know enough of your history to know it's wrong for you to be alone—forever."

"He would never consent."

"Ask him."

"Thomas, I hate and despise this life I am forced to live. I will not ask him to share it."

"Then I will."

Victoria pushed free of his grasp and stood looking down at

where he lounged on the bed. The gambler, exuding confidence, handsome in his camel colored britches and dark jacket, blue eyes dark with concern.

"I forbid you to speak of this."

He got up and moved past her to the door, finally turning to speak.

"I am your devoted servant, Victoria. But I serve you out of love. You are not my master." He closed the door quietly as he left.

Victoria stared at the door until he reached the bottom of the stairs.

*Thomas! Thomas, please don't.* She shook her head, trying to banish thoughts her heart had already considered so many times. *It couldn't happen.* She reached into the armoire and pulled out the first dress she touched. No matter what Thomas and Eugene decided, she was still in control and she would never let it happen.

She dressed quickly then fought the wild curls without success and finally left her hair loose. She moved down the stairs into the noisy hall. The gored skirt of the slim fitting black velvet dress swirled around her legs. The soft swish of the fabric over her flesh filled her with physical pleasure and she smiled at every man who turned to watch. Their admiration surrounded her, overwhelming her with warring emotions— adoration, lust, respect. She drank in all they offered.

The bar girls greeted her warmly as she crossed to the Faro table and the dealer stepped aside without question.

"Place your bets, gentlemen," she announced and the flurry of enthusiasm excited her even more as the game began.

Late in the evening, Thomas returned.

With Eugene.

They joined the poker game in progress at Winston's table and suddenly Victoria's night took on a different kind of thrill. They conspired against her—for her—and together their desire stunned her. She stepped back, grasping the rim of the table to steady her senses. The banker crowding the players pushed closer. Her control of the group was gone.

Winston lay his cards aside and rose. He stepped in as the banker reached for her.

"Give the lady a break. Can't you see she's worn out from dealing with your bad manners all evening." He called one of the other dealers to take her place and escorted her away, ignoring the irritated grumbling of the crowd.

"What's wrong, Honey? I've never seen you like this."

The look in his eyes told her he approved the change.

The men at his table stood, welcoming her into their circle. Randall vacated his chair. She sat beside a stranger and gazed across the table at Thomas and Eugene. Winston slipped his hands down her bare arms and leaned close.

"You've let your guard down," he whispered. "Which one is it?"

*If only you knew*, she thought. *If only you knew how much I love them both.* Thomas had the grace to look away before he smiled but Eugene would not let her go. He barely bothered to look at his cards as they played another half-a-dozen hands before the game broke up.

Winston held her chair as everyone left. "At least I won't worry about you going home alone tonight." He lifted her hand to his lips and kissed it.

Thomas slipped the cape over her shoulders and Eugene held the door as they left. Outside, they walked away without speaking, the fog muffling the sound of their footsteps along the wooden walkway. Eugene took her hand, and the heat of his skin destroyed what was left of her caution. He felt it, she knew he did—so did Thomas. It was a game to them, she sensed the humor in Thomas as he indulged himself. Pulling her close, he kissed her, his usual chaste embrace touching her with wonder and surprise at his boldness.

"Do it," he whispered. "I know how much you want to."

She did want it. She needed it. Right here—right now, on the street, wrapped in the soft blanket of the fog, she wanted to fling herself headlong into the ocean of passion radiating from these two humans she loved. But all the centuries of pain and horror still haunted her, hurling ghosts across time to dampen her ardor with taunting, mocking faces. Faces that reminded her of other loves, of other lives lived in the hope of her promise, only to be lost in bloody darkness forever.

But Eugene was not to be dissuaded. His relentless demand could in no way be compared to Thomas. The strength of his kiss forced her into a dark doorway. The heat of his palm penetrated the velvet covering her breast, the tips of his fingers branding her flesh, marking her with his impatience. He still held her hand.

Then he was pulling her along the empty street. Thomas moved ahead, stopping in another doorway to slip a key into the lock. Eugene lifted her, carrying her across the threshold. Thomas lit a lamp, placed the key beside it and quietly closed the door as he departed.

The stairs were narrow and turned back half-way up but Eugene carried her into dark shadows. He stood before a brass bed and still would not let her go. Victoria could hear his breath ragged in her ear as his need sang to her, the torrent of blood flooding his heart making sweet music in the night.

"Tell me what to do," he whispered hoarsely.

"Whatever will lay your demon to rest."

"And yours?" he asked.

"Only blood will suffice."

"I want to see you." His voice was stronger.

"Light a candle."

He set her down on the bed and fumbled with a match. Victoria caught his hand and guided the small blaze to the short stub of wax. Then she blew out the match, her sigh ruffling the hair on the back of his hand. She stood before him in the soft glow, her fingers working the tiny buttons running down the front of the black velvet dress.

He watched, entranced by the pale display of flesh. She wore nothing else. His hands trembled as he swept the narrow straps from her shoulders, letting the dress slip to the floor.

Victoria shut her eyes and shared his pleasure. His gaze swept over her like summer fire, sending heat licking outward from her nipples to quickly encircle her breasts. Then his lips consumed her for real, his hands urgent and demanding, reaching low to stoke the fire of her own need.

Even Nikolai had not made her feel this way. Eugene created such splendor with his lips and tongue. The way he saw her in his mind made her shiver. She opened her eyes and reached for his belt.

*Thomas was right*, Eugene thought. She wanted this, as much as he did. Why had he waited so long. He could hardly stand as her fingers unbuckled his belt and started working down the buttons on his pants. Her urgent touch brushed his skin and his knees went weak. He forced her back to the bed. Then let her go long enough to shed his jacket and shirt. She slid to the floor and knelt, the wild fall of hair hiding her face.

"Let me help you . . . ," she whispered.

"No!" He buried both hands in her hair and gently tilted her head back until he could see her face.

". . . take off your boots." She could feel him shaking.

"I thought . . . ."

"I know. But let me help you with your boots first."

She leaned toward him till her cheek rested against his thigh. His hands moved in her hair, the fingers caressing, then clenching as she reached for the heel of one boot. It slid off and he held his breath as she shifted her attention to the other foot. When the other boot had been discarded, she continued to kneel before him. Her hands slipped along the back of his thighs. The muscles bunched under her touch like a cat prepared to pounce as she pulled him close.

She buried her face against the mound of throbbing hardness and for an instant he allowed it. Then he forced her back, quickly undid the buttons and stripped out of the tight trousers. He pulled her close, and their coming together forced her into even more intimate contact with that part of him that refused to be ignored any longer. His desire to please her battled with his need to bury himself in her flesh. To pour out his life inside her. To give everything he was or would ever be to own the ultimate pleasure of coming within her.

Victoria let Eugene's thoughts thrill her. She fell back across the creaking bed, pulling him down, welcoming him into the heart of her need. Her tongue traced the vein pounding in his throat and her judgment got lost in lust, colored by visions of an eternity filled with this long forgotten pleasure.

Eugene thought no act of loving her could ever lift him beyond this one pinnacle of fulfillment, then the stab of her desire robbed him of all reason. Yes! he answered to her unspoken question. The substance of his life flowed into her again as she quenched her thirst. Yes, he would suffer the pain of this passion every moment for a thousand lifetimes in order to spend those lifetimes at her side.

The echo of Thomas' words drifted across the overwhelming relief of release, and Eugene longed to die—for her, in her—right here, right now—with no regrets, lost in the splendor of the moment.

The candle had long since burned down and Eugene sprawled across her in the darkness. Unwilling to give him up for even a moment, Victoria held him, using his pledge of undying devotion to banish the dark visions from an unbearable past and an unseeable future.

"How long will it take," he asked, his words whispering against her hair.

"I'm ready whenever you are." Her fingers trailed down his side, slipping under the curve of his leg pinning her to the bed.

"That's not what I mean," he said, reaching for her hand.

"The simple act we have committed will not make you a vampire."

He kissed her hand, one finger at a time. "Then what will?"

"No matter how the two of you conspire, I'll not consent."

Her voice was soft in the darkness but there was no despair, no anger in her words. Eugene felt as though he'd won at least this confrontation. He set aside his ultimate desire to consider the moment. Dawn was still far in this night's future. And he was definitely ready.

Outside, dawn struggled to break through the gray mist. Victoria rubbed Eugene's back as he stretched and groaned.

"What is this place?" she asked, glancing around the narrow room with its four dormer windows.

"Thomas found it. Used to be a seamstress shop. She moved on to a bigger place."

"So you took it for your shop?"

"Thomas took it so I could be near you." Eugene rolled over and looked at her. "He knows how much I love you. I thought I would never get a chance to show you."

"How much did he tell you?"

Eugene rubbed his neck. "Enough to know I would do anything for your love. Enough to know I would choose to die rather than live without it."

She left the bed and started dressing.

"Victoria, I will not apologize for what happened here. But I never want to hurt you. Or Thomas."

"I know. Much more than you can possibly think. But there is much you have to understand. About Thomas. About myself. I have to go."

She stepped out the door. By the time he reached the top of the stairs she was gone.

"None of that matters," he called, suddenly realizing it didn't. "None of it matters at all." He went back to bed and sprawled across sheets covered with her bright, clean scent of wild flowers—and the musky warmth of love—and slept.

And dreamed.

Of a darkness so deep it went on forever.

## Chapter Twenty-Seven

The early afternoon sun poured through the unshuttered window, waking Eugene. He rose and dressed hurriedly. He had a lot to do before sunset.

The orphanage was bustling with after-dinner activity when he arrived. He tied his horse at the porch rail and wandered into the parlor where Betsy supervised half-a-dozen boys and girls reading.

"Where's Thomas?" he asked.

"Out in the chapel."

"Thanks." Eugene headed for the kitchen where he paused long enough to turn up his nose at leftover fried chicken. He poured a mug of coffee and carried it with him.

Thomas stood in the framework of the building, a cigar glowing redly as he smoked. Eugene crossed the yard and came up behind him.

"Sorry I couldn't make it out earlier."

"It's okay. I would imagine you've been busy."

"Yeah. Busy." He set the mug down without drinking. "I have a couple of documents for you." Reaching into his breast pocket, he took out two slim bundles of paper.

"What's this?" Thomas asked, as Eugene handed them over.

"My Will. In case the old man changes his mind and leaves me half of his side of the Charles River."

"You don't have to do this now."

"I know. But I want to be prepared."

"She hasn't agreed."

"She will. The other is the Deed to this place. I can't believe the two of you have done all this work and never made sure no one could take it away from you."

"I never thought about it." Thomas sat in the wide opening

where double doors would soon hang, turning the documents over in his hands. "Thanks, Gene."

"No. Thank you. I'd still be banging my head against the nearest brick wall without your intervention."

"I just opened the door. You have make her take you in."

"I intend to be very intense about what I want. Are you sure it's what you want?"

"Yes. She needs us both. In very different ways."

Eugene sat beside him in the comforting darkness. "I love you, Thomas. More than I ever loved my father, as much as I love my sister. Almost as much as I love Victoria."

Thomas put his arm around Eugene's shoulders. After a moment he spoke. "I love you, too, Gene. But the depths of my gratitude is going to depend on how much you won last night."

Eugene laughed. "Well, I'm afraid I didn't do too good in the casino, but I certainly had a taste of something far richer than gold before the night was over."

"So did she, my friend. So did she." Thomas rose, stuck the papers in his hip pocket and started across the yard.

"Wait, Thomas. Where are you going?"

"To work. Since the two of you have other things on your mind, I guess paying for the church will be left to me."

They walked together toward the house.

"I sold two pictures to the paper today. And I have an assignment tomorrow. Can I borrow Billy for the rest of the week? To help me set up the shop?"

"Sure. But do me a favor? Don't let him see all those bruises on your neck. He asks a lot of questions these days. Some aren't easy to answer."

"Maybe he's not asking the right person. Oh, I found seven guys to help you here starting tomorrow."

"Thank you, God."

"You're welcome."

Winter was deceptively mild. Thomas, Eugene and Victoria spent a great deal of time together both in the City and at the orphanage. The Chinese cook finally learned how to make fried chicken, to mass approval. The chapel turned into a real church with hardwood pews and polished mahogany floors. The piano arrived safely along with another surprise from Eugene's sister. The young woman had come to play for as long as it took to teach someone else but she was so taken with the City and the children, she stayed, making music an integral part of the education available at what was fast becoming the best private school in San Francisco.

Thomas sometimes stood behind the podium and preached. But most Sundays he allowed other visitors the privilege of conducting services and confined himself to teaching.

Billy worked a part of each day in the photography shop. His assistance became essential when Eugene got word of a mine explosion. They traveled to the disaster and worked for three days, recording the pain and anguish of the victims and the families and the pictures appeared in newspapers as far away as New York.

Eugene always made sure the boy was not there when Victoria visited. And she visited often, feeding her need for passion even when she had no thirst for blood. Sometimes, Thomas and Eugene would spend the evening gambling and Victoria would join them in the early hours of the morning. They spoke of many things, the children, improvements to the home, the need for a new teacher. They didn't talk about the future, each one content to dream his own dreams of what might unfold from the darkness surrounding them.

One day early in the new year a steamer trunk arrived from Europe. Eugene tore open the letter from his sister and hurriedly read it. Then he unlocked the trunk and unpacked the latest in photography equipment from across the ocean. A new camera, smaller and more compact than the other two he now owned. And a flash-pan for taking pictures indoors and at night. He grabbed a kid off the street and paid him to take a message to Thomas and Victoria.

Thomas arrived first. The soft days of winter had left his overlong hair a burnished golden brown almost the same color as the pants he wore. And he looked every bit the gambler, in a fitted jacket so blue it looked black.

"Sit here, Thomas," Eugene directed, pushing him toward an ornately carved chair in front of a backdrop of gray satin. The new camera stood on a tripod about six feet away.

"What's this, Gene?"

"My sister, bless her ever loving heart. She's doing Europe again. She says this time she's going to stay. Something about marrying a mad scientist and living in the South of France. She sent me this new camera. Look. It's all self contained. It will revolutionize photography. I have to experiment with it."

"Inside? How will you get enough light?"

Eugene bit the end off a small cigar and puffed on it repeatedly. "Dammit, Thomas. How can you stand to smoke these things." He went over and stuck it in Thomas' mouth. "Keep it going, will you. Victoria should be here any minute."

"I'm surprised you haven't rigged the thing so you can be in the picture, too."

"I'm working on it."

"So, where does the light come from?"

"Oh. It's a flash-pan. You fill it with dry chemicals, in just the right mix, and there's a trigger on the handle that sets it off, creating a big flash of light. No more sitting still endlessly."

The bell over the door jingled and Victoria hurried in. "More pictures. I do love pictures, Eugene. Thomas. How did he talk you into this?"

"I didn't know what he was doing. I'm not sure he does either. We may all go up in a puff of smoke."

Eugene walked her to where Thomas lounged in the chair.

"Sit up straight, Thomas. Put the cigar in your other hand. That's right. Now. Victoria. Did I tell you how beautiful you are tonight?" he asked, smiling and kissing her hand.

"Yes, you did, thank you."

"It's written all over your face, Gene. It's one of the reasons you don't play good poker."

"Shhh, Thomas. He's almost ready to take the picture."

Eugene added an ingredient to the flash-pan, checked one last time that the camera shutter cord was attached to the trigger. Then he surveyed the scene. Thomas took a drag off the small cigar before moving his hand back to the arm of the chair. Victoria stood smiling, a dress the color of old blood the perfect contrast to the shiny backdrop and Thomas' pale hair.

He tripped the trigger and the small room filled with bright light. He shut his eyes for an instant, blinking at the negative image on the back of his lids.

Thomas and Victoria were still in their places.

"One more," he admonished.

Thomas rose out of the chair, blinking. "No, thanks. Once was enough." He moved past Eugene and handed him the cigar. "I see now why you had me smoking. Smells like rotten eggs."

"Victoria, you'll stay? Just another shot? I need to get this right before I start selling it to the public."

"Yes, I think you need the practice. I believe I have sunburn."

"Make an extra one for me, Gene?" Thomas asked.

"Absolutely," Eugene assured him as he left, the closing door setting the bell jingling.

Victoria sat in the ornate chair.

"Not there. Come back here." Eugene picked up the tripod and carried it to the back room, setting it in front of a red brocade fainting couch. "Take off your dress."

Her laughter filled the small room. "Whatever you say, sir."

The place looked like a Chinese laundry, the walls plastered with handbills and draped with layers of sheets and clothing. Fine silk hung across a swathe of heavy velvet casually arrayed over a screen behind the small sofa. Victoria stepped out of her dress and left it lying in a heap on the floor.

"Make yourself comfortable."

Eugene went back into the other room for the flashpan. When he returned, she lay on the chaise, facing the camera, one booted foot and black stockinged leg displayed to the knee under her soft white petticoat.

He whistled softly. "Almost perfect." He arranged the eyelet ruffle to fall in delicate folds across her thigh and off the side of the couch. "Don't move."

Victoria laughed again. "You're mad. This is not for Thomas."

"Of course not. He doesn't think of you as a flesh and blood woman with needs and desires. You're the mother of his children." He turned and surveyed the scene. "It's not right."

Moving around behind the sofa, he adjusted the petticoat as he went. His hand touched her hair.

"You wouldn't. No, Eugene. Leave my hair alone."

He started throwing hairpins on the floor. With his fingers, he combed through the soft curls until the dark red tresses fell over her shoulders and the back of the chaise.

"You have no idea how long it takes to do it all up again."

"I'll help you. Later."

Kneeling on the floor in front of her he drew part of the heavy hair forward over one camisole-covered breast and bare shoulder. He sat back on his heels.

"Now." He hurried to the camera, checked through the viewer and pulled the trigger.

Victoria sat up, blinking. "For heavens sake, open a window." With a quick twist, she captured the unruly mane in a rough braid hanging over one shoulder. Both straps of the camisole slipped off and lay on her upper arms.

"You are so beautiful, it takes my breath away."

The late spring breeze cleared the air. He moved slowly from the open window and knelt in front of her, untying the ribbon at her breast. The camisole fell away leaving her naked to the waist. He pressed his face to her breasts, his lips teasing first one nipple then the other.

She leaned back against the brocade, drawing him with her. His day old beard grazed her skin, making her shiver all over as his lips moved up to the hollow of her throat. With a quick impatient gesture his shirt was gone, pulled over his head and tossed aside. He lifted her hair and nuzzled behind her ear, biting at her earlobe.

Victoria ran her fingers through the short hair curling across his shoulders. The pile of clothing on the floor grew and the slow languid movements of play were replaced with the storm of their love. The golden glow of late afternoon faded into purple twilight darkness as the lense of the camera stoically watched the passion played out on the chaise.

They lay in the dark in each other's arms, the musky odor of love mingling with the scent of sweat drying on their bodies. Eugene pulled away first and walked naked to the table. He lit a lamp and stood in the circle of light.

"We have to stop doing this, Eugene."

"No. Never."

Outside the evening traffic to the saloons had begun. She left the chaise and moved to where he stood.

"We must!" She touched a finger to the slow dripping puncture wound on his neck. "When I drink your blood shared in passion, it hurts you."

"It hurts me more when you don't."

She watched his blood drip from her fingertip a moment before raising it to her lips. "I can make you forget."

He picked up a revolver that lay on the table and thrust it into her hand. "You'd have to kill me to make that happen." He held her fist tight around the pearl handle, forcing the barrel into the soft flesh under his chin. Just above her wounds of the heart. "Do it now before I have to have you again."

He forced his thumb through the guard on top of her finger. It took all her strength to keep his pressure off the trigger.

"No! Stop!" *Not another sacrifice.* Nikolai had forced her to kill Felix. But this didn't have to end that way. In dark and bloody death. Eugene could be different. He was strong. Even Thomas believed they could all live happily ever after.

"Eugene, let go," she whispered. "It's all right." She kissed his fingers. "Let it go!"

He took a long shuddering breath and the pressure on her hand diminished. Laying the gun aside, she led him to the chaise. She lay back and drew a sharp nail across her breast near the nipple. Blood welled darkly in a fine line on her pale skin. She shut her eyes and pulled his head down. His soft moan of pleasure wrenched her heart.

"Do this for me now. And soon it will be forever."


A pale sliver of moon rode across the sky. Thomas paced the porch. Where was she? Surely she knew he waited.

"I'm here, Thomas," her soft whisper echoed in his mind and his ear. She stood at the bottom of the steps, dressed in pants and a loose shirt.

He held out his hand.

She took it and drew him away into the yard.

"I'm sorry," she said as they walked into the dark shadows of the oak tree.

"I'm not. You've always needed more than my devotion. I'm glad you finally allowed Gene to fill that void. We both love you, although his will always be a bit more earthy than mine." He laughed and drew her close. "If you have to wear his clothes, couldn't you pick something cleaner?"

"I will always be grateful for your devotion, Thomas. Our closeness of mind and heart will never be torn apart by what Eugene and I share. Will it be the same with the two of you?"

"Yes. Is it over?"

"No. I have only just begun. It will take some few days to prepare everything."

"Tell me what to do and I'll see to it."

"Tomorrow will be soon enough. First I must reconcile myself to the enormity of my decision to bring him over." They stood hidden from sight under the tree, savoring a moment both felt would last forever. Dawn brought a gradual lightening to the grayness surrounding them. Thomas still held her, reluctant to release her to the growing light.

"Go to him. Tell him to be strong for me."

Victoria clutched at Thomas, kissing him hard on the lips, a most passionate goodbye and faded slowly from sight.

Inside the house, the stairs presented an unsurmountable obstacle so Thomas lay down on the sofa in the parlor and slept, his dreams filled with pictures of Victoria once again in that dark place from which her spirit could only travel by night.

## Chapter Twenty-Eight

Thomas was in the shop with Eugene when the first alarm sounded. Grabbing the new camera, Eugene headed for the docks. The fire department pumped endless streams of water from the bay but they couldn't keep ahead of the storm created by the fire itself.

The Sliver Slipper and the photography shop were far removed from the immediate danger but the smothering pall of smoke forced evacuation of the area. Thomas loaded equipment and supplies on the horses and headed for the orphanage. Then he returned for Eugene.

"I can't leave, Thomas. Not without Victoria."

"She's safe. The fire is nowhere near her."

By the time they reached Victoria's Hope, the fire had divided and spread in both directions along the dock. It made for an odd sort of holiday. The children perched along the fence and leaned out the upstairs windows, wherever they could find a good view.

It was near mid-afternoon when Thomas first felt Victoria stir, far too early for her to rise. He stood on the porch alone and watched the minuscule flames leaping into the dark shroud hanging over the bay. She was dreaming—and he smiled at her remembered joy. Eugene kissing her in front of the camera. Then somewhere from far away a voice whispered softly in the darkness. The sudden hot, stifling darkness.

*Rest now, Victoria.* The voice echoed through her tomb. Victoria felt very warm and drowsy. Eugene knelt before her, laughing, adjusting the focus of the camera that captured their act of love for all eternity.

*Do not be frightened. I am always with you.* So familiar. So dear. That sweet voice. Victoria lay in the small space unable to move. A faint smell of smoke seeped in.

In her vision, she stood on the forecastle of the Sea Witch, Jeremiah at her side. A cold wash of spray swept over the rail but heated air still scorched her lungs.

Victoria opened her eyes. She was in the coffin. She pressed the latch but the lid remained tight. She pounded on the soft lining with her fists.

"Mother! Dear Mother! Help me."

*Do not fight, my sweet. It is better this way.*

"No, Mother! Not now!"

The heat of the Sahara warmed her cold flesh. And she was lost once again in the passion of Felix's love. Her mind knew it was unreal but her heart wanted it so badly. The last true release she had known, until now, until Eugene. But Felix was dead. Nikolai demanded it—but she had wielded the dagger with her own hand. So many innocents sacrificed at the altar of her dark desire.

"Mother, I cannot go now," she begged. "Not when there is the smallest chance of happiness." The coffin shifted, jarred by something heavy falling from above.

*It was not meant to be, Victoria.*

The heat became unbearable. *This is hell, and I shall burn in it forever.* Once again she lay on the porch of the house in Cape Town. Nikolai's harsh howls echoed in the coffin as he threw her treasures down upon her. But the sounds of terror ringing in the closed space were her own.


Thomas slid down the fluted column and shut his eyes, but her life continued to flash before him, filled with madness and murder and blood—so much blood. An endless stormy sea swept her away to hot sands cooled by night, the quick flash of a dagger and another river of blood flowed from her hands to her lips.


She lay in the coffin imprisoned by that small death she endured each day while debris rained down. Nikolai's presence was so strong. Too strong to be a memory. With great effort she found the strength to look into the future one more time.

A black ship stood offshore, shrouded in the mist sweeping in from the sea. Nikolai stood on the bow, a dark shadow in the red tinged haze, watching San Francisco burn. Before him the shoreline blazed with a brilliance that shamed the sun into early submission.


Heavy smoke roiled skyward, blending with the fog rolling in from the bay until Thomas could no longer distinguish between the two. And out of the growing darkness he perceived in her mind, he saw what she saw. A black ship anchored far out in the bay, an even darker shadow striding back and forth on the deck.

He stood suddenly.

"Victoria!" There was nothing he could do to help her as the building that sheltered her coffin crashed down and she sank into a obscure world he could not comprehend. "Victoria," he whispered. "I love you. God forgive you. God forgive us all."


The voice of her mother whispered from far away. *Have no fear, my child. I give you sweet peace at last.*

She felt Thomas' presence, his words surrounding her like his comforting arms. Music of oblivion rang in her ears so strongly she barely heard the earthen walls crack under the pressure of burning debris. The general store crashing down from above combined with the external force of the sea came to her rescue at the last possible moment, filling her grave with mud and water, extinguishing the fire that would have truly ended her long and painful existence.

Beyond the gate, Eugene and Billy moved from camera to camera, taking picture after picture of the destruction. Eugene ground his teeth in anger and frustration. He didn't need Thomas to tell him Victoria was gone. A dark presence took the place of the joy he had know since she made him part of her life. And even as his mind and hands worked, his heart broke and bled.

## Epilogue

*All that remained of the wharf was blackened rubble. Miners, gamblers and saloon owners worked by day, cleaning up the debris. Very little if anything had been salvageable and most of what remained was simply shoveled into the sea. Rebuilding started right on top of the old wreckage. On the heels of disaster, a new and better San Francisco evolved.*

*I moved through the shroud of fog covering the waterfront into an area of small unpretentious buildings and stopped in front of the photographer's shop. Everyone to whom I spoke knew the young woman whose likeness graced the small oval portrait I carried. Several people even identified her by name. But none knew her intimately. It had taken two months to find this man, this Eugene Gordon. But even here in this place she visited often there was no satisfaction. The blood in my veins cried out, too late, too late. Only once had I felt her presence from the heart of the conflagration and then nothing more.*

*Crowded in the store-front were many illustrations of the photographer's work. Far down on one side, set apart from the others by its ornate package stood a daguerreotype of a woman. The style of dress and hair differed greatly from the last time I had seen her but there could be no mistake, it was my Victoria.*

*I rapped on the door several times before he answered.*

"Go away," he shouted. "The shop is closed."

*I could hear him moving about in the back so I persisted and eventually the door opened. He stood there half naked, a photograph in each hand.*

"Who are you? What do you want?"

"I am Nikolai Valfrey. I seek the woman in the photograph in the window." *My words caught his attention. A quick spark of interest flickered in his eyes then died.*

"She's dead. Buried under the rubble out by the bay."

"No. She is only sleeping." *I spoke softly, willing him to look at me. Instead he lifted one hand and gazed at the small elaborate portrait he held. His eyes raised to the level of mine as he presented the picture for my viewing.*

*I took his hand, holding it firmly while I gazed at the picture of Victoria reclining on a small sofa, clad in a white petticoat, black boots and stockings. She was smiling.*

"Come inside. There are others." *He stepped back and I accepted his less than gracious invitation.*

*He led the way to a room at the rear of the building. The display was small but all the gleaming portraits were of Victoria. He replaced those he held and picked up another. The one nearest the front drew my attention. Sharp, clear details filled me with anger and a pain too harsh to bear. Victoria lay on the same small couch that stood in the corner, the aftermath of passion evident in her face and posture. Naked, eyes closed, she reclined on the small sofa, her hair spread across the back, and near one nipple a hairline of blood showed dark enough to mar her perfect body. I controlled my fury and turned to Eugene Gordon as he stared at the blatant display of his desire for my wife.*

"So you, too, have tasted her passion." *He stood perfectly still while I advanced toward him. My hands closed around his neck as he spoke.*

"Kill me," he whispered hoarsely. "I want to be with Victoria."

*I considered his words.*

*My hands slid up his cheeks, thumbs caressing the warm sun-browned flesh beneath his eyes. He stood rigid while I kissed him hard on the lips. When I drew away with fangs bared, his blue eyes became bright with fear—and longing.*

*There could be no gentle persuasion here, not for this one so enamored of my Victoria. I ripped at his clothes until he was a naked as my wife before his camera. He did not resist as I forced him down across the back of the sofa nor did he cry out as his soft flesh tore under the hard cruel clarity my act of dominance signified. When my lust was finally spent, I pulled him down beside me on his bed of love and lifted his wrist to my lips. The small collection of veins just under the skin released his blood slowly and I sipped it like fine wine as I watched him die the mortal death. And as I made him my slave, my heart and soul cried out.*

*I will have you back, Victoria, even if I must wait forever.*

# ABOUT THE AUTHOR

ELAINE MOORE, a freelance public relations and advertising specialist, is a published poet and past president of the North Texas Professional Writers Association. Her work appears regularly in print media and on the Internet.

COMING JULY 2004

# ETERNAL EMBRACE

## THE "DARK MADONNA" TRILOGY
### Book 2

### by Elaine Moore
ISBN: 0-7434-8689-7

Locked in oblivion for well over a century, Victoria MacKay rises from a deep vampire sleep into a newer, faster-paced world, screaming her reluctance to leave the peace of Mother Earth. Adrift in a city filled with freaks far worse than herself, Victoria is befriended by humans, and pursued by her own kind.

She longs for a normal life, but the bloody, addictive nature of vampirism throws her back into a dark world of murder and madness—a world that shelters her husband, who will never allow her to escape his eternal embrace again, even if he must destroy her....